AMULET OF VISIMAR BOOK II

Night of the Wolf

Eugene Weaver

Eugene Weaver Publishing

For Chad, my horror
"brother from another mother"
who gets my quirky weirdness.
This one's for you, buddy.

Contents

Preface

Books and movies that deal with werewolves have always captivated me. The first movie I ever saw that specifically dealt with such creatures was Joe Dante's, *The Howling*. I marveled at the fantastic practical effects by Rob Bottin and wondered how they could possibly look so lifelike. This was followed up with the equally, if not more impressive, John Landis-directed classic, *An American Werewolf in London*.

Since then, I have been enthralled by werewolves in cinema and on the page. Truth be told, Neil Marshal's 2002 soldiers versus werewolves tale, *Dog Soldiers,* is how I envisioned my own creations on these pages and in the previous novel in this series, *The Amulet of Visimar.* That is, large and imposing human-wolf hybrids that tower over their human counterparts and are nearly impossible to defeat.

There have been many other werewolf tales I have loved and watched countless times over, all of them more or less "research" for this book which deals heavily with the subject matter of lycanthropy. And while some of the old tropes remain, I decided to play with a few as well, tweaking them to fit this tale better.

I have always found that werewolves and witchcraft and the supernatural go hand in hand, not a simple "man is bitten by wolf and then turns." I wanted to create a lore that involved numerous creatures of the night and the evil things that create and unleash them upon unsuspecting people who are ill-prepared to do battle with the unholy abominations.

So, when I decided to tackle a sequel to *The Amulet of Visimar,* I didn't want to just rehash the same thing I wrote in the first novel. What might you, dear reader, find intriguing about this gothic, old world I have created? What have the powers of darkness concocted this time around and to what end? Well, that's for you to find out.

It's time to jump back hundreds upon hundreds of years once more and enter a time of witchcraft, superstition, and evil forces bent on humanity's destruction with a ragtag group of decent people desperately taking a stand against it. Welcome to the longest night of horror anyone could imagine facing. Welcome to *The Night of the Wolf.*

ly·can·thro·py lī-ˈkan(t)-thrə-pē
The assumption of the form and characteristics of a wolf held
to be possible by witchcraft, magic, and/or the supernatural.

Resurrection Rites

Carpathian Mountains, Romania

"He failed you where I will succeed, master. You have given me another chance and I will not fail you," the icy cold voice uttered, standing atop the ruins of Castle Visimar. The cloaked figure looked up to the sky. It was nearly cloudless, unlike the many years the mountain on which he stood and the town below had been blanketed in fog. A bright moon shone down upon the rubble. In the distance, wolves' howls echoed throughout the valley.

Beside the man stood a single gray wolf, much bigger than any normal wolf. A *gift* from his master. It watched the man intently, studying him, looking for any weakness. This man would not fail as the previous inhabitant had.

Inside the cloaked man's head, a voice, barely a whisper but easily discernable as his true lord and master, spoke. *The scrolls have been recited, not by Antonin Visimar, but by a lowly servant, Marcel Metzinger. He succeeded where his master Visimar had failed. Visimar was defeated by a girl named Lily-Rose Burns with help from her sister Juliette.*

Those that assisted live in the village below, unaware that the beast lives still under the ruins of the castle, waiting for another host body to complete its transformation and begin its reign here on earth before I, the lord of this world, am granted access to all on the final days.

"You have called me forth, the original retriever of the gift from the magi to the Christ child. It rests with the bitch woman and the priest below. What do you ask of me, my lord?" the cloaked figure said, peering at the vast ruins of what was once Castle Visimar.

You will wait on the woman that travels now to a town known as Kortbeke. She is to kill her offspring. Her act of loyalty to me is what I command. When she proves herself worthy, she will return with his remains and offer them up as the host body for the Pricolici. The mother, turned to a wolf, will give her son for me. Much like Abraham was willing to give up his own son Isaac on the altar for his god. If she fails, however, it will be her that is offered up as a sacrifice to bring back the beast. She was given the gift of eternal life and if she cannot do as I command, it will be taken away from her. However, she will still be of use in other ways. But a blood sacrifice atop the altar must be made.

The cloaked figure waited for his own task. It had been countless ages since he was here. But at long last, the Traveler had been called back once more to complete what Antonin Visimar had failed to achieve. "Master, what of me?" he asked the slippery, hissing voice inside his head.

Did you collect what I asked from the forest below?

"They were difficult to retrieve and had been all but lost in the dirt, but they are here and accounted for, my lord."

He lifted his hand; in it was a sackcloth. The man spilled its contents across a chunk of stone that lay on its side, retrieved from the rubble. Half of a pentagram remained scrawled on the side of the broken piece of altar that still had blood stains from unknown and long forgotten victims.

Dirty and charred bones now lay spread out on the altar haphazardly. An altar that had seen much death since its creation, yet still, though the castle had been destroyed, remained. Ready to accept more sacrifices. And tonight, a sacrifice would be made.

Beside the man, the large wolf licked its fangs, its yellow eyes gazing at the bones then up to the veiled man beside it.

My angel shall be given another chance. I offer second chances, even to you, my faithful Traveler.

The original inhabitant of Castle Visimar known as the Traveler, whose human name was Marwan Haddad, bowed his head reverently, then uttered quietly under his breath a prayer to the god of this world, the unholy one who was with him in his thoughts, deep inside his subconscious. The *Pricolici.* So close to being brought back in all of its otherworldly glory, only to be thwarted by the foolish humans below in the town of Burnmere. Yet, a part of it still lived in a sort of hibernation, far below the castle. But not for long.

Now, do what I ask. Bring forth the sacrifice unto me. Prove your worth to me once more, ancient Traveler.

When he was done with his prayer, he picked up another sack from the cold ground at his feet. Unlike the bag of bones, this one was moving. He opened it and pulled its contents out, lifting it into the air above the bones.

The wolf looked hungrily at what the man held in his left hand, baring its fangs and snarling. Its tongue hung out of its mouth in a slight curl, wiggling, as if expecting to be fed immediately.

A long, thin knife was pulled from the waistband inside the man's black cloak. Bringing the knife up to the squirming, crying infant, chosen at random and taken from its cradle in a nearby village, he quickly ran the blade from its neck down the length of its stomach, instantly spilling its contents atop the dirty bones. The crying ceased almost immediately, its body becoming still.

Blood continued spilling forth onto the altar, covering the entirety of the dirty, burnt bones. The last bits of the child's blood dribbled onto fragments of what had once been a skull. When the body was drained completely, including the tiny heart that continued pumping blood onto the altar, the man quickly discarded it. He dropped it in front of the wolf that didn't hesitate, eating quickly and greedily.

The man cleaned his knife of the infant's blood with several quick swipes across his black robe before hiding it back inside his cloak, never taking his eyes off the now blood-soaked bones. His mind drifted to how easily he had swiped the infant from its crib in Crownhaven while its unsuspecting parents slept soundly in the room beside it. A shapeshifter, he prided himself on gaining entry, undetected, in tight places such as chimneys, something he had perfected over the centuries.

The moon shone down on the unholy sacrifice, exposing the malevolent deeds being committed. "Come forth, live once more," the man uttered as the blood atop the bones began to draw forth steam, growing thicker and more intense.

Seeing the sacrifice was working, the man closed his eyes and began once more to pray to the prince of darkness that had brought him out of exile, back to his home, after Anton Visimar's failure to resurrect the Pricolici. His lord, the fallen angel, Lucifer, had no further use for him after he had procured the beautiful stone hundreds of years ago in the Syrian region, and he had been vanquished from his castle in the Carpathian Mountains of Romania by invading Hunn armies.

But this was a different time. Now, the scrolls had been read in their entirety and the Pricolici had taken form, but not completely. Somewhere under the rubble of Castle Visimar lay the still-living remains, waiting for a new host body that would be perfectly suited for re-animation. Preferably, a holy man, further mocking the god that had exiled him in the beginning of time from his heavenly realm.

The Traveler had retreated back into the shadows upon his own defeat, long before Anton Visimar's arrival at the castle. Years had bled into decades that became centuries. And then, he heard the soft whisper inside his head once more, beckoning him back. *I need you once more, my servant.*

The blood bubbled and appeared to be seeping into the bones themselves. What were once filth-covered and charred now gleamed crimson red. Once the entirety of the blood had been soaked up, the hissing steam ceased. All was still for several minutes while the man patiently waited.

The bones shook where they lay until rolling together, carefully lining up in their intended positions, creating a perfectly reassembled skeleton. The spilled organs began wiggling, growing, then sliding into their proper places inside the skeleton, filling it perfectly in size. It was as if they had never belonged to the unwitting host and were made specifically for this new creation.

Once the bones and organs were positioned properly, tendons, ligaments, arteries, veins and finally, muscle began to spread across the skeleton that was now beginning to resemble a person. The tiny heart had grown significantly, connecting to the new arteries and veins. Once properly connected, the spilled blood began to slowly pump through the heart, moving to all other parts of the body.

The skull had reconnected itself and smoothed out, attaching to the spinal cord securely. Inside the skull, brain matter twisted and turned until the skull cap was filled perfectly. While muscle tissue continued to wrap around bones, white liquid puddled up inside eye sockets. Soon the liquid became a jelly substance before two bright blue pupils were brought forth, sitting atop the newly created eyeballs.

As the facial features were created, muscle tissue covered it. Cartilage built up, creating a nose along with ears. Lips swelled up, covering perfectly placed, white teeth.

This process went on for several minutes while the man stood silently and reverently by. The wolf finished its meal and licked its chops before turning its attention to the new life taking its final form. Its yellow eyes, unblinking and motionless, continued staring.

Sex organs were created last, including mammary glands that quickly filled against the chest wall. Once that was complete, a thin film covered the body like a nearly see-through blanket. The invisible film thickened and turned to soft, supple skin, grafting itself onto the body.

Finally, flowing, long blond hair spilled forth from the bald scalp, completing the regeneration process. With the heart pumping blood throughout the body, it took several more minutes to complete the reawakening.

Eyelids fluttered before opening. Newly created eyes peered up into the moonlit sky. The female figure moved her head back and forth slowly, getting familiar with having just been reborn. Once acclimated, fingers and toes wiggled, and limbs moved on their own accord.

Slowly, the woman lifted herself to a sitting position, swung her legs from atop the altar and got to her feet in front of the cloaked man. Her eyes went from him down to the wolf who was snarling, baring its fangs at her. Ignoring this, she looked once more at the man.

The man spoke stoically, staring at her nakedness. "It is done. You have been called forth from your eternal torment to help fulfill what Anton Visimar failed to do before he expired. Pray to your master that you do not fail this time, for if you do, there will not be another chance given. Only the fire in which you existed before I gave you your earthly life back. Do you understand the words I speak, Ingrid Brassard?"

A smirk formed across her thick, red lips as she looked down at her body. It was just as beautiful as it was before her demise. Thinking of this, her smiled faded and was replaced with a scowl. "Whatever thy bidding is and that of our master, it shall be done. As long as it ends in the slaughter of that town." Her eyes went from the cloaked man down to tiny lights in the far distance at the bottom of the mountain.

He responded coldly, "The woman once known as Everly Seiler will fulfill her obligation to our master. Willingly sacrificing her son in the name of our lord. But unlike the coward Abraham and his son Isaac on Mount Moriah, she will not fail. And when her deed is done, the mighty Pricolici will once more reign over the earth until Lucifer is finally released from his bonds. This world will be his and we will reign under him."

They both fell silent, staring at the town of Burnmere. The gray wolf sat still beside the man, a thin snarl across its snout and eyes that glowed yellow in the moonlight.

Chapter 1

Hell Comes to Kortbeke

Kortbeke, Switzerland 1876 5:45 PM

Gabriel Lambert, the law of Kortbeke, was called away in the early evening hours on a cold September day. The police chief had received a telegraph via Morse code at the station relaying that there had been a report of cattle mutilations in the nearby town of Granhal three miles west of them. The decision was made that Lambert would travel on horseback the short distance with his deputy Jules Erni to see what the fuss was about.

Granhal was barely a town at all, with so few inhabitants. Beautiful mountains surrounded the tiny village with only one road in and one road out. Being such a tiny town, its law enforcement consisted of one elderly gentleman by the name of Hanz Fritz. Fritz couldn't handle such an occurrence on his own, and on numerous occasions when he sent these sorts of telegrams, Lambert would comment to his deputy that the man was past his prime by a good twenty years and needed replacing.

Fortunately, almost no real crimes were ever committed in Granhal as the town consisted of roughly fifty people, all of whom got along quite well. When situations did arise, Lambert was always contacted via the telegraph. He had already grown to despise it. Although he saw the benefits of this new form of communicating with nearby towns, Granhal was one town that didn't need it. But old man Fritz had insisted one be installed so he could call for help if the situation called for it. And a situation had occurred.

And so, the seventy-three-year-old lawman had sent a telegraph on the cold Sunday afternoon that reached the station in Kortbeke several hours later at 5:45 PM, just as the sun was beginning to set behind the mountains.

From atop his horse, Lambert glanced over at Erni saddling up his own horse from the stables behind their police station. "Ready? This won't take long. Going out to old Fritz's to check out cattle mutilations is a complete waste of time. I like the man, but he simply cannot do the job anymore. It feels like we are policing a town three miles away."

"Well, we basically are, and have been for quite some time. And for what seems like no reason. We get called out there for the silliest things that take time away from our own jobs," Erni answered, adjusting the dark blue hat on his narrow head, covering his thick brown hair.

"I know, I know. Poor old bastard needs to be replaced but they love him out there. Hell, I'm quite fond of him too. Rest assured, he'll be quite happy to see us come out, check out the scene, then write up a few notes to document what happened," Lambert replied, rubbing his whiskered chin.

At fifty years old, Lambert held himself well. Always dressed for the job, he took it seriously in his buttoned-down and well-groomed blue police uniform. His wife having passed away from cancer three years prior, Lambert had sunk himself headfirst into the job of making sure Kortbeke remained relatively crime free. And on a cold September Sunday night, absolutely nothing happened. So, they had decided that both of them would head over to Granhal, to speed up the process so they could retire for the night before it got too dark. Especially considering the dreary weather, a light mist drizzling all day, blanketing what was typically a beautiful mountain vista in the rural hills of Switzerland with a dull, gray, chilly fog. They had surmised that the both of them could easy have this wrapped up and a report written up in no time, likely before even hitting the sheets and calling it a day.

Kortbeke was a town that had seen much growth through the years. The old Catholic church had remained relatively untouched since it had been built some one hundred years prior, but the buildings and houses that branched off in every direction from it were structurally sound and remained relatively well maintained as the years went by.

Kortbeke was situated on hilly terrain, with cobblestone streets like rolling hills that lead to different parts of the town as one traveled them over the roughly three-square miles of town.

The town of just slightly over one thousand people were made up of mostly immigrant families from France, Germany, and Belgium who were lured by the prosperous and rich farmland in this region of Switzerland. Situated snugly in the Swiss Alps, it offered beautiful vistas from nearly every vantage point. Farming and agriculture were considered the main source of income in Kortbeke, and much of its produce and crops were exported to more populated rural towns and cities, primarily Zürich.

Erni gave his horse a light kick on the side and took off, following his boss. Three miles on horseback would certainly not take long. Catching up, he asked Lambert, "You think there's anything to this cattle mutilation? I assume he wants us to go to Florus Widmer's place at the edge of Granhal? Only place in town that's got cows."

"Doubtful," Lambert answered. "If it's a wolf attack then it'll have to be dealt with like the rest of them. Those old timers over there all have guns and know how to use them, especially against wolves, which they've dealt with from time to time when those bastards coming down off the mountains get too aggressive, looking to pick off some of the livestock, hitting Granhal before Kortbeke. However, if a wolf's got the taste of blood, it'll stick around and then it'll only be a matter of time before it gets its ass shot off. End of story. We're just checking it out so Fritz doesn't have to go out in this shit weather and get himself another bout with bronchitis. I'd warn him that he's smoking himself into an early grave, but that ship has sailed. The man's living on borrowed time. And once he kicks off, they're gonna have to hire someone else. Which I am positive we'll be involved in, one way or another."

"That I do believe," Erni replied as they continued to trot toward their destination. "Should we check in with Fritz first?"

Lambert answered, "No, let's just get to Widmer's, save us some time. This being a Sunday and late afternoon, no less, not much going on in Kortbeke. Plus, we still have a bit of daylight left peeking through those clouds even in this shit weather. We'll be fine. I know it'll be a sonofabitch riding back in the dark, but we've ridden through worse. Mayor Kessler knows we'll be gone for a spell, although that doesn't amount to a pint of piss. That man isn't capable of doing anything worthwhile other than kissing the ass of Uma Karlen, if that's something to consider worthwhile. And I do mean that literally."

Chuckling, Erni replied, "When is her tub-of-lard husband Nils going to figure out she's rotten to the core? Not that he's any better, I suppose."

"Don't know and, quite frankly, don't care. They are certainly two peas in a pod. What with their winning personalities and pleasant demeaners," Lambert answered with a laugh.

Erni was glad for the back-and-forth banter which took his mind off the lousy weather they were riding in, thankful that Granhal was approaching soon. The spritzing mist smacked his face and made visibility a bit more difficult than either were anticipating, especially considering the speed at which they were riding.

After a bit of silence with nothing more than the wind blowing and the horses' hooves clopping on the dirt road, Lambert observed, "Almost there. Goes without saying, but let's make this snappy. I might even suggest to Fritz when we check in to keep the telegraphs to a minimum, if possible. We've got our hands full with the town drunks at Maximilian's and Hubschmid's."

Erni chuckled at the joke. Sure, there was the occasional scuffle, but they were typically dealt with by the bars' owners.

"Hey, at least we haven't had any issues with the big man," Erni stated.

"Ahh, you mean Chadwick? Well, he seems a bit better now that his Lydia gave birth. What is she now? Two years old?" Lambert asked.

"That she is. Cute little thing. Though I do believe Lydia and the child may be out of town. Saw them leave the other day. Which means he may be getting drunk over at Maximilian's tonight. I don't trust that guy. Our town's small and rumors travel fast. That man is a wife beater, sure as I'm sitting atop old Bertha here," Erni replied.

"Well, be that as it may, he hasn't given us grief in a while and we won't be gone long enough for anything to happen. But if it does, Uma will nip it in the bud. I am sure of that. Even Chadwick won't cross her, much less her useless husband, for fear of being barred from Maximilian's," Lambert quipped.

The three short miles normally didn't take long on horseback, but the drizzling rain slowed them down slightly, stretching the trip to roughly an hour. On a clear day, it could take significantly less time than it took to walk from one end of Kortbeke to the other, which is why Fritz considered them to be almost one large, extended town. Something no one in Kortbeke, especially the town's mayor, agreed with or wanted, Lambert and Erni included. Granhal was a Protestant town, while Kortbeke was strictly Catholic. On top of that, the folks in Granhal didn't want the kind of progress Kortbeke enjoyed and were stuck in their old-fashioned ways. At least they minded their own business. Something they all could agree on.

They arrived at the edge of the tiny town consisting of a single row of houses spaced apart by several yards each. It was quiet as Lambert and Erni rode in on their horses. Which was no surprise; this being a Sunday night and the weather being what it was, everyone had likely stayed indoors.

They rode past the houses, then the small Protestant church in the center of town with white paint peeling from its wooden structure. In short order, they made their way to Florus Widmer's place near the edge of town and circled around back to where he kept his cattle.

"Whoa, boy," Lambert said, pulling back on the reins.

Erni followed suit as both horses came to a stop but appeared agitated.

"Calm down, there, Brutus," Lambert said, patting the dark horse's neck. "What's gotten into you?" Big Brutus gave a whinny and a hasty snort in reply, shaking its large head nervously.

It was beginning to get dark outside. The small bit of sunlight that had been peeking through the dreary rainclouds was now long gone and quickly being replaced by nightfall. What they could see, however, was troubling.

Hopping off their horses, the two men tied the reins to the fence and opened the gate. Both horses struggled with the reins and their owners.

"Will you both calm the hell down?" Lambert said again, growing agitated with his horses. "What has gotten into you? Christ almighty, you'd think the ground was covered with snakes or something."

"Or something," Erni replied, concern quickly replacing curiosity, looking warily at his horse before following Lambert as they walked toward the first cow lying still on the grass several hundred feet away. They crouched down to inspect the damage.

The dairy cow at their feet had its skin ripped from its body, all the way down to its hooves. Its stomach was sliced open, with five long claw marks running from its neck down to its utters and its entrails splayed out in a bloody display on the soaked grass. Laying on the other side of the animal was its skin. Almost as if it had been placed there deliberately.

"Lord, have mercy," Erni said, wiping cold rain off his wet face.

Lambert grimaced at the ghastly sight and put his hand to his mouth. "Well, shit. I suppose old Fritz did have reason to contact us after all. Wasn't no wolf that did this. Or if it was, it's bigger than any wolf I've ever seen that could tear a large animal up to this extent, that's for damn sure."

"What in God's name did do this, then?" Erni said, repulsed at the brutality with which the cow was dispatched.

"I don't know. I just…don't know. Bear, maybe? Some wild cat up in them mountains behind us?" Lambert answered in a near whisper, suddenly frightened.

They peered across the large, fenced-in area to see several more cows lying still on the grass. "Without inspecting them, I can guess the rest of this lot look like this here poor beast," Lambert said.

"Why does this look like something wanted to draw our attention to it? Like, a rational, thinking mind?" Erni asked shakily.

"Ain't no rational mind did this. But it *was* cunning and calculated. The five slices on its stomach are in a near perfect, straight line. And these animals aren't eaten. Simply slaughtered for the sake of slaughter. What in Christ's name are we dealing with here?" Lambert said shaking his head, then instinctively glancing up toward the town.

The horses' whinnying caused both men to look up. Bertha broke free of her knot and immediately took off in the opposite direction. Avoiding the road leading in and out of town, she instead took to the grassy landscape beyond the town's borders.

"Oh shit!" Erni cried out, watching his horse take off in a full gallop.

Just then, Brutus pulled back hard enough to break the old board attached to the fence post it was hitched to and followed Bertha's lead, taking off into the grassy plains beyond Granhal, also at a full gallop, whinnying in fright as it went.

"I think they sense what did this. Shh, listen," Lambert said, falling silent.

Soft footsteps could be heard in the darkness, along with the blowing wind. Erni's eyes darted back and forth, trying to see what he assumed was still lurking in the area.

"It's still here, Erni," Lambert said, now in a full whisper. He glanced from the fleeing horses back to the field in which they stood, then over toward the deadly silent town.

Both men instantly pulled out their flintlock pistols holstered at their sides and began loading them with a lead ball and gunpowder. Once the single-fire weapons were loaded, Erni looked at Lambert for direction in this strange turn of events.

The tall grass nearby that had been flowing in the wind seemed to shift directions. As though something was inside, waiting, watching, *hunting*.

"We've got to get to Fritz's place, now," Lambert said gravely, adding, "Something here is horribly wrong."

Erni saw the fear in his boss's eyes, something had never seen before. Despite several rough interactions with drunken patrons at their town's two bars in the past, his boss was always one to take it on the chin. A tough cookie. Especially since his wife had passed.

Neither man hesitated, breaking into a sprint back to the town's entrance where old man Fritz lived. Passing through town, this time both men noticed the distinct lack of lighting inside the homes and the utter silence throughout all of Granhal, something that hadn't crossed their minds earlier when making their way to Widmer's.

Slowing to a trot and attempting to catch his breath, Erni glanced back and forth at the houses on either side of the single street. "It's too early for everyone to be asleep on a Sunday, right?"

"You'd think so," Lambert replied, also slowing down. "There's not a sound here. No dogs, no insects even. Just this damned drizzling rain and whatever was back there in the tall grass. I know I heard something."

They both fell silent as they hurried the rest of the way to Fritz's tiny wooden house.

Quietly walking up to the door, Lambert pounded and waited for an answer, both men out of breath from the run.

Erni shook his head at the lack of response, waiting.

Lambert knocked again, harder. "Fritz! You in there? What the hell is going on here! Open up, come on now!"

Still nothing.

Both men heard a sound like padded feet on the dirt behind them, followed by heavy breathing.

"What was that?" Erni called out, trembling as he quickly spun around.

"Shut up, Erni!" Lambert whispered loudly.

They both peered into the darkness. No lights on in any of the houses made the scene even more ominous.

"Where…is…everyone?" Erni said, this time in a whisper.

Lambert merely shook his head, equally puzzled.

"That sound again! What is it?" Erni asked as his eyes darted back and forth in the darkness.

"There, something off to the side of the road, I saw movement," Lambert said as he raised his pistol in its direction.

Erni, taking his cue, also raised his weapon.

The large, looming shape walked on two legs as it moved slowly with a low, guttural rumble. It was hunched over slightly with large, muscular arms that were outstretched, as if stalking its prey.

"Whatever it is, I think it's snarling," Erni said, growing more terrified by the second.

"Is it on its hind legs? What animal around these parts walks like that? Christ! It looks huge, whatever it is!" Lambert said, himself growing more alarmed.

Glancing over, he saw Erni getting ready to fire but whatever was out there was too far away for a clean hit.

"Erni, do not shoot your—" Lambert said but was cut off by the loud blast from Erni's flintlock.

The blast briefly lit their immediate surroundings enough to get a fleeting glimpse of what looked like a mutated wolf's face with long, pointed ears. Eyes glowed yellow above a long snout with rows of long, pointed fangs, thick saliva dripping from its mouth. Over seven feet tall, completely covered in thick, white fur, it stood on its muscular rear haunches.

Darkness fell across Granhal once more, shrouding the beast in darkness. Only its heavy breathing could be heard through the blowing wind.

"Lord! Oh, dear Lord! What is that thing!?" Erni cried out.

Padded footsteps in the pitch-black darkness moved closer, dirt crunching under its huge, clawed feet.

In a panic, Lambert turned to Fritz's door and twisted the knob to find it was unlocked. Just as he opened the creaking old door, the footsteps behind him stopped and Erni screamed out. Glancing back, he saw his deputy lifted into the air by the shadowed figure. Erni's screams were instantly cut off by the loud crack of what sounded like bones snapping.

Bursting into Fritz's darkened house, Lambert turned and tried to close the door just as Erni's body crashed through it with incredible force, knocking Lambert to the wooden floor.

Lambert cried out in pain, landing hard on his hip, then looked over to where his deputy lay—without his head. Legs and torso were folded completely backward and twisted in a position no human could survive. *Snapped in half like a twig,* Lambert thought with horror.

Lambert quickly crawled on all fours to the opened door, dragging his flintlock along with him. He slammed it shut and forced himself to his feet, hastily locking it and whimpering out as pain shot up through his hip.

Unable to stand up any longer, he lost balance and dropped to his knee. He quickly looked around the house for a place to either hide or better protect himself from what had just killed his deputy. Seeing his options were quite limited he decided to crawl toward the small bed in the corner where a shape lay.

He stopped in his tracks and pulled himself up to get a look. On the bed was old man Fritz, what was left of him. His stomach was ripped open, similar to the cows in the field. His intestines were placed on a pile atop his body, eyes forever frozen in utter terror at what was being done to him. His head had been severed from his body and placed near the stump.

Lambert suddenly realized why everyone's houses were darkened. Whatever that thing was, it had likely gone from house to house, killing all inside. Men, women, and children. Quickly, efficiently, and silently, just as it had quietly crept up on them minutes earlier. Like a silent butcher. Only the horses seemed to sense its presence earlier.

Outside, he heard the padded, muffled footsteps again, now on Fritz's small front porch. Spinning around, he fired his flintlock toward the closed door, causing wood to splinter and shatter.

As dust floated in the air, an eerie silence fell over the small house. Lambert held his breath, unsure if his blast hit its mark. The sound of footsteps had ceased.

The door's lock had been destroyed by the gun blast, and it now slowly opened on its own accord, the wind pushing it inward. Lambert squinted to see in the darkness what lay beyond the opening.

Two yellow eyes glowed, peering at him. Whatever had been standing on its hind legs earlier now crouched on all fours. It made its way past the busted doorway into the darkened room, staring at the lone inhabitant of Granhal. Its current population now reduced to one police officer.

Lambert watched in wide-eyed terror as the wolf came to a stop in front of him, its snarls growing louder, saliva dripping from its opened jaws exposing rows of the largest fangs he had ever seen. Yellow eyes remained fixed on his. He screamed as the wolf's body began to contort and change shape, and he closed his eyes in terror.

Seconds later, he opened them and saw its yellow eyes blink, now revealing bright blue eyes. Lambert's screams ceased as he stared in wonder at what stood before him.

A hand reached out, grabbing his throat and squeezing. Instantly, he was lifted to his feet then off of them. His windpipe closed from the iron-tight grip of the murderous being in front of him, he was unable to utter a word.

"You'll do nicely. Yes, indeed. You will do just fine," a soft, soothing voice whispered.

Outside, the night sky once more fell silent as the shape made its way out of the opened doorway. Now slim and standing on two feet, the figure walked to the town's entrance from which it had come earlier.

The plan was falling into place.

The figure smiled, proud of her work in this nothing, nowhere, and now, literally, dead town. She glanced back, thinking of her handiwork and the ease with which she had slipped into each home undetected.

Her mind focused on the task at hand. *Remove the law,* she thought as she had many times on her treks across Europe. It always started this way.

The slender figure began walking silently toward the town of Kortbeke.

Chapter 2:

†

hubschmid's Pub

10:00 PM

The woman lay on the cold ground, her mouth covered in blood. She looked at him with an evil smile then blinked and her eyes suddenly turned yellow. A voice said softly, "You will meet her and her kind, and you will do battle with them."

Davide Hubschmid, owner and operator of Hubschmid's Pub shook his head as he had periodically throughout the day, trying to get rid of the grisly and puzzling image from the previous night's dream that had caused him to lose valuable sleep. He had woken from it in a cold sweat. Trying to shake the foreboding dread that had been with him all day, he ran a hand through his dark hair, glancing at his wristwatch. It read 10:00 PM, one hour before closing up for the night.

It had been a long day tending the small bar in the north end of Kortbeke. It was September and the weather, typically warm until October, was cooler today. The light drizzle outside drew far more business than he was prepared for as many of the locals decided to warm themselves with a pint of Kulmbacher Bier, poured fresh from his large keg behind the bar.

The tall man was ruggedly handsome and, at thirty-five-years-old, hadn't lost any of his youthful good looks. Growing up in the Alps working the family dairy farm had made him strong, and it wasn't until he reached sixteen years old that his father decided to relocate and open a restaurant in the small but thriving town of Kortbeke.

Hubschmid's pub was one of two bars in town. The second, located on the other end of town, was called the Maximilian Inn, but all in Kortbeke simply referred to it as Maximilian's, named after the town's founder, Maximilian Rastorfer. Maximilian Inn was quite a bit larger than Hubschmid's Pub and drew a significantly higher-class clientele, which is exactly how both of its current owners liked it.

Maximilian's owners were the husband-wife duo, Nils and Uma Karlen. Nils, forty-two, married the malicious, power-hungry Uma, a woman with a dark past who was four years younger. Nils ran the bar most nights while Uma pushed her way onto the town counsel in Kortbeke, ensuring that many of its laws and ordinances were reviewed by her and would also need to be approved by her. The couple had been married for fifteen years and had never been able to have children, nor had they wanted to.

As the years ticked by, Uma became more enamored with power in their small town. Sticking her nose in nearly every aspect of the town's business and pushing her agenda forward, her involvement was usually to the detriment of businesses in the north side of town, while heavily favoring businesses on the southside. Better maintenance of roads and buildings in the south end of town, as well as higher-end goods sold at high prices, were just part of her ongoing agenda to push out the working-class citizens from Kortbeke. Between having Mayor Klaus Kessler's ear and enjoying tenure on various committees that pushed her initiatives through, she was thus far succeeding.

Coming from a family of inherited wealth, Uma's grandfather, Jügen Stoller, a land baron in his day, had snatched up as much real estate as possible, quickly selling it at sometimes three times the amount at which he had acquired it, typically strong-arming his way into the many deals. The apple not falling far from the tree, the Karlens had bought out Maximilian's previous owner for far less than the property was worth, by making sure all other offers were squelched before reaching him.

The prices of the drinks went up almost immediately once they took over, as did the rather "snooty" atmosphere. Nils could be found most nights at Maximilian's schmoozing with the bar's clientele. Puffing on his expensive cigars, he would gossip about any number of topics, most of which revolved around what he called "the stain on their town," Hubschmid's Pub.

When one visited Maximilian Inn, one dressed their best while indulging heavily in the bountiful and expensive spirits lining the back wall of the bar. You would be laughed out of the building at Hubschmid's for such attire, but you would be kicked out of Maximilian's if not wearing proper attire.

Most of the patrons of Maximilian's were decent people, but the atmosphere inside the bar had changed such that a sort of "better-than-them" attitude had formed in the establishment. This toxic atmosphere that seemed to permeate the bar was palpable.

Hubschmid's, however, was quite literally, the opposite of such a place. And that was part of its charm. Much smaller than Maximilian's, it offered nearly no street presence other than a door and two windows peering into the quant single room adorned with worn but comfortable wooden tables and chairs. The ten tables and small bar were usually sticky from dried spirits, but the atmosphere inside, with its dark mahogany wood and warm lighting, was usually festive. On many nights, loud singing could be heard from passersby heading home from jobs ranging from meat packers to barbers, seamstresses and small store operators in the relatively small town of Kortbeke.

There were occasional fights that broke out, as with any bar when large quantities of spirits are being consumed, but they were rare occurrences, given how Davide Hubschmid chose to run his establishment. His small but deadly wooden club kept behind the bar had only been used on a few occasions, and those on the receiving end would never forget the cracking sound it made when it smashed against their skulls.

Davide, even in his youth, was an imposing and, at times, intimidating figure. Never one to bully or pick a fight, he held his own and wouldn't back down from a tussle if he was backed into a corner with no other options. His usually calm demeaner, however, diffused most situations inside the bar—yet another reason he was good at running the establishment.

Davide had owned the bar for ten years, inheriting it from his father upon his death. The one-time restaurant was quickly turned into a watering hole for the working-class citizens of Kortbeke. Catering mostly to farmers and small business owners, Davide had no intention of becoming competition for Maximilian's when he transformed the restaurant into a bar, but Nils—and Uma, especially—saw it as an outright declaration of war and instantly began spreading rumors and gossip about those that frequented Hubschmid's, doing everything they could to make David's life and his business hell.

Regardless of the Karlens' attempts to shut down the establishment that catered to the working-class citizens of Kortbeke and drum up controversy where none existed, such as the time they started a rumor that rats had been found near the kegs behind the bar, it remained open and its patrons supported it almost religiously. With its far less expensive beer and liquor and laid-back atmosphere, it was a hit with most of the locals. Offering bare essentials like bread, cheese, pretzels and, if Davide was feeling generous, locally-made jerky for the patrons to soak up the alcohol after a full night of indulging.

Up the street from Hubschmid's, facing the businesses and shops, was St. Raphael's parish, a Catholic church in a Catholic town, and a beloved iconic building regardless of one's faith, with its beautiful architecture and status as one of the first structures erected in Kortbeke when the town was founded one hundred years prior.

The Sonderbund War of 1847 between conservative Catholic cantons and liberal Protestant cantons had little to no effect on the strictly Catholic town of Kortbeke, all going about their business and attending their own preferred Masses, week in, week out. As progressive and growth-oriented as Kortbeke was, most the people remained set in their ways when it came to their religious beliefs, another reason why the town of Granhal was to remain a separate entity while still maintaining relatively friendly relations toward each other.

Those that believed they had to atone for the numerous sins committed inside Hubschmid's did so at reconciliation every Saturday morning, directly following the eight o'clock early Mass at St. Rafael's Parish at the end of the street. Some would say it was God's way of keeping his eye on the rowdy crowds that frequented Hubschmid's every night except Monday when Davide was closed to clean up after the weekend crowds left their mark on the place.

Father Nordin Steffen, a good man and even better priest serving the town of Kortbeke for nearly twenty years, presided over the Mass every morning at six-thirty for those on their way to their daily jobs, along with weekend Masses starting Saturdays with a five o'clock vigil then Sunday mornings at eight and eleven. Fr. Steffen's parish reflected the modest population of Kortbeke, and his only parochial vicar, Fr. Simon Kries, had been called away on this particular weekend to assist Fr. Almen at St. Mary, Mother of God, a significantly larger parish than St. Raphael's five miles away in Salzben.

"Where the hell is Fr. Steffen? He should have been here by now. Hell, he should have been here thirty minutes ago! He's never late for his Sunday evening nightcap and knows how slow things are around here," Davide muttered from behind the bar as he wiped down the smooth, treated wood top. He glanced worriedly at the door leading out to the cold evening streets of Kortbeke.

Ruppert Sprenger, a local man and nearly permanent fixture at Hubschmid's every open night of the week, took another gulp of his golden-brown ale from the large beer stein sitting in front of him at the bar, glanced over to the door and shrugged. "Must have had a lot of customers today," he said with a smirk.

Davide glanced at his longtime friend, for better or worse, and rolled his eyes. Ruppert was the furthest thing from a religious man. Once the thirty-one-year-old's wife of twelve years up and left him four years earlier for another man and took off for Germany, he lost not only his faith, but his two children as well. She had blamed it on his increased drinking after their second child, but he knew in his heart she had been swept off her feet by the strong and financial stable German banker who had been courting her privately while residing in the nearby town of Birkensbüld.

Now, the once handsome man, before years of drinking started to show on his weary face, lived alone right up the street from Hubschmid's in a one-room loft. Below his room, during the day, he worked for the town butcher, Lorin Wirthlin, of Wirthlin's Meats. The job paid for his loft and the copious amounts of alcohol he consumed throughout the weeks, months, and finally, years since his family abandoned him.

Davide and Ruppert had been friends even before the sad turn of events in Ruppert's private life, and Davide knew without his stability and friendship, Ruppert would likely further delve into depression, possibly becoming suicidal judging from several off-handed comments he had made from time to time. Therefore, Davide was there to lend his ear and keep tabs on the pitiful man every night at Hubschmid's, and because of this they had become quite good friends. Davide always sensed there was something more to Ruppert. A spark still shone inside the tired, sad man who drowned his evenings in copious amounts of beer. It just hadn't been brought out yet, dulled further by the loss of his wife and children.

"I think it's about time you call it a night, Ruppert. What are you on? Your fifth pint?" Davide replied, leaning his elbows against the bar top and glancing around at the other patrons. It was relatively busy at ten o'clock on a Sunday night, but with the looming Monday-morning daily grind rearing its ugly head, this wasn't out of the ordinary. A busy bar meant money in the pocket, even though it also meant much of Monday would be spent cleaning up as much as he and his assistant could manage.

"Five pints? That's what I'm at? That's it? Davide, you know as well as I do that I'm good for ten on a good night!" Ruppert answered with the slightest of slurs.

"You call that a good night? I think your liver would have something to say about that," Davide answered dryly.

Shrugging off the slight dig, Ruppert answered, "And that, good sir, is what bread is for. Soaks it all up and makes room for more!" He took another swig, finishing off his fifth pint and pulled out his nearly depleted pack of cigarettes. Pulling one out, he put it in his mouth and looked wearily at Davide.

Sighing, Davide pulled a match out from behind the bar, struck it against the side of the nicked and dinged-up bar top and a flame shot forth. He held it forward so Ruppert could lean into it with his tobacco. After several quick puffs, the cherry on the tip was well lit and Ruppert sucked in the cool nicotine then exhaled away from Davide's face.

"Well, speaking of bread, here. Soak it up," Davide replied, setting down a small round loaf from behind the bar in front of a visibly pleased Ruppert. "Closing in an hour and it'll take that long to get everyone else in here to finish up and get 'em all out the door so I can get some sleep. This weekend has been one sonofabitch, if I must say so myself."

Ruppert began tearing the bread apart while his lit cigarette dangled in his mouth. He glanced up at Davide. "You and Emila fighting again?" he asked, putting a bite of the local bakery's bread into his mouth and nodding at its taste.

Cocking an eyebrow at Ruppert, Davide sighed, replying, "I wouldn't call it fighting. Just a disagreement on my evening hours. You know, serving you sorry lot copious amounts of ale while she's at home with our girl. I get it, I do. It's just, I'm not sure how to remedy it."

"Take it from me, women. You let them and they'll rip your balls off and leave you with fuck-all if you piss them off just right," Ruppert said bitterly, taking another drag then pointing to his empty pint.

Sighing, Davide took the glass and begrudgingly filled it up with Kulmbacher Bier. As the sudsy golden liquid and foam spilled over, Davide grabbed his nearby foam scraper beside the keg and wiped it off perfectly. He set the fresh glass of beer in front of his friend and cocked his eyebrow. "That's it for you tonight, Ruppert. And I do mean, *that's it!*"

Taking a gulp of the ice-cold alcoholic beverage, Ruppert wiped the foam from his top lip and smiled wide. "Thank you, good sir. Best damn bartender in all of Kortbeke! What would us drunks do without you!?" He turned to face the few remaining patrons of Hubschmid's and raised his glass. "Here's to our illustrious bartender, Davide Hubschmid!"

Most of the remaining patrons tiredly lifted their nearly empty glasses in unison. A mumble of thanks and praise wafted through the air. Davide merely grinned, shook his head, and went back to cleaning up behind the bar. He hoped to have things all closed up right at eleven and, if he was lucky, be out the door thirty minutes later heading back home to his wife Emile and daughter Frida.

It had been rough at home the last several months with Emile, his dear wife, sick of his late nights and coming home reeking of beer and cigarette smoke. It was an environment she liked less the older their daughter got. On top of that, and most importantly, was Uma Karlen, owner of Maximilian's on the southside. The bossy, pushy woman had caused Emila and Davide much strife on numerous occasions. His wife wanted nothing to do with the vile woman, yet her husband and Uma owned the only two bars in Kortbeke, so they were unfortunately connected in this way, for better or worse, and had to deal with the same alcohol distributors and competing prices.

Uma insisted their establishment got preferential treatment, due to their larger footprint in Kortbeke, and the spirits they sold were always of a far higher quality than the alcohol found in Hubschmid's. Uma continually did all she could to raise the prices of kegs being sold to Hubschmid's in the hopes that, at some point, the cost would simply be too high to sustain a profitable business and they would be forced to close their doors for good.

Davide had agreed, it wasn't ideal, but this was his business and he wanted to ensure the locals had an alternative to the Maximilian Inn. Which was its own source of contention at the Hubschmid household. The longer both establishments were open, the more it seemed as though Nils and Uma Karlen grew openly hostile toward the Hubschmids, going out of their way to not only avoid looking in their direction when they would meet on the street, but Uma was known to lob insults their way as well. Primarily at Emila and her long, flowing red hair.

"Looks like I'll need to stock up on some more ginger beer for the bar!" was one such comment Emila had heard in passing, along with, "What's this town coming to, letting someone of filthy Irish descent in here? Next thing you know, the coloreds will want to move in and take over this town we've done much to build up with our hard-earned wealth!"

Emila had gone so far as to attempt to have an actual discussion with Uma, but it fell on deaf ears. Uma refused to speak with her, only interacting with Davide when absolutely necessary, and even then, it was single words and glares that got the point across as to where people like the Hubschmids fell in the hierarchy of the town.

Davide noticed this hadn't gone unnoticed by the local town chief of police, Gabriel Lambert. Lambert kept a watchful eye on his town since being elected five years ago. He often frequented Hubschmid's Pub after a long day on the job, finding the conversation there engaging and down-to-earth, even if it was simple chitchat about the current weather and whose cattle were producing the most milk that season. He had no interest talking of wealth, power over others that were *lesser*, and hatred for those of other ethnicities and skin colors over at Maximilian's.

Mayor Kessler, however, enjoyed drinking at the Maximilian Inn with its lush and elegant interior and top-shelf spirits lining the back wall, even if topics of discussion always seemed to be hostile or leaning that way. Joking was always done at others' expense and lobbed at those considered poor or weak. The relationship between police officer and the mayor of Kortbeke was, at times, icy, but they seemed to make it work as best they could, avoiding each other when possible and interacting on mainly surface level topics. Especially ones that the Karlens didn't need to be a part of.

Sunday nights were typically slow in Kortbeke, with the work week starting bright and early the next morning and many farmers up at the crack of dawn to tend to their farming. Which is why Davide was concerned that Fr. Steffen hadn't shown up for a nightcap. "Why am I concerned about Steffen?" Davide muttered aloud while he wiped dry several pint glasses he had just washed.

Ruppert took another large gulp of his beer and set the glass down, glancing at the door then shaking his head. "No clue. The guy is a man of God. Maybe he's doing, I don't know? God stuff? It's Sunday, Davide."

Smirking at Ruppert's attempt at humor through the haze of alcohol, Davide placed the clean glasses back with the rest of his arsenal of glassware along the back wall behind the bar.

Running his hands through his hair, Davide nodded. "Every Sunday night. Without exception, he's here for a weekend-capping beer to shoot the shit with me. You see him too. But not tonight, though he was leading Mass today. He's a man of ritual and when that ritual is changed, I take notice."

Through the fog of alcohol, Ruppert simply nodded his understanding at his friend's puzzlement over the absent priest.

Davide came from behind the bar, inspecting everyone's glasses and collecting the empties. He had exactly one employee, the young and spirited Nina Gesser, who was off tonight as well as every Sunday. Another reason his bar saw a lot of the same men, night after night, the twenty-four-year-old blond woman was easily one of the prettiest girls in all of Kortbeke, but she never acted as such. In fact, she had always thought of herself as a bit of a tomboy. However, she did realize her looks could be used to her advantage which is why a bar maiden job at a pub was perfect work for her.

The tips were great, made even better by the light flirting she had mastered with the patrons, while never giving the wrong impression that she would consider going home with one of them. An only child, she lived with her aging and quite poor parents Richard and Lucie Gesser several blocks south. Sunday, however, was her night off. A stipulation agreed upon by her conservative parents who had initially frowned upon their attractive daughter working at an establishment that catered to drunken, and at times, horny men.

She knew her employment at Hubschmid's was frowned upon in Kortbeke by many of the woman in town, but her parents had run into financial trouble years ago after several bad investments left them not only broke but with failing health, and they were forced to rely on their daughter for most of the income. Davide took her under his wing at Hubschmid's and she quicky proved to be a fantastic barmaid, going above and beyond keeping the place clean and moods up.

As feisty as Nina was, she cared little for what those around her thought of her and focused more on her parents and her boyfriend. Her goal was to someday be out on her own, away from the relatively small town of Kortbeke. Davide knew this well and did his best to pay her what she was worth, and then some. He hoped she would indeed someday be on her own, away from the prying and jealous eyes of women and the lustful eyes of men in town.

Sunday was the Lord's Day and thus, Nina and her parents went to morning Mass then spent the rest of the day at home. While Davide would have certainly liked help on Sundays, having her every other night continued to bring in numerous patrons hoping to have a go with her.

She was always friendly, with a big smile across her beautiful face, but she promised her parents that the man who would eventually sweep her off her feet wouldn't be someone she had met at Hubschmid's Pub, or any other bar, for that matter. She promised this, of course, with her crossed fingers hidden behind her back, thinking of her love on the other side of town begrudgingly working behind the bar at Maximilian's.

"Damnit all to hell," Davide said, back behind the bar, tossing his wet towel onto the bartop. "I wish Nina was here. I'd run down to check on old Fr. Steffen myself. He was complaining earlier about his old ankle injury flaring up again. He should be using a cane, stubborn old bastard. Regardless, it's got me a bit concerned he may have had an accident because that old timer is never, ever late."

Ruppert nodded as he extinguished the remainder of his cigarette into the ashtray sitting in front of him then lifted his beer glass to take another swig of beer. "Yeah, I get it. Hey, I can watch the place if you want to head down to the parish."

Davide laughed out loud at this suggestion. "You must be joking. I'd come back and you would likely be behind the bar helping yourself to more of my beer."

"Payment for services rendered," Ruppert shot back, setting his empty pint glass down on the wet coaster in front of him. He burped then said with a grin, "Check, please."

Davide smirked as Ruppert pulled out his francs to pay his tab. "The butcher shop, and more importantly, Lorin, the boss man, beckons me in the early morning hours so you, good sir, are now going to be rid of me."

Once more, Davide glanced at his watch then to his front door. It was close to closing time. And still no Fr. Steffen. "Hey, Ruppert. Tell you what, wait up a bit. I'm closing up shop early. What say you and I take a quick stroll down to St. Rafael's, if you've got a few minutes?"

Tilting his head and rubbing his hand across his whiskered chin, Ruppert responded, "Down to the church? Shit, man, this has really got your knickers in a knot. What about Fr. Kries? Surely, he can help the old priest out with his bad ankle. Hell, that's one of the reasons he was hired in the first place. To replace Fr. Steffen when he retired."

Davide glared at Ruppert, as if to say, Are you coming or not?

But Ruppert was in no hurry to leave the bar, it seemed, and continued talking. "Speaking of Kries, I gotta say, something about him has always struck me as slightly off. I mean, he's friendly, even to a drunk like me, but he's hiding something, I just can't figure it out. His eyes, maybe, they remind me of, well, they remind me of me. Damaged," he finished softly with a slightly slurred tone.

Davide knew what Ruppert was saying. Fr. Kries was a good man, wise beyond his young years. But he always seemed to be holding something back. Davide could never put his finger on it, exactly, and had always chalked it up to the life of a priest and the many difficulties it presented to a young man.

The parochial vicar, however, was out of town at the moment and not wanting to continue this back-and-forth with his inebriated friend, Davide waved him off then clapped his hands loudly several times. Clearing his throat, he shouted to the few remaining patrons of Hubschmid's Pub, "Closing up early! Everyone, time to go!"

Grumbles and mumbles of disappointment echoed throughout the bar as beer glasses were emptied and hastily slammed back down onto their tables. The ten random Sunday night drinkers got up and slowly shuffled off, out into the chilly and still drizzling night, off to their nearby houses on the northside. The old wooden door closed behind them until only Davide and Ruppert were left.

"Well, it's only 10:45. Fifteen minutes of lost business. Want me to help you clean up?" Ruppert mumbled, starting to grow weary with the numerous pints of beer sitting heavily in his stomach, along with the bread he had cleared from the plate.

"No, I don't want you dropping any of my glasses. I don't want to have to clean up broken glass on top of spilled beer when I get back," Davide answered, making his way out from behind the bar, looking around his establishment now empty of patrons.

"Fair enough. Lead the way, I suppose," Ruppert said, standing to his feet slowly.

Normally, Davide would have done a quick check on his friend Steffen by himself but tonight, he felt having someone with him might be for the best. Even if it was the town drunk. Once more, he thought back to the bad dream he had awaked from that morning. It had haunted him most of the day as he went about his routine.

In it, he had found himself walking through a town he had never been to before in the dead of night. In the town, horrible things had apparently just happened. Murder by gunshot. A thick fog surrounded the old, depressing town near a large foreboding mountain as people came out of their homes, seeing the carnage and screaming at the grisly sight.

One of the people that lay bleeding on the street was a hideously ugly woman, shot in the stomach and bleeding out. Yet she seemed to be smiling even as she lay dying in front of a tiny house. As her lifeblood pumped out, she had looked at Davide and uttered, "Don't bother sending for the priest, I killed him." She laughed and coughed up a mouthful of blood.

Then she reached up and grabbed hold of Davide's throat, pulling him down to her waiting, bloody lips. She opened her mouth revealing a row of sharp, pointed fangs. Her eyes had turned bright yellow, filled with evil. A long, wet tongue slipped out of her open mouth, running over his face, covering it with fresh blood.

He had awakened in a cold sweat, lying beside his sleeping wife. He kept the dream to himself; it was too horrific and too real to share. At his age, bad dreams rarely, if ever, happened anymore. But this one felt so *real*. The maniacal laugh. It was a cackle. A mockery and a threat followed by another voice, this one gentle, *You will meet her and her kind, and you will do battle with them.*

Thinking of the dream and replaying it in his head again, Davide made haste toward the front door to his pub with Ruppert following close behind.

"Is there a reason you're taking your ass beater with you?" Ruppert said, looking down at the wooden club Davide had retrieved from behind the bar before exiting.

✝

Chapter 3

Desecration at St. Raphael's Parish

9:45 PM

Fr. Steffen glanced at his watch. It was nearing 10:00 PM. *I'm running late. Davide will wonder where I am.* Steffen wasn't a fast man. Not anymore, at least, since he had broken his ankle several years earlier in a mishap that could have been avoided. But at his age, following the accident, he was unable to move around nearly as well and his weight had increased some, causing him to be more prone to accidents.

Before the injury, he had been wanting to help out with some of the cleaning duties around the parish as his caretaker was himself getting older. Oskar Bryner had been a good and loyal caretaker for the parish for nearly as long as Fr. Steffen himself had been a priest in Kortbeke, twenty years. Steffen himself had hired him on.

When Oskar began to show signs of arthritis, Fr. Steffen decided to help his friend out by taking over stained-glass window washing, a task he would later regret attempting. As he wiped away the dust from baby Jesus's innocent body displayed on the beautiful glass, the rickety old ladder he was using gave out from under his weight and he fell to the hard floor below, instantly breaking his ankle.

Shortly after the incident, during the long and painful healing process, he realized he needed a parochial vicar to help him out with the many Masses he led each week. Soon, a new and much younger priest, Fr. Simon Kries, was hired from out of town to help lead the church. Kries had numerous other obligations in other towns nearby, so his time was limited, but in the three-plus years since he had been hired, the stress of leading a town spiritually that had solely rested on his shoulders was now lightened enough to tend to parish day-to-day life much better.

Fr. Simon Kries was a good man as well as an attractive one, with dark, well-groomed hair combed back over his head and a radiant smile to go along with his tall physique. Because of his youthful good looks, he had to squelch the sometimes flirtatious advances of some of the more forward women in the parish. His history was rather scattershot and vague, but he had gone through seminary and was ordained in Austria and had checked out. St. Raphael Parish was his favorite parish to preside over Mass. He liked the people and, most importantly, the relatively drama-free small-town life that Kortbeke offered.

Tonight, on this rather chilly September Sunday evening, Fr. Kries was out of town presiding over Masses in the town of Salzben a few miles away. He enjoyed travelling to and from Salzben to Kortbeke, choosing his bicycle as the primary means of transportation during the warmer weather months. If weather wasn't cooperating, he would walk. A brisk walk would get him there in roughly two hours. And in the winter, when it was snowy, he found one of the locals in town to give him a carriage ride. When he was called away to St. Mary's, he typically wouldn't return until the following Monday morning, staying in a small room near the parish in Salzben.

The townspeople of Kortbeke liked the young man. All, that is, accept Nils and Uma Karlen. His homilies tended to speak a bit too much about the need to help out those less fortunate and the feeding of the poor and hungry, which he described as "the meek inheriting the earth." The Karlens considered these acts of kindness as giving handouts to those choosing to be unproductive citizens, mooching off the backs of the hard workers of the world, not caring that their generationally inherited wealth was similar to those they openly mocked and all but barred from Maximilian's. Not that the Karlens attended Mass, ever. They both found it to be a "boring waste of time" and a "money-grabbing scheme."

This weekend, Fr. Steffen wished his parochial vicar wouldn't have been called away on church business as his ankle was giving him grief. The sudden bout of cooler weather brought on an achiness that made it difficult to navigate around his parish while presiding over all weekend Masses. The townspeople would hang around after Mass to chitchat with each other and usually commend him on his homily of the day, thus keeping him on his feet longer than he would like.

Now, the Sunday Masses had ended and the day was officially over. It was time for his pint at Hubschmid's. Oskar had gone home early with a bit of a cold, not wanting to infect the elderly Fr. Steffen.

Fr. Steffen had happily accepted his early departure and would see to it that final shutdown and tidying up would be taken care of himself, something he hadn't been looking forward to with his weary body and throbbing ankle. Oskar could always tell when Steffen was uncomfortable by the way his typically warm, jovial smile became thin and forced. But his head cold wasn't improving and would only get worse the more physical labor he performed. A long night in bed after a tall hot toddy of Irish Whisky, honey, and touch of lemon would do the trick.

St. Rafael's was a parish of fifteen-hundred-square feet that held two rows of wooden pews, twenty per row, with a thirty-five-foot cathedral ceiling lined with wooden beams. The altar itself was a large marble slab that had been used since the church opened its doors one hundred years prior. Above the altar hung a large wooden cross with a crucified Christ, his head tilted to the side and eyes open, looking compassionately down at his followers. The stained-glass windows were of equal if slightly smaller-scaled beauty. Lining each wall were the stations of the cross, representing Christ's Passion.

The tabernacle stood directly behind the altar in close proximity to the priests that would consecrate the Eucharist at each Mass. Fr. Steffen and Fr. Kries's sacristy was located off to the left-hand side of the entrance of the church and was where both men prepared themselves for Mass. The candles were lit, several of which he blew out after setting up the altar for Mass the following morning. The building still needed to be swept after the numerous parishioners had occupied it, especially with the on-and-off drizzle occurring this particular Sunday.

Fr. Steffen knew this added task would squelch any attempt at a nightcap at Hubschmid's Pub. But not sweeping would cause even more work in the early morning hours before Mass the following morning at six-thirty. He simply didn't have an extra thirty minutes in the morning to spare without Fr. Kries on hand to help out. He wouldn't return from Salzben until mid-morning at the earliest.

Fr. Steffen carefully swept the floors between every pew, where dirt from so many shoes was scattered about. While the streets in Kortbeke were relatively clean and well maintained, on bad weather days, dirt was inevitably drug into the parish.

As he swept, Fr. Steffen recalled the amendment brought to the town council regarding upkeep on their roads. Only one had dissented to the amendment, and it was no surprise to Fr. Steffen who that person was: Uma Karlen, the president. She had argued that the money could better be spent in the upkeep of buildings around town. Businesses that couldn't afford the financial burden would have had their doors shuttered if her idea had seen the light of day. It was voted down swiftly, something Fr. Steffen knew Uma wouldn't soon forget. Because of her role as president of the counsel, she assumed that her say was final, but many of her ideas, all of which benefitted her and her husband in some way, were either squelched or heavily amended.

Fr. Steffen tried to push Uma and Nils out of his mind. He was a priest and it was his duty to love the community, both the good and the bad. They, however, seemed to be a stain on an otherwise good town and did their best to pit the locals against each other. They were fiercely nationalistic and hated outsiders, both inside Kortbeke and in all of Switzerland as well, for no good reason other than that was simply how they were. Anyone and everyone seemed to be an immediate threat to their comfortable lifestyle, no matter how insignificant the individual might be. One such person was his parochial vicar, Fr. Kries from Austria. He was an *outsider* to them, and his homilies, especially, of love and acceptance for neighbor and fellow man, had hit a sour note to the always sour Uma.

He was nearly finished sweeping. Glancing at his watch, he saw his opportunity for that beer at Hubschmid's was closing. It was 10:35 PM, and by the time he limped to the pub on his bum ankle, it would surely be 11:00 PM. He knew Davide Hubschmid would happily let him in and have a beer with him, even past closing time, but Davide had a wife and child to get home to. He didn't want to be a burden, something he felt more and more as the years continued to stack up behind him and his health continued to deteriorate.

Glancing up at the large cross hanging over the altar, Fr. Steffen mumbled, "Forgive me, my Lord, for my foul mouth, but, *shit*." He smiled up at Jesus hanging on the cross, sure that the good Lord up in heaven was smiling down on his servant that had earned the ugly word he had just muttered.

"I really should go see the good doctor about this ankle. I could use a higher prescription of meds with the pain of winter just around the corner," Fr. Steffen muttered to himself. A conversation he wished he was having with Davide.

He dumped the dustpan into the trash can, then glanced once more at his watch and shook his head sadly.

Suddenly, he heard a noise that seemed to come from near the altar, like something had dropped to the floor. He glanced up but it was hard to see with his declining eyesight and only a few remaining candles lit.

Did my Roman sacramentary atop the altar fall?

Continuing to stare up toward the altar nearly shrouded in darkness, his curiosity quickly turned to fear when he heard a low, almost undiscernible snarl followed by a dark shape moving quickly in the darkness behind the altar. A chill went through his large body as his eyes nervously shifted back and forth, trying to see what made the noise.

Slowly, Fr. Steffen made his way down the center walkway toward the altar. His peaceful and, more importantly, *holy* church suddenly feeling ominous and foreboding. He called out again, "Hello? Is someone up there?" *What if an animal got in here? A stray cat, maybe? Surely not a rat.*

Still wearing his black cassock, Fr. Steffen didn't have a crucifix on him, just his trusty old rosary he had carried every day since his younger years, which he pulled out of his side pocket. "A priest's best weapon of defense against Satan and his minions," Fr. Steffen would sometimes tell his congregation before concluding Mass. "Pray your rosary!"

The closer he got, the more he saw of the altar. In front of it, the large sacramentary which he read out of at every Mass was opened and laying upside down.

Behind the altar, something moved. A figure, shrouded in darkness. "Who's there? What is the meaning of this?"

Fr. Steffen's golden chalice sailed out of the darkness, clanging to the floor in front of him. He looked down at the cup that had held the consecrated blood of his Lord and Savior countless times, now nearly flattened, looking as if its sides had been pushed together then twisted. He desperately wanted to bend down and pick up the chalice he held near and dear to his heart, but something was clearly wrong, and his ankle simply wasn't up to a task that may require quick movements, depending on what was behind the altar in the darkness.

Looking up in fear and anger, Fr. Steffen shouted out, "Show yourself! You have defiled the altar in the house of God! How dare you perpetrate such blasphemy!" His hand holding the rosary was shaking; he had to clench it tightly so it wouldn't spill from his hand. "Hail Mary, the Lord is with thee. Blessed art thou among women, and blessed is the fruit of thy womb, Jesus. Holy Mary, Mother of God, pray for us now, and at the hour of our death," he whispered.

Something easily leapt up in the air and on top of the altar, and instantly, Fr. Steffen assumed it was a woman, judging by her legs that were visible in the dimly lit church. The rest of her body still remained shrouded in darkness as her bare feet stepped forward until she was on the edge of the altar, facing him.

His body shook with fright at what appeared to be something utterly evil and supernatural. He made his way forward, rosary gripped tightly. His morbid curiosity was taking over his sense of safety, and something else. He was strangely drawn to whatever was atop the altar.

Several steps more and he could clearly see the shape on the altar. Not just a woman, but one completely devoid of clothing with long, flowing, silky-blond hair that bordered on white. Perfectly smooth, unblemished, fair skin. Large, firm breasts and her pubic region exposed as if she never had worn an article of clothing in her life.

She's flaunting her nudity! Proud of it!

He pried his eyes off of the strange woman's almost supernatural beauty. Shaking his head he stuttered, "You, get down from the altar of our Lord at once!"

"You mean, *your* lord. Not mine. My lord rests and waits for me to do his bidding. Now, what was it you said? Pray for me at the hour of my death? Very well, may the almighty god of this world and his faithful servant see to it that this man meets his end." She paused, then added, "Imminently. *Amen.*"

She leapt down from the altar and in several graceful steps was in front of Fr. Steffen. He could now easily make out her facial features and her beauty was even more evident up close. His fear of her was quickly replaced with lust and arousal. Her lips were full and red, her eyes seemed to change color, from yellow to blue and back again, when she blinked. As if she were able to change them at will.

Another short step and she was now directly in front of his face, breathing on him. Her breath was alluring and hot and, while he had never experienced it, he imagined it smelled like sex. She watched the old priest intently, seeing the arousal mixed with fear in his eyes. Slowly, her tongue worked its way out of her mouth and licked the top of her lip, wetting it before sliding back into her just slightly opened mouth.

"Tell me where the other priest is, the young one. The *handsome* one," her cool, calculated voice said in an almost whisper.

"Huh? What? Who?" Fr. Steffen blurted out.

"I don't believe I stuttered. Did I? Or do you take me for a fool? Are you mocking me?" she shot back, her tone filled with contempt and now anger.

Fr. Steffen tried to avert his eyes from her gaze and realized he was looking at her nakedness. He closed his eyes tight and attempted to take a step back, then felt the woman's hand on his face, pushing him, causing him to instantly fall backward on his bad ankle. A crack reverberated through his foot as his ankle snapped under the heavy weight of his body crashing to the ground.

He cried out in pain and immediate shock. His head throbbed as it made contact with the painfully hard solid wood flooring beneath him. Instantly, he felt blood bubble up in his mouth and knew he had bitten into his tongue at his hard landing. He spit onto the floor beside him and realized he didn't just bite into his tongue, he had bitten the tip of his tongue completely off as a small chunk fell from his mouth, covered in his blood on the floor beside him.

"Please," he tried to say but all that came out was a garbled mess of sounds.

Smelling his blood, the woman walked over top of him, her legs on either side of his body.

"Once more, where's the priest? The young one?" She stared down at him, her womanhood hovering above him mockingly.

"Fr. Kries…he is not here. He…" Fr. Steffen paused; he would give out no more information to this wicked woman.

"Where is he, you worthless pig? I have travelled far in my quest to find him, and my master waits for me to fulfill my task!" she said, this time much louder and angrier.

Finding his courage, Fr. Steffen spit a mouthful of blood out, looked her in the eye and shook his head. Then, through blood once more filling his mouth, he uttered, "Our Father, who art in heaven," while still grasping his rosary.

The woman shook her head at hearing the Lord's Prayer recited. She opened her mouth and instead of a human voice, a low snarl escaped.

A wolf! That sounded like…a wolf! Fr. Steffen thought, once more peering up at his assailant.

"Very well," she said snidely. Her naked body was beginning to change. No longer an arousing, sexually-charged young woman, she began growing larger as hair sprouted rapidly out of her body. Fr. Steffen's eyes widened while blood oozed from his opened mouth, watching her change before his eyes. He realized instantly it wasn't hair but fur, white fur, that was spreading across her body, covering it completely.

Arms extended while bones popped and cracked. The front of her face seemed to cave into itself then instantly extend outward, revealing a large snout. Human teeth were pushed out of the way, making way for large, carnivorous fangs. Human ears pushed upward and became pointed at their tips. Her silky-blond hair had pulled back into her scalp and what was left had changed to white, blending in with the rest of the fur now covering her entire body.

Now fully changed from the woman, the creature bent down and wrapped its large hands around the priest's neck. As it did, large claws pushed out of the tips of the fingers, sinking into his skin.

"Hallowed be thy name, thy kingdom come, thy will be done..." he uttered through a mouthful of blood.

Squeezing tightly on the priest's throat, the creature pushed its claws in further, grabbing hold of muscle tissue as the dying Fr. Steffen tried to cry out. In one quick yank with both of its claws firmly inserted into the priest's neck, it ripped his entire neck open, lunged forward and sunk its fangs into the exposed throat until his head was completely severed.

Once finished feasting, it stood up on hind legs atop large, thick paws with claws of their own. It peered down at the dead man on the ground whose throat was now almost entirely missing while blood gushed from the large, open wound. Blood dripping from sharp teeth and yellow eyes filled with rage, it looked toward the door where it had quietly slipped in earlier while the old man had been busy. The creature was stealthy and could make herself almost invisible and utterly silent, something she had learned the last several years roaming the forests and small villages in Eastern Europe, stalking various prey.

In a final act of desecration, the wolf-being scooped up the headless, dead priest's body and threw it up onto the altar where it landed with a thud, spraying blood across the white sheet that blanketed the marble slab. The beast then picked up what remained of the priest's head, throwing it against the altar. It smashed against the front of the stone, fell to the ground, and rolled several feet before coming to a stop.

She turned and walked to the entrance. One she reached the front she looked up at an old wooden crucifix with a tarnished gray Christ figure perched atop it hanging above the door. Reaching her large, clawed hand up she swatted it easily off the wall, landing it in one of the two large holy water fonts located on either side of the entrance.

Satisfied at what she had accomplished in her massive wolf form, she opened the door as bones began crunching and shifting inside her body as it shrunk down to the size of a smaller, white, fur-covered wolf. Now on all fours, she slipped out the cracked door into the darkened night. Light rain fell as it kept to the shadows on the cold Sunday night.

No one was outside except for two people all the way down on the end of the street. With its yellow eyes, she peered at them walking in the direction of the church. Her incredible vision at night instantly saw the wooden club the larger of the two men was carrying.

She dashed off silently through a side alley and off the main road, heading south toward the other side of town. Her work in Kortbeke had only just begun.

Chapter 4

✝

What the Hell
Did This?

11:15 PM

The light drizzle on top of the chilly wind sweeping through Kortbeke added to the misery of walking any significant distance. For most the year, the town and mountains surrounding it were beautiful. Lush trees climbed the Swiss Alps and mild, pleasant weather graced the spring and summer months. In the fall, however, the weather turned cold, and this Sunday in September was no exception.

Davide and Ruppert put on their jackets and left the bar, passing Wirthlin's Meats and Ruppert's loft on the opposite side of the street several buildings up. Ruppert had looked wearily at the shop, wishing he was inside his tiny loft, however depressing it was. *At least I wouldn't have to be out in this lousy weather, even if I have to step inside that damned church building,* he thought.

They continued down the street, both keeping their jackets pulled up over the bottom half of their faces in an attempt to block out the wind that blew tiny, sharp rain drops against their cold bodies.

Glancing up through the drizzle, Davide elbowed Ruppert, pointing to the church. "I could have sworn I just saw something move in the shadows beside the church. Did you see anything?"

Squinting through beer-fueled eyes, Ruppert replied, "You're seeing things, Davide. Nothing out there but miserable, dreary rain to end the weekend and usher in the Monday morning doldrums."

Davide continued to stare into the rain at the approaching church. Whatever movement he saw was gone now. *Maybe Ruppert is right. My eyes are playing tricks on me.*

"Sonofabitch, this is some miserable weather!" Ruppert said as the effects of the large consumption of alcohol couldn't shield him completely from the cold and rain.

"Come on, we're almost there," Davide replied through gritted teeth, shaking off the notion that he had seen something move a second ago.

"You know, Fr. Steffen is older, and his ankle is fucked. Maybe he just didn't want to walk down in this shit," Ruppert said with more than a hint of agitation now that he was exposed to the poor weather instead of either sitting in the bar or, better yet, back in his small loft above Wirthlin's Meats.

"Maybe," was the only reply from Davide as they neared the church.

Ruppert shook his head, seeing he wasn't going to get any sympathy from his friend. "You really like that old timer, don't you?" Ruppert said, glancing over at Davide.

"I most certainly do. He's done much for this town and would literally give his life for his congregation. He's helped me through some rough patches myself. He's been there for me and now as his health is diminishing, I want to be there for him. Feels like not only the Christian thing to do, but the *right* thing to do," Davide answered.

Ruppert continued watching his friend as they walked, then looked down at the ground, feeling a bit ashamed of himself suddenly. For the life he had led and continued to lead ever since his wife had left him, taking the kids along with her. He missed them every day, which is why alcohol was consumed as frequently as it was. To drown out the pain and sorrow he felt and the aching in his heart for what he once had.

He thought often about what it would be like to get his hands on the man that stole his wife and children from him, Andres Stirner. He had no way of tracking them down any longer and hoped that one day, when his boys were old enough, they would come back to Kortbeke to see their old man again.

What kind of God allows something that unjust and unfair to happen to someone? Where is the justice? I'm a loser in a one-room loft above a butcher shop, of all places.

Ruppert rarely, if ever, set foot inside St. Rafael's Parish in the center of town. He had sworn off God, and even the thought of setting foot inside felt wrong, like a cop-out in his ongoing feud with God. If he couldn't make his cheating wife and that slimy bastard Stirner pay, then God would have to suffice.

Davide glanced over at Ruppert deep in thought, his eyes on the wet, smoothed over cobblestone street. He was well aware of Ruppert's disdain for the church in all of its various forms because of what had happened to him four years prior. Even before the split, he had never been much for organized religion, choosing to make his own way through life.

Davide had surmised that Ruppert had been relatively aimless while married, likely one of the reasons Chloé had up and left him after a short affair with the German gentleman. Once that happened, though, Davide saw Ruppert taking a further downward spiral with his drinking and felt partially responsible for it as Hubschmid's was his primary source of indulgence. However, if not for Hubschmid's, Ruppert would simply sit alone in his loft and drink himself into an early grave. At least inside Hubschmid's, Davide could keep an eye on his buddy and make sure he got home safely up the street.

"Ready to take a peek inside?" Davide asked, sensing what his friend was thinking by the expression on his face.

"Oh, what the hell. I agreed to come down here with you so let's get this over with. I'm sure old man Steffen is probably fast asleep somewhere in there, probably on one of the pews," Ruppert tried to joke.

Davide turned the knob and pushed the heavy, unlocked door open. It creaked as it opened, something Davide was used to over the years as the church was one hundred years old and showing its age.

He stepped inside and looked around the dark building. The few remaining candles still lit cast shadows over the entire interior of the chapel. Ruppert entered behind him, almost bumping into him as Davide stopped, staring at the center aisle between the two rows of pews.

"What? What is it, Davide?" Ruppert asked.

Pointing, Davide responded with a whisper, "Up there, close to the altar, on the floor."

Rupert peered up at the altar area. "Does Steffen put shit, I mean, stuff on the altar other than his cup and book and whatever else is up there? Looks like something big is up there. Can't tell for sure." Also whispering, he then added, "Why are we whispering?"

Davide looked at Ruppert, his facial expression telling the quickly sobering man all he needed to know. Something was very much, *not right* at St. Rafael's Parish.

They both moved forward toward the darkened altar until coming to a stop in front of something wet on the floor. "Oh shit, is that blood?" Ruppert asked, looking down at the mess in front of them.

Davide bent down to inspect it. A chill went through him. "That's blood. We need to check the altar."

"Steffen! You in here?" Ruppert called out.

"Shh, quiet! We may not be alone!" Davide whispered loudly.

Falling silent at the reprimand, Ruppert waited for Davide to move forward.

"Try not to step in this," Davide said, walking around the blood toward the altar, following its splattered trail. Several feet away, he froze. "We need to get Gabriel Lambert over here, now."

"Holy shit, Davide! Is that—" Ruppert said, standing beside him, peering at the bloody, ravaged head on the floor and the body spilled over much of the altar.

Davide, careful not to touch the headless body laying atop the altar, moved closer to inspect it.

Aghast at the grisly sight in front of them, Ruppert exclaimed, "His head and neck look like they were gnawed through! His foot is snapped completely sideways! Oh Lord, what the hell happened here!?"

"Something killed our priest, and whatever it was crept in the shadows outside the church. I knew I saw something. We need to get to the police station. Don't step in the blood, Ruppert!" Davide cautioned again, not taking his eyes off the murdered priest.

"Y-yeah. Okay," Ruppert answered, backing up carefully.

Davide, pulling his eyes from his dead friend, turned to follow Ruppert who had now stopped near the blood.

"Davide, look here!" Ruppert said, pointing at a bit of the priest's blood splatter near a pew, away from the majority of the carnage.

Kneeling down, Davide inspected the blood. In it, he saw what could only be described as a wolf's paw print.

"It looks like a wolf's paw but it's twice the size," Ruppert observed.

Clenching his club so tightly his hand was beginning to throb, Davide stood to his feet, his teeth gritting as he thought back to what he saw. *It was a wolf in the shadows. I know it was a wolf.*

Ruppert, now completely sober, quickly moved to the entrance of the church, wanting to get out of the building as fast as possible.

The two men quickly walked outside and stopped, collecting themselves. "What the bloody hell is going on here, Davide? What in the hell *did* that?" Ruppert said, wiping his eyes, suddenly realizing he was crying at the absolute evil desecration he had just seen.

Davide breathed heavily, appalled and enraged at what he had witnessed inside the church. The ferocity of the murder was nearly too much for him to take in. "I don't know, Ruppert, I just don't know what could have done this, wolves are dangerous for sure, but this brutality is something on a whole other level. And I sure as hell don't know how this town will take to hearing one of its own, and a man of the cloth, no less, was brutally slain inside a building that has always been a safe place of refuge. This town has never experienced anything like this."

"So? Police station?" Ruppert said, shielding his face from the rain standing in front of the parish.

"I need to get back home and let my wife know what's going on. I don't want her to venture out looking for me if I don't show up. Ruppert, you need to let Chief Lambert know he has to get down to St. Raphael's immediately," Davide said urgently.

"Davide, I reek of alcohol. He's just as likely to throw my ass in jail for disturbing the peace at this time of night with that crazy story!" Ruppert replied shakily.

Looking Ruppert in the eyes, Davide answered, "You tell Lambert and Erni to get their asses down here. There's been a murder and the culprit is still on the loose. Tell him I sent you, now go! I'll meet you back here at the church in a few. Take this." Davide handed his club over to Ruppert.

Nodding grimly, Ruppert took the club, pulled his coat up over his cold face and hurried away from the church toward the Kortbeke police station.

Watching him until he disappeared into the shadows, Davide thought back to the dream he'd had in the early Sunday morning hours. Of the woman peering up at him, her eyes filled with hate. Shaking it off, he turned to quickly make his way back home to his sure-to-be waiting wife. He glanced down at his watch. 11:30 PM. This was going to be one long night. Davide sighed as he headed home.

His house sat on a side street past his pub, near the edge of town on the far north side. He liked the privacy this location offered him. Few people lived nearby, though his view of the beautiful Swiss Alps was incredible. His walk to work usually took ten minutes, but tonight he would do his best to make it quicker. Ruppert needed him for backup once he dragged what was sure to be an angry and tired Police Chief Lambert out of bed and down to St. Rafael's.

Davide jogged down the street, past his darkened pub. *So much for cleaning up in there.* He thought of his wife and how she would likely take this news. Of his innocent little girl Frida, sound asleep. He would try to keep the grim news of Fr. Steffen's grisly murder from her young ears. However, if his thinking was correct, there was something lurking in or around this small town. Something on all fours that had the wherewithal to open church doors, slip in unannounced, rip an old man's throat clean out then fling his body up on the altar. All of which sounded premeditated and nothing a feral animal could or would even be capable of doing.

He wondered why it hadn't continued to eat the dead man, and how his body got from the ground up to the altar. *It couldn't have been a wolf! But I know what I saw, dammit! And the head, it looked like it was thrown and smashed against the front of the altar after being gnawed off!*

After his near sprint through the damp and darkened streets, Davide reached his home. He was barely winded after the run, thankful he was still in good shape at his age. His adrenaline was on overdrive, his mind racing.

A small trail of smoke wafted up from the chimney. *She's waiting for me.* He paused at his door, catching his breath then looking around at his surroundings. All was quiet, and nothing in the shadows moved as he had seen back at the church. Seeing nothing out of the ordinary, he turned and entered into his small house.

Once inside, he quickly closed the door behind him and latched it. Breathing heavily, he rested his forehead against the door to collect his thoughts before…

"Davide? Are you alright?" a voice from the living room spoke out.

Turning, he saw his lovely wife sitting in her thin, black, low-cut nightgown, waiting up for him as she usually did, especially on Sunday nights when she knew he didn't have to work early the next morning. They had been married long enough that the Sunday-night sex had become a pleasurable habit. It was Davide's stress wind-down that often built up throughout the week.

Tonight, she could tell immediately from his face and how he breathed heavily things were different. As if he had run home instead of the leisurely stroll after Fr. Steffen's Sunday night beer, regardless of good or bad weather.

Emila, whose hair was long, red and curly, was trim and almost petite, even after having their child. Light freckles dotted her cheeks and, with her fair skin, she looked even more beautiful at the age of thirty than she had in her early twenties. Likely from the love she had for her family and her deep, caring nature.

She instantly stood to her feet, suddenly feeling slightly awkward in her alluring attire chosen for tonight's sexual escapade once Frida had been tucked in for the night and she had gotten a bath in preparation for Davide to arrive home.

Rushing over to her husband, she placed her soft hands on his grizzled, handsome face, looking him in the eyes, her green piercing eyes searching his. His hair was a mess from the wind and rain, and he felt cold.

Davide shook his head, then gently wrapped his arms around Emila. He needed to feel her warmth and her love. He recalled the argument they had this very morning about late nights at the bar once they were back home from the morning Mass. Arguments that had sprung up more and more as the years went on and Frida grew older. But all of that would have to wait.

"Davide, please. What is it? What's wrong?" Emila asked with growing concern. She grabbed a blanket from the sofa in their tiny living room and tried to drape it around his cold body, but he pushed it away, instead turning and glancing out the front window into the darkened street.

All was quiet inside the house while Davide continued peering out the window. "Davide, you're scaring me. What the hell is…"

"Fr. Steffen's been murdered," Davide said gravely as he turned to face her.

After a brief pause, Emila's only response was, "Wait, what?"

Rushing forward and taking hold of the sides of her arms, he repeated, "Fr. Steffen has been murdered inside St. Rafael's and I think I saw what did it. Listen, honey, I have to get back to the church. Ruppert was with me when we went to check in on the old man after he hadn't shown up for his Sunday night beer with me. I got a bit concerned after an odd dream I had last night that's been bothering me all day. So, I closed up shop a bit early and we went to check on him."

"A bad dream? Our priest murdered in his own church? What? You're not making any sense right now, Davide!" Emila responded, now with true fear in her voice. She glanced past him at the window then quickly wrapped the blanket she had intended for her husband around herself.

Nodding, Davide replied grimly, "It's true. He's dead and Ruppert went to fetch Gabriel Lambert at the police station. He's not going to like being woken up at this hour, but this is bad, Emila." He glanced down at his watch. 11:45 PM, inching closer to midnight.

"What are you going to do? You're not going back out there, are you? Who killed him?" Emila said, now trying desperately to control her near panic at this horrible and terrifying news.

Kortbeke was a safe and almost boring town. Only minor bar fights and the silly feud between Maximilian's Inn and Hubschmid's Pub. Otherwise, the town was like any other town in Switzerland. Pretty in the summer and dreary in the winter. But, if what her husband was saying was gospel, things were about to be turned on their head in Kortbeke.

"I need to get back to the church and answer any questions Lambert may have. I have to go now. I wanted to let you know. Keep the door locked, do you understand? I'm not sure when I'll be home, but rest assured, it's going to be a late night," Davide said urgently.

Emila didn't respond, but just stood in their small and usually cozy living room that now felt suffocating, trying to grasp the news and what she would do next. Frida needed protecting and her husband was leaving again. "Davide, if there is something out there, you can't go outside!"

Quickly walking over to the small, crackling fireplace, Davide reached up above the mantle and pulled the double-barrel shotgun from its resting place along with the box of shells sitting below it. He broke open the chamber, pulled two shells out of the pack of ten remaining and stuffed them into the barrels, slamming it shut. His face had turned from panicked, cold, and scared to angry.

"Someone killed our priest and my good friend, and whoever," he paused, "or, whatever, did it, is going to pay."

He leaned forward, kissed Emila quickly on the lips, then turned and walked out of the house.

Emila stood in the middle of the living room, stunned. She rushed to the window and looked out to see her husband already running up the street. Within seconds, he was out of sight.

Breathing heavily, Emila wiped her face with her hands. *What do I do? Get dressed and wait on Davide. He's going to be fine! He said someone or something. What the hell did he mean by something? Maybe I should pray…yes, praying is what I need to be doing!*

A tiny voice from the small, darkened hallway inside the Hubschmid homestead called out, "Mama? Why did Papa leave?"

Emila quickly turned to face her daughter who was rubbing her eyes and yawning. *Protect your daughter, that's what you're going to do, Emila.*

†

Chapter 5

Maximillian's Inn

12:00 AM

While Ruppert and Davide were witnessing the sudden and grisly death of Fr. Steffen, night life continued into the midnight hour down at the south end of Kortbeke at Maximilian's Inn. Located between Finnigan's Fine Clothing and Walter Peakins Bakery, all three establishments catered to the wealthier people that frequented Maximilian's more than those that lived in the northside, or, *poor* end of town.

The shops had opened at Uma's behest when Nils and Uma took ownership of the bar and the buildings on either side. Both paid hefty rental fees which drove their prices up, which kept much of the northside folks away and closer to their own home turf. Something that delighted Uma. If it were up to her, she would split the town in two completely. Uma hated having to visit the northside, repulsed by their common clothes and penny-pinching ways along with their ugly children. *Christ, how can those people breed and create so many offspring?* she would complain to her husband.

But significantly more levelheaded people intervened at a town hall meeting, insisting that it would do nothing but cause more infighting among people that, at one point, before Nils and Uma began throwing their weight around, got along just fine. Even Mayor Kessler, as biased as he sometimes was, saw to it that her suggestion was squelched. Although he did so quietly, weeks later, with the signing of a law stating that Kortbeke would remain one entity and everyone needed to get along as best they could, like they used to before the Karlens came to town, spreading their hatred and bias like a plague.

Inside the well-appointed room with lush furnishings, beautiful, dark mahogany wood tables and chairs filled the room and were lit up tastefully with gas lighting, a new and modern lighting system. The interior reflected the price of the drinks served, which consisted of fine liquors, wine, and cocktails. Beer was served as well, but most customers darkening Maximilian's doors considered that to be the poor man's drink of choice and suited more to the tastes of the lower-class citizens that frequented Hubschmid's Pub. Although those same individuals had no qualms stocking their ice boxes with bottles of Kulmbacher Bier purchased at the Kortbeke Market one block east of the police station, central to both sides of town.

Only a few patrons remained, and Nils was always keen on keeping his establishment open longer than Hubschmid's on principle alone. If Hubschmid's closed at eleven, Maximilian's remained open until midnight. Not that any of Hubschmid's customers would make their way to the only remaining bar open in Kortbeke after it closed for the night. The few that tried were swiftly told Maximilian's was open the extra hour for invited guests only—yet another way of keeping the unwanted crowd out of their bar permanently. These townsfolk were quickly spotted by their inferior attire, and the Karlens' knowing who was who in the town of Kortbeke. Their regulars also helped in picking out northsiders. Turning away good money was something the Karlens were willing to do to make a name for their upscale bar, ensuring its exclusive experience for those they deemed worthy of patronage.

Nils downed the final gulp of his J&B blended Scotch whisky. It wasn't Maximilian's top-shelf liquor, but this was a Sunday night, not a roaring Friday when he had to impress the wealthy of Kortbeke with his extensive knowledge of fine bourbons and Scotches from around Europe. He set the glass down on the bar top which Leonz Laurer, the bartender on duty for the evening, quickly scooped up and washed. Nils paid little attention to the help at Maximilian's; they got paid and that was all he cared about. No special treatment would be given to those that had the luxury of serving under the Karlens' employment.

But Leonz, the handsome, muscular, twenty-four-year-old Black employee with thick, black curly hair was someone Nils kept an eye on. Nils had seen Uma flirt with the young man who seemed to avoid interacting with her whenever possible. Word was, he was well known in town, mainly because he was one of only a handful of Black people, yet no one looked down at him. Least of all, young Nina, Davide's barmaid at Hubschmid's Pub, whom he was apparently madly in love with. They kept their relationship relatively quiet, no doubt to avoid rustling any feathers over working at essentially the other's competition, along with the color of his skin, something many townsfolk could likely not get past.

One of Nils' employees told him that Leonz planned on marrying young Nina—when he had saved up enough money—and then she would no longer have to work at a bar with drunken, lustful men staring her down. She was ready for marriage and had expressed as much but funds were tight, and Leonz wanted to give young Nina the best life he could. Especially since Leonz had been an orphan, brought up in a local orphanage over in Salzben.

As long as he works hard here, that's all that matters to me, Nils thought, rubbing his large belly and pulling a comb out of his back pocket, running it through his blond, greasy hair. "Three people left. What time do we have? Ahh, good, nearly midnight." He glanced at his expensive watch adorning his wrist. He wore black pants, slightly too tight, along with a white button-down shirt and a black vest. It was his version of a tuxedo.

This being a Sunday night, Uma wasn't around, but likely fast asleep at home on the opposite side of the cobblestone street to Maximilian's in a well-appointed, if sterile looking house whose furnishings were more for looks than comfort. Just the way Uma had wanted it.

The remaining three patrons stood to their feet, bid Nils farewell with a nod of their heads, and left the building. As the door closed behind them, Nils walked to their table and saw one of them had spilled the remaining bourbon from his glass and attempted to quickly wipe it up but left the wet napkin sitting on the booze-soaked table.

"Why, you lousy, no-good clumsy git! Can't even hold his liquor, that damned Chadwick!" Nils spat out angrily, looking toward the door. "Leonz, get your skinny, Black ass over here and clean this table! Actually, wipe them all down. I shouldn't have to tell you this."

"Yes, sir," came the reply as Leonz quickly came from behind the bar with a wet rag.

Nils and Uma, typically not ones to hire a person of color, had agreed to take him on with reduced pay until he "proved himself," something he had done time and time again, to no avail. Nils knew Uma secretly found the handsome man quite alluring, his skin color attracting her "forbidden lust," which he had turned a blind eye to many times in their marriage. Their patrons paid him little mind, seeing him essentially as their slave and making them feel all the more powerful because of it.

✝

The white wolf glided through town on all fours, keeping to the shadows. Its mind calculated what its next move would be, after the massacre at Granhal and the removal of Kortbeke's law, followed by the swift and efficient butchery of Fr. Steffen at St. Raphael's.

Fr. Kries wasn't here in Kortbeke, but she was. He would return, and when he did…

I shall cause chaos. I will see to it that the town that houses the young priest will fall into utter despair and ruin before I depart back to my homeland, but not before he meets his end, in front of everyone. They will all suffer. Everything he loves…will suffer. Then he shall be my sacrifice to the lord of this world. He will be so pleased with his servant.

Now on the southside, the large white wolf whose eyes shone yellow saw lights on up ahead. It stopped and looked at the establishment open late on a Sunday night, seeing three men stumble out, swaying as they closed the door behind them.

Bar. It's a bar.

The first man, a towering and stocky bearded fellow, slipped on the wet sidewalk and immediately fell forward onto the cobblestone street, crying out. The other two men, significantly smaller than he, began laughing and pointing at their drunken friend.

The wolf's ears perked as it listened intently to the conversation.

"Don't laugh at me, you worthless git! Help me up, damn you!" the large muscular man called out, obviously not caring about the time of night.

Quickly, the skinnier men shrugged and helped the large man to his feet.

"You bloody drunken idiot, Richard! Your house is the other way!" one of the skinnier men with a thin mustache exclaimed to the other skinny man who was balding.

"Well, excuse me all to hell, look at this miserable shit weather! What do you expect from someone that's likely finished off half a bottle of that fat bastard's swill inside there?" the balding man retorted as he swayed on the street, pointing up at the Maximilian's sign above.

"Why don't you both shut the fuck up? Go home, the both of you!" the bearded man said, brushing himself off.

The balding man glanced at him. "Chadwick, aren't you going home?"

"I'll go home when I'm damn good and ready!" the angry drunk called out, attempting to put a cigarette in his mouth. Once it was lit, he added, "The lovely miss Uma's bedroom light appears to be on. I could sure go for a row with that one."

The three of them continued talking about the things they would do to Uma Karlen and wondering why in the hell she was married to the fat slob inside Maximilian's, when everyone knew she was fucking the mayor and trying to seduce the young colored fella that worked the bar for them.

"And speaking of that pretty boy bartender, you've seen him fancying the little lady Nina, the barmaid at Hubschmid's? That pretty lassie is enough to visit that shithole bar on the northside!" the mustached man named Jonathan stated.

Chadwick grinned. "What that little filly needs is me, on top of her, training her to behave like a good little slut!"

"What would your wife think of that?" Richard said chuckling.

Chadwick quickly swiveled where he stood and grabbed hold of his bald drinking buddy's coat, pulling him in tight. "You shut the *fuck* up about my wife, you hear me? What she doesn't know won't hurt her none, but what you know will. So, keep your fucking mouth shut!"

"Fine, fine! I get it!" Richard said, backing down instantly, trying to get away from the large man's strong, tight grasp.

Chadwick let go of the man's coat and glanced at Jonathan who quickly averted his eyes. He knew well that when Chadwick's drunkenness took a turn to the dark side, and it just had, this is what often happened. Someone would say something seemingly harmless, and Chadwick would be set off, threatening the offending party with any number of painful beatings.

Due to the man's size, they would back off quickly, never standing up to what they knew well was a bully. And a wife beater, having seen the poor man's wife Lydia Kern on numerous occasions with bruises on her body that she desperately tried to hide from prying eyes. Most of the town knew what was going on but kept silent for fear of retribution from the man with the violent temper.

The door to the house directly opposite Maximilian's Inn opened, which caused the three men to hurry away. Several more curse words were thrown to the wind along with laughing and glancing back as they all made their way down the road. Down to where the wolf sat still in the shadows in between two nondescript buildings.

The men passed the animal shrouded in darkness, never once seeing it watching them. Their banter had ceased after the altercation and now all three had fallen silent.

The large one, he might do. Yes, I think he will do nicely. At least, for this night.

The wolf watched them pass, then its eyes went to the opened door of the house opposite Maximilian's. A woman walked out. Her hair was long and black, she wore a beautiful white coat and walked with an air of confidence. Confidence and power. The wolf instantly liked this woman.

✝

Nils watched Leonz cleaning the tables. He saw the way his wife looked lustfully at the attractive man, and he knew it wouldn't take more than her being alone with the lad to threaten him with all sorts of humiliation and gossip if he didn't pleasure her.

Nils's wife was admittedly attractive in her own way, even at thirty-eight years old, she kept herself up, while Nils had let himself go. Content to live luxuriously and to excess, consuming large quantities of rich and buttery foods to go along with the copious amounts of liquor ingested every evening. Uma, on the other hand, was strict with her diet and appearance. She was trim, her black hair usually pulled back in a bun, along with make-up to keep her skin looking easily ten years younger. She liked wearing tight, low-slung tops, revealing her large and still firm breasts in front of the Maximilian's patrons that ogled her.

Sex with Uma was incredibly rare and typically only occurred when they were both celebrating a special occasion and had drunk to excess. Even then, it was a robotic and quick experience, lasting no more than a few minutes. Nils found himself masturbating more frequently the older he got and the less sex he had with his wife.

He had considered an extramarital affair, and could have on several occasions, but he knew if discovered, Uma's wrath would be swift. The money they had inherited had come from her grandfather, skipping over her weak father who had died when Uma was only fifteen years old along with her mother in a house fire. "No loss there, they were abusive and treated me terrible! Too bad about my poor brother, though, only seven years old! So young to perish in such a horrible way!" Uma would utter through forced, fake tears whenever her parents were brought up, knowing full well what really happened to her family, happy to accept the sympathies from those she told. In truth, Uma's parents had been kind people that did their best to raise their daughter and younger son right. They had all indeed perished in a house fire. A house fire that had gone unexplained. A house fire that Uma herself had escaped from in the middle of the night.

When the fire department had arrived on the Stoller farm, the house was completely ablaze as poor Uma Stoller sat outside softly crying at the sudden and mysterious death of her entire family. Quickly, Jügen Stoller, her grandfather, took her in and the rest was history. It had been determined that the fire had been caused by a lit candle in the kitchen that Uma's mother had forgotten to blow out. If Uma's story was to be believed. And it had been. Why would a young girl lie about something as heinous as her entire family being burned alive in the middle of the night?

Jügen raised her to become the woman she was now in Kortbeke, power hungry, devoid of empathy, and quite wealthy. At a young age, Uma had always seen things differently. Her lust for power started at seven years old when she realized that begging just wouldn't suffice for her poor parents, learning the art of temper tantrums and attempting to pit one parent against the other. This had worked until her younger brother came into the picture. It was then that young Uma knew she had to change her situation, eventually. Especially with her grandfather whispering in her ear when he would visit on rare occasions, all but ignoring her younger brother and showing disdain for the son he wished he never had and the weak wife he had married. In his eyes, Uma was the only good thing that had stemmed from his bastard son and bitch wife he shacked up with.

He quickly saw in Uma a younger version of himself and thus, the grooming began. Going so far as to suggest he could raise her much better than her weak parents if only he was her caretaker. Uma's already aggressive nature, stemming from the genes passed down from her grandfather and skipping her father completely, was honed and fine-tuned, much to her grandfather's liking.

Marrying Nils at the age of twenty-four after several months of lust-filled courting, she had found him to be a handsome fellow at the time before quickly packing on weight once their marriage was sealed.

Nils smirked while continuing to watch Leonz clean the last table in the bar hurriedly. He enjoyed watching other people do menial tasks. And knew the best was yet to come for Leonz, cleaning the toilets in both the men's and women's restrooms. *Speaking of which…*

Nils smirked and made his way to the men's room feeling his stomach rumble and gurgle from his four glasses of J&B mixed with the buttered bread and peanuts he had been snacking on all evening while schmoozing with patrons.

Once the tables were wiped down, Leonz glanced up to see Nils walk down the hallway toward the restroom. He looked at his watch, 11:55 PM. "You couldn't wait to do your business until you walked across the street, could you? And I always wipe everything down without you telling me.

Lousy son of a…" Leonz mumbled to himself, knowing well this power move on the part of his boss.

Leonz lived by himself on a side street that ran between the police station and Maximilian's. It wasn't much, but it was inexpensive and allowed him to continue saving up for his eventual marriage to Nina, and then they would set off to other parts of Europe. He had lived in Switzerland his whole life and hadn't seen any other part of the world except Salzben, then Kortbeke, and several smaller towns in the surrounding region. The world would be his and Nina's oyster, just not yet. *Good things come to those who wait,* he thought as he continued cleaning up Maximilian's for the night, anxious to get out of there and off to bed. Tomorrow, he would see his love.

The door to Maximilian's opened. Without looking up, Leonz stated, "We're closing for the night. Sorry, come back when we—"

"It's my bar, silly boy. I will come and go as I please," a cool voice said from the entrance.

Leonz swallowed hard. *Damnit, damnit to hell, not her! Not tonight!* Putting on a friendly face, Leonz looked up and forced a smile, "Good evening, Mrs. Karlen."

Moving in past the door and closing it behind her, she stepped forward until coming to a stop in front of Leonz, inspecting him. Her slightly damp black hair was down instead of in the usual bun, and she was wearing her expensive long white coat. Purchased at Finnigan's Fine Clothing, likely the most expensive coat on display before she snatched it up at her heavily discounted pricing.

Glancing into her dark eyes, Leonz saw that she appeared to have put on red lipstick and perfume. Her eyes peered at him with both contempt and lust. He remembered well how she had attempted to bed him down on more than one occasion while he'd had to fend her off. Usually, it occurred when Nils wasn't around and he was left to close up himself. Regardless of the occasion, Uma always attempted to look her fake, vapid best to go across the street to torment the young man that refused her advances.

"So, what brings you by tonight?" Leonz asked shakily.

Seeing his discomfort, she leaned forward, her mouth near his. "Like I said, I come and go as I please." She paused, letting her warm breath hit his face. He took a small step back, away from her. *I win again*, she thought smugly. "If you must know, silly boy, I am here to see my husband. Where is he?"

Leonz was about to answer but fell silent when he heard the door to the men's room open and Nils stepped out, peering at his wife, coughing a bit as he walked forward, glaring at Leonz. "Why are you standing so close to my wife, boy?"

Uma smiled thinly.

"Well, I um," Leonz began.

"Oh, hush up, I'm just fucking with you! Finish your cleanup and go home. Don't forget the washrooms," he said with a smirk.

Biting his tongue and clenching the mop in his hands, Leonz nodded quickly and went back to his current task of floor cleanup. Then it would be off to deal with the toilets.

Nils leaned forward and kissed Uma lightly on the cheek. "Why are you not at home in bed, my dear? Isn't the weather outside miserable?"

Sighing heavily, Uma turned away from her husband, glancing over at the young stud Leonz quickly, eyes still filled with lust. "If you must know, I could not sleep. So, I thought I would come fetch you. I heard talking and laughing outside our house and it added to my, hmm, my *restlessness*." She kept glancing at Leonz who was doing his best to avoid her ogling eyes.

How can Nils not see what she is up to? Leonz wondered, thankful for a change that he had to clean the restrooms, which would be out of her sight.

He made his way back to the restrooms with his cleaning supplies as Uma watched him. She turned to face her husband again.

"I imagine what you heard were the last three customers of the night. Chadwick, Jonathan, and I believe, Richard. Damn drunks spilled a drink on one of our tables," Nils replied.

"Those losers would be better served at Hubschmid's. However, their money remains good here. For now," Uma said casually, before adding with what looked like the possible hint of a smile, "Come home, Nils, let the boy finish up."

Nodding, Nils smiled at the sudden if still highly unlikely possibility of sex. He shouted back, "Leonz! I want everything tip-top before you leave! Anything less than spotless will be taken out of your wages! We pay you well! Earn your damn keep for a change! And don't you dare forget to lock up, you hear me?"

Leonz poked his head from out of the recently defecated-in restroom, glanced at his employers, gave a quick nod then said, "Certainly."

Uma smiled slyly at him once more as their eyes met briefly. *One day, I'm going to ride you, my little orphan boy. I'll make you my own little personal love slave* she thought as he darted back into the restroom and out of sight. Much like her grandfather who never took *no* for an answer, she never took her eyes off of what she wanted. Eventually, she got her way, by persuasion or by force.

Chapter 6

†

The Drunk and the Mayor

11:30 PM

Ruppert snuck quietly through the street, staying in the shadows and clenching Davide's small wooden club on his way to Lambert's. He hated how loud his shoes sounded when they hit the cobblestone streets, feeling as though they were drawing too much attention. His eyes shifting back and forth, he was terrified at what was out there lurking in the darkness. He hadn't seen what Davide had in the shadows outside the church, but he had seen Fr. Steffen's mutilated body inside, and that was enough to give the thirty-one-old a bigger fright than he had experienced in his entire life up to this point.

After inadvertently knocking over several crates stacked up outside the local flour mill and making unwanted noise, he collected himself and continued on as quietly as he could. He made his way along the main street and avoided any shortcuts that would take him back increasingly darker alleyways.

Once he made it to the police station, roughly fifteen minutes after leaving Davide back at the church, Ruppert caught his breath, feeling the need to relieve his overflowing bladder of the copious amounts of beer he had consumed at Hubschmid's. Before knocking on the door, he went around the side of the building. Leaning against the brick structure, he put his weary and slightly spinning head against his resting arm, breathing in the cold air and catching his breath. As he drained his bladder he had to admit, even in the midst of this terrifying ordeal, it felt wonderful.

"What in the hell do you think you're doing?" a voice all but shouted from the main road several feet away.

Quickly attempting to cut off the stream of piss, Ruppert stammered, "Oh shit! Um, hold on." He knew that voice well. It was the mayor of Kortbeke, Klaus Kessler.

"You realize public intoxication and exposing yourself in public is against the law, right?" Klaus said, his voice full of condemnation as he inspected Ruppert, caught with his dick out near the chief of police's headquarters.

Klaus Kessler, at thirty-five-years old, was young for being in charge of the entire town, but he had been voted in thanks to the efforts of one Uma Karlen. She wanted someone she could easily persuade to her way of thinking, and who would push through laws she thought would best benefit her and, to a lesser extent, her husband. After Kessler was voted in, she had found his services valuable, although he wasn't quite the pushover she had hoped for, pushing back on her more radical ideas and initiatives. Still, she got her way more than not and the sex was good for both of them.

Klaus Kessler was single and wanted to keep it that way. *Why be tied down to one woman when the world was full of them?* he told his drinking buddies back in his early twenties. While they all eventually got married off themselves, he chose the path of pleasure and indulgence. He could be quite smooth when he wanted to be, and he used it to his advantage over the past two years as the town's mayor.

His predecessor had retired and moved to France. He had been beloved by all, and the town had hoped his replacement would be equally likable and honest. But that wasn't to be. Instead, they got an Uma Karlen puppet who would likely be voted out in the next election unless the Karlens could fudge the election counts.

Ruppert hated the mayor and the way the Karlens had him in their back pocket. He also despised the man's face, always in a half grin. Staring at it now, Ruppert glared back at him. *Oh, how I would love to wipe that fucking smirk off your face, you arrogant...*

"Well? Are you going to answer me? Let me guess, getting drunk again over at Hubschmid's? Typical. Why are you carrying a weapon?" Klaus said, pointing to the small wooden club in Ruppert's hand.

Collecting himself, Ruppert tried to hold his head up and replied, "Listen to me Klaus, we need to wake up Lambert, now! Davide gave me this to protect myself!"

Suddenly intrigued and forgetting about having seen Ruppert pissing all over the side of the local bakery, Klaus asked, "What in God's name are you talking about, Ruppert? Protect you from what, exactly?"

"I'm not drunk, not anymore at least, and I'm going to Lambert's. Fr. Steffen has been murdered inside his church!" Ruppert exclaimed in as quiet a voice as he could, given his terror, then added, "And his killer is still out there somewhere!"

The mayor of Kortbeke stared at him, trying to gauge what to do with him.

Before he could speak, Ruppert fired a question of his own. "What are you doing out here?" The man looked like he was ready for bed, not out strolling the street at night.

As if taken aback by the question, Klaus replied, "I couldn't sleep, so I had my window open and was smoking a cigarette when I heard something fall. I assume that was you?"

Damnit! Ruppert thought. He nodded quickly in response.

"Of course, it would be you. Drunk and stumbling through the streets, proclaiming our priest has been murdered! The little room you call home is across the street from Hubschmid's, so what the hell were you doing at the church in the first place? Not that I believe a single word of this nonsense," Klaus stated.

We are getting nowhere with this, I need to talk to Lambert, not this clown. "Fuck this. I'm going to see Lambert," Ruppert said impatiently and pushed past the mayor.

"Excuse me? You can't just—" Klaus began.

But Ruppert was already walking away.

Mumbling under his breath, Klaus said, "Why, you arrogant sonofabitch," and followed Ruppert to the chief of police's home only several buildings up from the station.

Ruppert began knocking on the officer's door. At this hour on a Sunday, Lambert was likely sound asleep. But tonight wasn't any ordinary night, not anymore.

"Come on, wake up, Lambert!" Ruppert called out, avoiding looking over at Klaus.

"I'm sure he's asleep, like you should be right now. Why should I believe a word of this? I've heard worse from you in the past. Remember that time you were exclaiming to all that would listen that you were convinced the Free Democratic Party in Switzerland were German foreign operatives out to corrupt and ruin our country from the inside?"

"I was drunk! My wife and kids had just left me! I barely remember that!" Ruppert retorted.

"Exactly, you barely remember that or anything else that comes out of your mouth when you drink down at that damned Hubschmid's Pub, and that likely includes right now! I know you, Ruppert, and how much alcohol you can put down on any given night. The whole bloody town does! So, unless you have some proof…" Klaus said, growing more agitated and wishing Lambert would open the door and deal with this drunk so he could be rid of him and crawl back into bed.

"The proof is inside St. Raphael's, which I intend to show Lambert once he opens the door. And if not, I'll go to Erni's place." Ruppert attempted to twist the knob of Lambert's door, but Klaus laid his hands on him and pushed him back.

Klaus, trying to keep his voice down, uttered, "Get your hands off that door, *now!*"

Instinctively, Ruppert raised the small club above his head. "Don't touch me, damn you!"

Klaus backed up and raised his hands slightly. "You don't know what you're getting yourself into here. You've been busted before for public intoxication and now threatening an elected official?"

Ruppert lowered his club and continued with the door handle that turned open, unlocked. He pushed through and looked around the darkened room, finding a lantern and matches on a nearby table and lighting it. With his free hand, he held the lantern up, peering around the room.

"Where's Lambert?"

Glancing back, he saw that Klaus had followed him. *Sonofabitch, I'm not going to get rid of this guy and I've got to get back to the church to meet Davide.*

"I don't know, but he's not here," Ruppert answered after scanning the empty house.

"He should have been back from Granhal by now. Told me him and Erni were making a quick trip out there. Old man Fritz sent another one of his damn telegrams. This time about a few of Florus Widmer's cows being killed by what was likely a wolf or something," Klaus said, still scanning the empty house.

"Wolf, huh?" Ruppert mumbled, thinking of the grisly sight inside St. Raphael's and the shape that Davide had seen earlier.

He quickly pushed past Klaus and walked out of Lambert's house, making his way several houses down to Erni's,

Klaus once again following him. After several knocks on the door, he tried the handle; it was locked. More knocking and waiting followed, neither man saying anything.

"It appears they never came back. How long ago did they leave?" Ruppert asked, staring at Klaus impatiently.

Klaus thought for a bit. "I don't know. Earlier this evening, maybe even late afternoon. Why?"

"Why? Because our priest is dead, and all signs point to it being some sort of large animal. Our chief of police and deputy appear to be missing, investigating cattle killings possibly done by a wolf? I'm not very bright, Klaus, but this is pretty easy to deduce here!"

He motioned for the mayor to follow him, feeling more sober by the minute.

"Where are you going now?" Klaus asked with a hint of nervousness in his voice.

"To check on the horses. If they aren't here, this town is without a police force," Ruppert responded as he headed around the back of the house to where the officer's stables resided.

"Shit! What the hell is going on here?" Klaus whispered as he followed close behind, now with more than a hint of uncertainty and worry in his voice.

Ruppert held out the lantern and shined it into the empty stalls where Brutus and Bertha would normally have been at this time of night. "They're empty. Both Lambert and Erni's horses are gone."

A hushed silence fell over both men, Klaus now genuinely scared. "So, what now? I mean, if they are still back in

Granhal? What do we do? You can't expect me to have all the answers all of a sudden, right?" he asked Ruppert.

"Well, last I checked, you *are* the one in charge here! And you're asking me, the drunk that makes shit up, remember?" Ruppert said bitterly, angry that this was the best the town of Kortbeke could come up with for leadership in such a trying time.

Klaus contemplated firing back his own set of insults, but figured it was best to hold his tongue as he stared into the empty horse stalls, spooked and now quite concerned.

Ruppert thought for a second then replied, "We go back to the church. Davide was going to meet me there once I grabbed Lambert and Erni. They're not here, so, I suppose it's a good thing you are. Follow me."

Heading toward the church, he looked back and saw that Klaus wasn't following him. He stopped and held out his arms. "Well, come on!"

"Now, wait just a minute. How do I know you didn't fly off your rocker and do something to Lambert and Erni? And now you want to take care of me too?"

Is this man really that stupid? was the thought that raced through Ruppert's mind as he stared dumbfounded at Klaus. He approached the frightened man and looked him in the eye. "Klaus, we need to go, now. This town is in serious danger and you're the mayor. Now, damnit, *let's go!*"

Shocked at hearing Ruppert speak with such uncharacteristic authority, Klaus nodded his head and began to follow him down the quiet street toward St. Raphael's.

✝

Uma and Nils went back to their place across the street, leaving Leonz to himself. He would certainly be working later than he had hoped but was certain Nina would still wait for him. Because she had Sundays off and Hubschmid's was closed Monday, often times she would quietly make her way over to his place. They were keeping the relationship relatively under wraps for the time being, not just because of Leonz's employment at Maximilian's, but also because her parents wanted someone for her that would be staying local. And that wasn't Leonz. He, along with Nina, wanted out of Kortbeke.

While Leonz was busy with numerous closing tasks, Uma had decided after peering at his handsome body that she was feeling…warm. And when she felt warm, she typically found a way to have Mayor Klaus pleasure her. However, it was Sunday, and it was late, and her fat husband would have to do.

"Nils, darling, I'm feeling a bit warm," she said as she slipped off her coat, revealing a beautiful nightgown underneath.

Nils smiled, understanding what she meant. Tonight would be his lucky night. Instantly, he felt an erection forming in his tight pants. "Why, of course, darling, I'm always up for a good tussle!"

She rolled her eyes as she made her way to their bedroom in the back of their beautifully decorated house with its paintings and furniture far too expensive for a town such as Kortbeke.

As she walked to the bedroom, she dropped the straps holding up her nightgown draped atop her shoulders. The gown slipped off to the floor revealing her naked body.

Following suit, Nils began stripping off his attire hastily, looking lustfully at her naked beauty.

Once at the bed, she turned to face him as she sat down on it. Her husband was struggling with his pants, but she shook her head. "You can take those off when you're done."

She laid back on the bed and he knew what to do, nodding his understanding and burying his face between her legs.

As she always did when her pig husband had any sexual relations with her, she imagined any number of other men pleasuring her instead. She knew with her money she could very likely have any man she wanted at her beck and call, but at least with Nils she could trust him to follow her commands. The tradeoff was that he continued to grow larger and larger. Once incredibly handsome, he had let himself go soon after the marriage was sealed and made no attempt to remedy it, only indulging in food and alcohol all the more.

She moaned in ecstasy at the oral sex she was receiving, all the time imagining Leonz performing it, but performing it *much* better. Then she would return the favor. But this man was not Leonz. Uma gripped the sheets tightly and grit her teeth for the few seconds of release, then relaxed.

Nils lifted his head, smiling, then stood to his feet, once more attempting to take his pants off.

Uma, however, rolled over, wrapping the covers around her and turned away from him.

"Why, you fucking little—" Nils began. This wasn't the first time she had left him with a hard-on.

"Careful what you say next, Nils. Go to the bathroom and take care of yourself. I'm tired. Goodnight," Uma said, grinning to herself.

She didn't look at him but heard him hastily shuffling out of the bedroom mumbling under his breath followed by the bathroom door slamming shut.

"That's right, follow my orders," Uma said as she closed her eyes.

Chapter 7

†

Game Plan

12:15 AM

While Emila recited fairytales to little Frida in an attempt to get her daughter back to sleep, Davide continued on silently through the quiet streets back to the church after speaking with his wife. He hated leaving them alone, but someone needed to get a handle on the situation. To his knowledge, the only people that knew trouble had come to Kortbeke were himself and, not the most reliable person, especially when alcohol was involved, Ruppert Sprenger. But tonight, Ruppert would have to prove himself, one way or another.

Come on, Ruppert, don't let me down. Please make some progress with Lambert or Erni! I'm counting on you, buddy.

He wanted nothing more than to be back home in the safety of their home with his wife and child. But that no longer existed in Kortbeke, not with this violent assault on

Fr. Steffen. It was up to him and his friend Ruppert to alert the proper people of what happened. It was his civic responsibility to the town, and that included keeping his wife and daughter safe. Furthermore, he owed it to his now deceased friend Fr. Steffen to see to it that justice was brought forth by the law in Kortbeke. Once Lambert and Erni were notified and, to a lesser extent, the mayor, they could determine what the next steps would be.

"Come on, Lambert, be home, for the love of God, be there! I'm a bartender and father, not a hunter!" he muttered on his way to Lambert's. The fear he felt was palpable and threatening to overtake him, but Davide did his best to remain calm and in control, something his wife had always admired about him.

Gripping his double-barrel shotgun tightly, his eyes darted around for any movement. Nothing seemed out of the ordinary on the dreary Sunday night in Kortbeke. Nothing except the mutilated body of Fr. Steffen and the way in which he had been dispatched.

As he made his way through the street, he thought back once more to his dream the previous night.

"Don't bother sending for the priest, I killed him." It was ominous and stuck with him. The slight grin on the haggard-looking woman's face. The eerie feeling as though she knew what was to come, the wound in her stomach a minor inconvenience.

"You will meet her and her kind, and you will do battle with them." What had those words meant? Who had uttered them to him in his dream? Was it simply dream logic or had something or someone wanted to send him a message?

And now, their priest was killed. And what about Fr. Kries? *Wherever you are, be safe. Your town is going to need you*, Davide thought as he approached the church once more, this time armed.

Sighing heavily, he was about to push the door open when he saw something in the shadows approaching him. Instantly, he raised his shotgun to eye level and pulled back on the hammers and waited.

He heard the slow clopping of hooves on the cobblestone street and soon realized it was a horse. "What the bloody hell?" He lowered the gun, staring at the large brown beast cautiously making its way up the street toward him. He stepped forward to get a better look and saw that it was not only saddled up, but bridled up as well, with reins hanging by its sides, dragging on the ground.

"Good Lord, that's Bertha, Erni's horse. What the hell is going on?"

Erni, on occasion, would visit Hubschmid's when coming back from Fritz's in Granhal, and Davide had grown familiar with his horse. Glancing around nervously, it took several steps forward, recognizing Davide, who rubbed the horse's muzzle with a soothing clicking noise.

"Where's Erni?" he asked, puzzled at the sight of the deputy's animal loose in the streets after midnight. The horse swished its tail, enjoying the nose petting. "What am I going to do with you? Ruppert's gone to Lambert's, I suppose I should…"

He stopped speaking. Two more figures, one holding a lantern, were approaching from the direction of the mayor's and Lambert's. Before long, Ruppert and Klaus stood in front of him.

Shit. Davide thought, staring at the puzzled Mayor Klaus wearing pajamas, lit up slightly by Ruppert's lantern.

"Ruppert, you made it back. And I see you brought the mayor along," Davide said with a hint of contempt.

Klaus looked warily at Davide, another individual on the Karlen's' hate list. He didn't mind the man so much, but being friendly with the likes of Davide Hubschmid would do nothing but cause more trouble than it was worth.

"Evening, Davide," Klaus said quietly.

Nodding and seeing the puzzled looks he and Bertha were receiving, he said, "Old Bertha here just came from the direction of the town's entrance, if you can believe that. Things are getting stranger by the minute in this town."

Klaus was going to chime in, but Ruppert beat him to it. "Well, you found one of the horse's because the stalls were both empty, so is Lambert's building."

Taken aback, Davide replied, "What do you mean, empty?"

"As in, our law enforcement is not here," Ruppert responded gravely.

"I think I know where they are," Klaus sighed.

Davide raised his eyebrow. "And?"

"Headed out to Granhal to investigate some cattle mutilations. Got a telegram from Fritz earlier today," Klaus answered.

All three men fell silent.

Davide took Bertha's reins and wrapped them around the gate leading into St. Raphael's. "Come on, Klaus, you need to see this." He pushed the door to the church open and walked in with Ruppert and an anxious Klaus behind.

Several more candles had burned down since Davide and Ruppert had found the priest's body earlier, and the eerily dim atmosphere inside the church only added to the horror of what lay up on the altar.

The three men made their way up the aisle leading to the front of the church, Davide and Ruppert in the lead with Klaus trailing behind. As expected, they soon came upon the blood. Klaus looked down at it as Ruppert held the lantern then pointed up toward the altar.

Klaus's eyes slowly shifted from the blood-covered floor to the front of the church. He instantly made out something large atop the altar and moved forward until it became clear what, and who, it was.

"Oh, my Lord in heaven," Klaus gasped, holding his hand to his mouth at the grotesque abomination sprawled on top of the altar. "Fr. Steffen, *shit!* Who could have perpetrated this sacrilege?" He looked at Ruppert, slightly ashamed about the drilling he had given the man earlier, especially calling him out for his drunken stories.

"Whatever did this, it's still loose and likely went through Granhal before making its way here. And Lambert and Erni are there. My strong hunch is, they might be in serious trouble," Davide said grimly. His eyes fell to Klaus.

"What the bloody hell are you looking at me for? You think I should go out there? That's someone else's job. It sure as hell isn't the mayor's! Furthermore, I don't think it's wise to go out to Granhal, we need to formulate a plan here. We have an entire town sleeping and a killer on the loose!" Klaus felt angry and confused as to the right course of action in their current situation. He hastily pulled out a cigarette and held it to a barely lit candle nearby, shaking and inhaling deeply.

Turning to face the mayor, Davide saw fear and indecisiveness in the man's eyes. *Son of a bitch, I'm going to have to go to Granhal on my own. Son of a bitch!*

He bit his tongue and nodded. "I suppose I can agree. We have a sleeping town and right now, only three of us. If we wake people up, there will be a panic. Half this town consists of women and children, all of whom will be getting up early to be shuffled off to school and begin their day, so we have to stay calm. However, someone has to go to Granhal, that much is certain. Our lawmen are likely in danger. So, it's imperative that we check on Lambert and Erni. They're in trouble, I can feel it in my bones."

"Well, suit yourself then, have at it! Off with you, but I stay put!" Klaus retorted.

Davide glanced at the man angrily. "Fine. I'll go. Someone has to and I suppose you are the mayor, so it's your call." Davide was doing his best to show respect toward this last bastion of leadership in Kortbeke, pathetic as it was.

"You damn right," Klaus retorted a bit too loudly, sensing what both Davide and Ruppert were thinking.

"You are, hands down, the most cowardly—" Ruppert began but fell silent when footsteps sounded at the entrance of the church.

"Excuse me," a soft voice said from the entrance of the church.

All three men spun around, Davide quickly raising his shotgun. "Who's there? Show yourself, now!"

"Davide? Is that you?"

"Nina?" Davide answered.

The young blond woman stepped forward holding out her own lantern inside the church.

"Stop!" Davide called out, not wanting her to see the horrors that lay atop the altar.

The three of them moved toward Nina, standing puzzled at the entrance of the church, a blanket wrapped around her, hair pulled back in a ponytail. Even without makeup, she was beautiful, her skin naturally soft and tan. She had filled out in her teens, becoming a woman some ten years ago, much to the lustful stares of many men. Her spunky attitude had also developed and she was easily able to fend off unwanted advances. All except Leonz, who had swept her off her feet almost at once when they first met.

"What on earth are you doing here?" Davide asked.

Nina looked at the three men, puzzled. "I could ask you the same thing. I'm on my way to see Leonz when he gets off work and saw the door open to the church and Erni's horse tied up outside. I got closer and heard talking inside."

"Listen, young lady, you need to—" Klaus began but was instantly cut off by Davide.

"You can't be outside. Not tonight, Nina. You've got to get back home. Something has happened and we're trying to figure out what to do next."

Seeing his shotgun and the grave expressions on their faces, Nina instantly became frightened. "What? What's happened? Come on, Davide! Out with it!"

Davide turned to face Ruppert and Klaus. Ruppert shook his head. All three seemed to be blocking the path between the rows of pews leading up to the altar.

Taking all of this in, Nina said, "Okay, fellas, what's up there? Come on, what is going on?"

"You don't want to go anywhere near the altar, Nina, trust me," Ruppert said.

"I can't go up to the altar, I can't go see Leonz, Erni's horse is tied up in the middle of the night outside the church—what the hell is going on?" Nina demanded, one hand on her hip and the other pushing her lantern out in front of her.

"Let her see," Davide said after giving it some thought.

"What? Are you crazy? No way, this young girl needs to get back home now!" Klaus exclaimed.

"I'm not a young girl," Nina said, glaring at the man she knew and had no respect for. She knew all about Uma and his secret relationship, and while she herself could be a bit flirtatious and outgoing at times, she would never, ever, cheat on the love of her life.

Feeling seen for the coward and cheat he was behind the façade of town mayor, Klaus looked away.

Nina pushed her way past the three men and set her blanket on a nearby pew. Seeing the blood splatter in the aisle, she gasped, quickly turning to face them once more. "What happened?"

Davide's eyes went from hers to the altar past her.

Nina carefully moved past the blood, up to the altar, and seeing the mutilated body of Fr. Steffen, let out a small cry of terror and disgust.

"Oh no, oh no, no, no, this cannot be!" she exclaimed, staring in horror at the mutilated body. "What, or who, could have done this?"

"There's a wolf's paw print in the blood, so we surmised that a large wolf did this. However, it doesn't explain how Steffen's body got up there, nor how his severed head was flung against the front of the altar," Davide answered.

"There's a paw print?" Klaus asked.

Ruppert pointed down in its direction as Klaus quickly inspected it and nodded.

Nina backed away from the altar, joining the three men that stood by the blood on the floor.

"I'm sorry you had to see that, Nina," Davide said softly.

"Me, too." She was shaking, trying to process the brutality she had just witnessed, inside a church of all places. She caught her breath, paused for a second to collect herself, then added, "I need to get to Leonz. He's likely by himself at Maximilian's closing up. Then he'll be walking back to his place, between Maximilian's and Lambert's."

"Just hold on a second, Nina, please."

Nina was about to reply that she was leaving, no matter what, but respected Davide enough to stay for now.

"I-I guess we should contact the doctor?" Klaus chimed in, uncertain.

"More like the coroner, at this point." Ruppert scratched his whiskered face, trying to make sense of it all.

Davide shook his head. "I'm not sure now is the best time for that. There's nothing they can do for Fr. Steffen. That will come later. We don't want to cause a panic here. We have roughly a thousand people in this town. The more people that are alerted to this, the more things are likely to spiral out of control, especially in the middle of the night. Someone needs to get to Granhal."

"But, why?" Nina asked.

"To find out what happened to Lambert and Erni. That's where they went earlier today, and that's likely where they are now. In the meantime, we need to figure out what to do about this wolf, or whatever it is, that has come to Kortbeke," Davide answered.

"Any ideas?" Ruppert asked, shrugging.

Shaking his head, Davide looked at his friend. "No, not yet. But I have a feeling Granhal will shed some light on what we're up against. Or, at the very least, shed some light on what happened to the police in this town and their whereabouts."

"Well, you all do what you need to do, I'm going to Maximilian's. No way in hell I'm waiting in here," Nina said.

"It's not safe out there!" Klaus exclaimed.

Looking at him with eyebrows raised, she replied, "And it's safe in here?" She pointed to the priest's body.

"Nina, you should go home," Davide began but he knew his barmaid's answer before she even uttered it.

"I'm going to Maximilian's, to Leonz. Right now."

"I'll go with her," Ruppert sighed.

"I don't need a bodyguard! I can handle myself, damnit!"

"Nina, please. Let Ruppert go with you. Klaus, you sure you don't want to come along with me to Granhal? I could use a hand."

"Are you out of your mind? No! I'm staying put! Not running some fool's errand." He paused then stammered,

"I-I'm the mayor and I think if anyone should be going out searching for Lambert and Erni it should be you, you were the one that suggested it in the first place. My duties lie here in Kortbeke! Furthermore, there's only one horse out there..." Klaus trailed off, sounding less convincing with every word.

Sighing with the realization that Klaus was going to be little to no help, Davide said, "Fine. But Klaus, I suggest you go with Ruppert and Nina. It's safer than staying here." He looked up at the numerous stained-glass windows adorning the high walls of the church. "That thing could come back for a late-night snack. At least Maximilian's can be barred up and Uma, love her or hate her, made sure that place was built with the best materials. Once you're there, stay put and I'll try to get to you. Lord only knows what I may find in Granhal, so, take care of yourselves and look out for each other."

"We'll be fine, Davide," Ruppert said, glancing at the wooden club Davide had given him back at Hubschmid's earlier.

Davide replied, "I really wish Fr. Kries was here. Having a priest on hand would be a bit reassuring, considering what happened to Fr. Steffen. We need a man of God right about now."

"I had a dream last night," Nina started. This caught everyone's attention. "I don't know why I'm telling you this, I suppose the strangeness of it coupled with what happened here..." She paused, contemplating continuing then decided to go ahead. "Well, it's been on my mind and I can't shake it. It was awful. And damned if it didn't feel like I was *living* it!"

She looked at them as they waited for her to continue.

"There was a woman, I think she was trying to break into someone's house. She opened the door and got what sounded and looked like a shotgun blast in the stomach, or chest. Not sure. All I know is that she fell over onto the path leading up to the front door of this really shitty-looking house, in a shittier looking village. And then it was as if I was looking down at her. Her eyes turned yellow, maybe. Then, she said—"

"'Don't bother sending for the priest, I killed him,' yeah. I had the same dream," Davide replied, trying to mask the sickening feeling of dread washing over him at hearing someone had the same nightmare he had. *What the hell is happening here?*

Klaus too, looked as if all the color in his face had drained.

"You had the same dream?" Nina exclaimed, holding her lantern up to Davide's face.

"Yes, only mine ended with some voice telling me that I would meet her and her kind, and I guess do battle with them," Davide answered.

Thinking on this, Nina replied, "Come to think of it, my dream ended with some mysterious voice telling me to 'make haste to the origin of the evil.' Whatever that means."

"What in God's name is going on here?" Klaus said, shaking his head.

Davide shook his head. "I don't know. Something unexplainable. Something…evil judging by what happened here. And right now, whether we like it or not, it's up to us to figure out how to stop it. So, I suggest we stick to the plan: get to

Maximilian's and I'll do my best to meet you there once I get back from checking out Granhal. I'm going to ride like hell."

Ruppert and Nina nodded then turned to face Klaus.

He extinguished his cigarette on the floor and looked up at them with terror in his eyes. "I had the same dream last night as you two. It's why I couldn't fall asleep tonight. It's why I was smoking a cigarette out my window when I heard Ruppert. That crazy-looking bitch lay dying, bleeding out on the street in some decrepit looking village in the middle of nowhere, and I couldn't force myself awake if I tried. Some voice in my head told me great sacrifice would be needed to stop the evil. Can't believe I remember those words, but damn, they were haunting. I mean, what the hell does that even mean?"

The four of them stood stunned, speechless and horror-stricken in the waning candlelight of the old church.

Quietly, Davide finally turned and left, shotgun gripped tightly in hand. Outside, he glanced up and down at the silent streets of Kortbeke while he unhitched Bertha, climbed up onto the leather saddle, then cautiously made his way back through town toward Granhal. All the while, thinking of his wife and little girl back home, terrified at what had come to their town. And terrified at what it may yet still do.

Push that fear away, Davide! You may not want to do this, but you're the only one fit to do it at the moment, so man up!

He kept his head bowed against the wind and made haste toward Granhal.

Chapter 8

†

Chadwick Enters the Fold

12:10 AM

Chadwick, Jonathan, and Richard staggered home drunkenly down the long stretch of cobblestone road. Chadwick's wife was out of town with their two-year-old daughter. Hence, the late-night drinking on a cold Sunday night. Not that it mattered if she was home, he did as he pleased and she obeyed, or else.

At least that's what Chadwick had wanted to believe after their last fight that left her with bruised ribs. He had been violent with her before, but after this last incident, in which she had inadvertently left a toy on the floor which he drunkenly tripped over, stubbing his toe then beating her for it, she had become distant. Then, unexpectedly, she left town, *for good,* she had said.

The three men worked jobs on the northside and, truth be told, would be more welcome at Hubschmid's than Maximilian's. But in a town the size of Kortbeke, status was important, and they desperately wanted to be part of the wealthy crowd, even though all three of them were most certainly not.

The men turned down a quiet side street off the main road leading through town. "Well, shit, Monday morning is going to hit me like a ton of bricks. I'm calling it a night. At least that miserable drizzle seems to be stopping," Jonathan said, sobering up from the chilly weather and wind whipping his face.

Looking up at the night sky, Richard, who had put a hat on to protect his balding head from the cold air, nodded in agreement.

"Did you hear that? Jonathan asked suddenly.

Shaking his head, Richard replied chuckling, "No, I heard nothing. Too much booze in your system, methinks."

"I could have sworn I heard horseshoes clopping down toward the jailhouse," Jonathan said, shaking his head.

"You damn drunk, you need to sleep it off. Hell, we all do!" Richard retorted.

Chadwick stopped, turning to look behind them at the noise he had just heard. Standing in the shadows at the entrance of a side street they had just turned on stood the largest wolf he had ever seen. So large, in fact, that he immediately thought it was a different animal altogether, but its shape and size made it clear that this beast was a wolf.

"Hey, guys, look," Chadwick said quietly.

Jonathan and Richard looked over in the direction he was pointing.

"Holy shit, is that a—" Jonathan began.

The white wolf took off in a sprint, all four massive legs working in tandem. The three drunken men had no time to flee before it was upon them. Richard, the closest to it, was the first to be attacked. Snarling, it jumped onto the man, knocking him to the ground where it ripped into his neck ferociously. In two quick bites, his neck was splayed open, blood rushing out of opened and torn veins, spilling onto the wet cobblestone street.

"Oh, my Lord! Oh no, God help me, no!" Jonathan exclaimed, trying to run but slipping on the wet cobblestone and landing hard on his face. Instantly, he felt warm blood rush out of his broken nose onto the street. He tried to stand to his feet but the hard blow to his head, along with the co-pious alcohol consumption, made him unstable.

The wolf landed on top of his back, wasting no time, its enormous sharp claws digging into the flesh on Jonathan's back and slicing it open with ease. Jonathan was about to cry out in agonizing pain but was silenced by a pair of jaws clenching down on the back of his head, easily biting through hair, skull and finally, brains. The wolf clenched its jaws like a vise-grip until fangs closed in on each other, its mouth full of a large chunk of the man's head.

The wolf peered down at the man lying face down and dead on the road. Its otherworldly, glowing yellow eyes quickly glanced around for the third man.

Chadwick had taken off in a dead sprint, away from the carnage and down the long dark side street. The wolf heard the man attempting to call out for his life, most of it unintelligible slurring. "Please, dear God! Please, someone help me!"

Once more, the wolf took off further down the dark street and away from the main road where light was almost nonexistent, the few people living on the street having been sound asleep for hours now. Chadwick arrived at his home and began fishing through his pocket for the key to unlock his door, but it took precious seconds he did not have. He pulled the key out and jammed it into the lock, twisting it as he frantically tried turning the knob at the same time.

The handle turned and Chadwick began moving inside just as the wolf leapt onto him, driving him forward to the floor of his small house and crashing through a table in the middle of the living room. Chadwick instantly turned around in an attempt to fight the wolf off, grabbing the fur around its neck tightly and pulling its bloody, snarling jaws away from his face. The wolf snapped and snarled at the man in its attempt to bite down, much as it had with his friends outside.

Chadwick, a large man weighing well over two hundred pounds, was able to leverage himself on his right leg and roll over until he was on top of the wolf.

The wolf, meanwhile, scratched at him with its large paws, digging into the man's stomach and slicing it open.

Chadwick cried out in pain as he felt the claws cut through skin and muscle. Blood began pouring out of Chadwick's open wounds onto the white wolf as the claws continued slicing.

The man was quickly losing his strength along with his adrenalin. The cuts were too severe and far too many. He began loosening his grip on the wolf's fur as he coughed up blood that dripped into the beast's open jaws.

Slumping forward, he came to rest atop the wolf, no longer able to fight it off and passing out from the massive blood loss and shock. His last coherent thought came to him in a fog: *I'm dying and when I die, I shall go to hell for my many sins. Father, please forgive…*

The man lay still atop the white wolf, now covered in the man's blood.

The wolf started to change, its legs extending. Fur retreated into the skin. The snout pulled back and, in its place, a perfectly shaped woman's nose. Yellow eyes turned a beautiful blue. Long, flowing, light-blond hair once more spilled over soft, supple skin. She rolled the body off of her and stood to her feet, naked and covered in the dying man's blood.

Wiping blood from her lips, she walked to the door and peered out. Nothing was stirring in the street. No one had heard the commotion.

Good, I shall continue to stay in the shadows, picking this town apart until the priest arrives. The streets of Kortbeke will run red with the blood of these worthless pigs.

She looked around the room and saw a child's toys. *Kid means wife, and that means…clothes.*

She made her way to the washroom, wiping the blood off her naked body and glancing around the small bedroom. Opening up a chest at the foot of the bed, she saw a few items of women's clothing. She perused the few garments, picking out suitable attire. A beautiful, light-blue dress that complimented her fair skin and blond hair. Once dressed, she looked at herself in the mirror in the washroom, satisfied at her appearance.

Back in the living room, she inspected her handiwork. The man lay still on the floor losing massive amounts of blood from the deep puncture wounds on his chest and stomach.

She walked over to him, peering down at him. "Wake up. I've chosen you." She bit into her wrist, cutting it open and instantly drawing blood. Bending down, she extended her wrist, letting the tiny flow of blood seep out of her wound into his opened, unmoving mouth.

Chadwick blinked his eyes. He heard a voice somewhere in the foggy recesses of his brain. *I said, wake up! Now!* He tasted something wet in his mouth. It was thick and warm. Pursing his lips, he sucked at the woman's open cut and drank until she pulled back.

His eyes now fully open, he felt wetness on his chest and lifted his head from the ground, instantly seeing that his sides and chest were covered in blood. "What, what is happening? What was I drinking? Am I dead?" he sputtered out in a slurred, deep voice, wiping the blood from his lips.

A voice above him answered, "You most certainly are. But I've allowed you to exist a bit longer. As long as you follow my orders and carry them out exactly as I instruct."

He looked up and saw that a lantern had been ignited in his living quarters, lighting up his surroundings. His eyes fell upon the most stunningly beautiful women he had ever seen wearing his wife's dress, her wrist bleeding.

She tilted her head to the side, inspecting her property. "Yes, I do believe you will do just fine, big man. Up, on your feet, now."

Chadwick's first instinct was to tell the bitch to shut her lousy bitch mouth, or he would shut it for her. But something told him that was be very unwise. He pulled himself up, blood from his wounds dripping onto the hard, wood floor.

"What happened to me? Who are you?" Chadwick asked, trying to not appear as frightened as he was.

He watched the woman approach gracefully, sexually. Her lips pouty and alluring, her bosom full, almost popping out of his wife's slightly too-tight dress. Her long, flowing blond hair, so light in color it was almost white.

Inside Chadwick's body, the blood he had unwittingly ingested was spreading throughout his organs and seeping into his own bloodstream. Like a parasite, the alien host quickly took over, mutating his red and white blood cells in rapid succession, changing his DNA.

Chadwick, feeling his body rapidly morphing, screamed out in pain. "Oh, God! No! Ahh!" He curled up in a ball on the floor, every part of him suddenly feeling engulfed in flames as the new blood forged a path of destruction and rebirth inside him. The burning sensation began to subside while new levels of torture took over. His organs began to grow, pressing against his ribcage, his lungs expanded, as did his heart.

He clenched his fists into tight balls as the wolf's blood pumped so hard and rapidly through his veins they bubbled up and exposed purple lines across his body. This continued for what felt to Chadwick like hours, but only mere minutes had passed.

Bones pulled on cartilage and shifted around his skeletal frame, growing wider and longer, while muscle tissue separated from bones, causing Chadwick even greater levels of pain and agony. When his skull contracted and then expanded slightly, his eyeballs felt as though they would pop like grapes inside their sockets.

Once the blood had done its job and his body had fully adopted the new invading presence, the pain began to rescind. Slowly, he relaxed, worn out from the internal struggle, still curled into a ball but feeling better by the second.

Seeing that the process was complete, the woman tilted her head to the side as if waiting impatiently for him to look up at her. "It's finishing. Your blood has been changed. You can get up now."

Chadwick looked up at her with a combination of fear and outright hatred. He had the sudden desire to leap forward and murder the woman that had violated him, yet his mind told him that was not possible. Something about this woman, the most beautiful he had ever laid eyes on, would rip him apart, limb from limb, if he attempted anything other than absolute obedience.

Still glaring at her, he slowly stood to his feet, inspecting his body that appeared to be larger in every way than it was before he had been pushed into his home by this crazed woman. "What just happened to me?" he muttered.

Ignoring his question, she stated, "You look like a man I was married to in another life. Maybe that's why I chose you. No bother. Where is your wife and what I assume is your offspring?"

"Just a minute, I have some questions that need—" Chadwick began, looking at his impressive new physique then up to her.

The beautiful woman instantly grabbed him by the throat, lifting him off the ground as she stared at him with blue eyes that flashed bright yellow. "You will answer me, or you will *expire*, this time permanently. Don't assume your larger stature has made me any less formidable."

Looking into her glowing eyes with terror, he tried to speak but was unable to, due to her tight grip.

Satisfied she had driven her point home, she dropped the bloodied man to the ground.

Rubbing his neck, Chadwick's demeanor changed. He was clearly dealing with something utterly alien and supernatural. Something that had contaminated him with its vile blood. And he would lose, no matter what he attempted, unless he blindly followed the woman's commands.

"My wife, she is visiting relatives with my daughter," Chadwick said but his voice sounded unconvincing.

Looking at him warily, her eyes back to a beautiful blue, she replied, "Answer me again, and do not lie this time."

How does she know? Staring at her in disbelief, Chadwick answered, "She has left me. Taken my child with her, that bitch!"

"That's what I thought when I went through her belongings. Judging by your temper, I assume you beat her? Good. Just what I need, remorseless."

"I don't beat her!" Chadwick exclaimed, feeling his anger rise.

"Save it. I don't care what you did. I care what you do *now*. For me."

"Please, lady, am I dead?"

Sighing, she looked at the bite on her wrist, nodding at the rapid speed at which it was healing. "Yes, you are. I killed you. But unlike your foolish friends who most certainly will not be making any returning appearances, you, I have decided, could be of use. See, it is I that penetrate you. Not you men with your pathetic sex organs. I give and I taketh away. You drank from me, so, I giveth. And with my gift, I have ensured you continue to live after death. I am very particular about who gets this gift, as most are merely slaughtered like the pigs they are. Human pigs. Not me, though, my master saw the greatness in me. And I have been repaying him for the past two years."

"So, what are you?" Chadwick asked, curious in spite of himself.

"I am *the* evil. The taker," The woman grinned, leaning forward and staring up into his eyes. "And I am here to claim my prize before going back to my master. If you obey me, you too may join me, for a time. But that requires absolute and complete allegiance to me. So, will you do what I ask and live on with powers you can only dream of? Or do I sever that stupid, wife-beating, alcoholic head of yours from your neck?"

"I suppose, well, I suppose allegiance," Chadwick stuttered, realizing it was literally his only option.

"Good choice. You just saved your wife and child's life. I would have hunted them down after my business here was complete and slaughtered them, bathing in your child's blood," she said with an almost gentle smile.

Chadwick shook his head in disgust, then looked at his bloodied clothes. He felt his chest. "I thought I was scratched?"

"You were, and it was fatal. But you've healed, thanks to me, I giveth and I taketh away. I took your life, easily I might add, and gave it back to you to through my blood. With my blood, and the blood of the beautiful beast that gave it to me, you can live forever. But you must feed and mind me. Much like I mind my master. That is why I am here in the first place, to do his bidding. You see, this is the way of the werewolf; you must die to be reborn in your creator's image. We cross from life to death, and back again. Much in the same way as the vampire."

Her tone became crisp and demanding as she ordered, "Now, first task, go take care of the filth outside on the street, bring them in here. We can't have any panic from the peasants in this town, not yet anyway. The panic will come later. Go, now!"

Unable to resist what felt like a spell or psychic link from her tainted, superhuman, supernatural blood now pumping through his heart, he nodded, quickly making his way to the door.

Chadwick walked outside and peered down the alley from which they came, his eyesight now fantastic. Better than fantastic. He could see in the dark almost as if it were broad daylight. He looked down to the ground and saw his friends lying in pools of their own blood. He quickly went over to where each body lay and bent down to inspect them. He felt nothing for their brutal deaths. What he did feel was hunger inside his expanded stomach. *That meat looks delicious.* "No!" he told himself. "The woman instructed me to bring them back inside, nothing more."

He reluctantly grabbed them both and hoisted them up with ease by their bloodied clothes. He carried the bodies to his house and once inside, tossed them on top of each other on the floor like rag dolls. Both heads were either removed completely or hanging on by mere strands of flesh.

My strength, I have so much strength! Chadwick felt his already large muscles bulging under his bloodied shirt.

"Good, you can take orders. Change out of those bloody rags. We have much to do in Kortbeke. There is someone else I very much would like to meet," the woman said, thinking of the black-haired woman she had seen earlier.

Nodding, he turned to go to his room, sensing that his life, whatever it was up to that point, was over. The new Chadwick had been created by this evil beast in his living quarters. His wife plagued his mind as he hastily took his bloodied clothes off and put new ones on. Thinking of her, he became enraged, smashing his fist against the mirror in front of him. Glass shattered to the floor and his hand was instantly sliced open. He held it up and watched as the blood flowed down onto his wrist. He licked it and instantly found the taste to be *delicious* as he recalled the sweet warm liquid trickling down his throat minutes earlier. He suddenly had a deep craving for more, much more. But not his own. He thought of his dead friends laying in his house and salivated at the thought of sinking his teeth into their soft bodies.

Shaking it off, he ran his hands across his flat and suddenly quite muscular stomach. Not only had the deep wounds nearly all healed up, he could feel his new muscles pushing forth. Hard and strong. He washed the blood off his hand and splashed water on his face, running his wet hands through his dark hair until it was slicked back.

Looking into the broken mirror, he saw his eyes were a darker hue now, almost entirely black. His facial features, while still resembling the Chadwick of earlier in the evening, were now hardened and chiseled. Appearing ten years younger, he saw how handsome he had miraculously become, even more so than in his youthful years. He smiled at himself then stepped out into the living quarters where the woman stood, looking out the window.

"I'm hungry, so hungry!" Chadwick said, his confidence returning.

With her back turned to him, she replied, "Later. First, tell me about Fr. Kries. Where is he? The frail, old priest in no longer with us."

"What happened to him?" Chadwick asked.

"I killed him. I needed to make sure a message was sent loud and clear once he arrives back here," she said coolly.

"The young priest is over in Salzben. He helps out over there with their parish. He's typically back by Monday morning on the weekends he travels there," Chadwick said, walking up behind her.

"How far is this Salzben?"

Chadwick thought for a moment then replied, "I believe it's around five miles at most. He'll likely be back by dawn."

She thought on this. *Do I go and find him in this Salzben town? Or do I stick with my plan and let him find the priest dead along with other townsfolk?*

"We have police in this town, two of them. They will certainly find out what's going on here," Chadwick said.

"No, they won't. I killed them and everyone in Granhal earlier tonight," the woman said nonchalantly.

With mouth agape, Chadwick replied, "You? You killed everyone?"

"Of course I did. So, we are now in charge. I am in charge." She thought back to walking the streets of her old town, armed with two guns. The thrill of blowing the schoolteacher's head off.

Chadwick, behind her, began shedding tears. Not of sadness but of overwhelming dread and horror at what his life had become, and tears for the hell they would soon be raining down on the unfortunate souls of Kortbeke. Seeing the tears, the woman smirked.

Seeing he no longer had control, all of it handed over to the beautiful woman in his empty house, he realized that to struggle for what he had become was pointless. Quickly wiping his eyes of the last tears he would ever shed, he replied, "The mayor. There is a mayor in this town. He would be next in command; the man is useless." Chadwick then fell silent, hanging his head as he contemplated what was happening to him.

Nodding and glad she had chosen this one, she answered, "Useless or not, you will see to it that he is dealt with."

"What is your name? So that I may call you by it," Chadwick asked reverently.

"My name is Everly. But to you, it's *master*," Everly responded, glaring at him.

"Yes…master," Chadwick answered, knowing his fate had been sealed by the woman's tainted blood.

"What will happen to me?" Chadwick asked, thinking of the shape-shifting attributes she had displayed earlier.

"You will find out soon enough." Everly smirked, knowing that what little humanity the man had left would soon be depleted as her blood and her curse would overtake him completely, rendering him nothing more than a servant. A *slave*.

"You may now eat," she commanded as she turned from him and toward the door.

Now she needed only to wait for the priest's return. *Then, when I have severed his head from his neck and feasted on his flesh, I will take his sacrificed, lifeless body with me as I make my way back to Romania to fulfill my destiny and that of my eternal master.* Her full lips turned to a smile.

Behind her, Chadwick obeyed her command happily, lunging on top of Jonathan's corpse, tearing him open, and feeding on his insides greedily.

Once satisfied her new slave had gotten his fill, she left Chadwick's house.

Chadwick quickly wiped the blood and drool from his mouth, jumped up and followed behind. He quietly closed the door behind them, shutting out his old life as well.

Standing outside on the narrow side street, she looked to the sky then to the puddles of blood where her crimes had been committed, satisfied at how everything was going thus far. Pausing a moment before moving out into the night, she spoke quietly to the darkness.

"Master, grant me further cover of night so I can best carry out my task before coming back to you with the sacrifice you require. Bring confusion to these lowly townsfolk and turn them on each other, so as to better succeed in my most unholy mission! You, who wait on your faithful servant for your triumphant return, help me to succeed. I will kill as many as is needed as long as it leads me closer to the priest! And then Burnmere will, at last, fall at our feet. The amulet will return to its rightful owner once the priest is killed by my hand and delivered to you."

Her blue dress flowing behind her, Everly began walking toward the building with lights on earlier. She was very keen to meet the woman with the long black hair. She had a good feeling about that one.

Close behind her followed Chadwick, dressed in black clothing, his large physique making him look all the more imposing. His black eyes stared at the back of the woman who called herself Everly. What was her story? How did she become the thing she was now? When did she fall so far from grace to lead her down this path that he was now most assuredly on?

His mind grew weaker the longer he was infected with the blood from her wrist. Though his body felt stronger, the thoughts pulsing through his head became more and more sinister. He thought of his wife and daughter, now fading from his memory. *What did they look like again? Does it even matter?*

As she walked down the silent street, Everly's prayer was being granted. Now that the rain had ceased, a blanket of darkness descended from the mountains above, shrouding her and her accomplice further into the shadows. She had called forth the blackness before, in other towns, as she searched for prey, getting familiar with the powers of darkness granted to her back in Burnmere several years prior. With the supernatural darkness brought confusion, untrust, and ultimately, murder.

Everly delighted in seeing the ruin of towns. All in service to her master, the one that had sent the wolf to lay with her back in Burnmere, the one who would raise up the mighty Pricolici once more and with it, rule the world. The lord of this world, the fallen angel himself, would one day rule supreme and she would be at his feet, worshipping.

He will accept my adoration; he will love me! No one in this filthy world has ever truly loved me, but he will. All I have to do is bring him a blood offering.

This night wasn't over yet, she had much death and destruction to bring to the poor souls of Kortbeke, nearly all of whom lay fast asleep in their beds. They were unaware that one of Satan's own had arrived in their town that very night whose mission was locating the young priest and bringing about his imminent demise.

As part of her mission, she would pick and choose at will who would live, who would die, and who would be turned into one of her own creations, descendants of the one that made her who she now was, a lycanthropic creature of the night. Damned to hell, but before getting there, her sole purpose, her very existence, was to create *chaos* while securing her ultimate sacrifice. A task she intended to fulfill this night.

Chapter 9

✝

Fr. Kries's Grim Discovery

12:15 AM

"**D**on't bother sending for the priest, I killed him." The
evil woman looked up at him and smiled a thin, evil
smile before breaking into a cackle. Her eyes turned yellow,
her teeth long and pointed, drool spilling out of the sides of
her mouth.

A soft voice, more of a thought, spoke into his subconscious after the woman faded from his dream and he was met
with blackness of deep sleep. "You shall be shown the means
to defeat the evil that spawned her. You must be strong."

Fr. Simon Kries woke up in a cold sweat in his small bed
in the single-room cottage on the outskirts of Salzben, close

139

to St. Mary, Mother of God Parish. The room was dark but he quickly got his bearings and wiped the beads of sweat from his face, running his hands through his messy dark hair, pulling it back behind his head. He felt soaked though it wasn't warm in his room.

Fall was coming, and thus, the temperatures were falling, especially this close to the Swiss Alps. The snow-topped mountains brought not just their majestic beauty but also cold fronts rolling off their hills. Today was one such day as it had been drizzly in Salzben on and off since the morning hours when he presided over Mass for the good people of the village.

Getting to bed early to make the trek back to Kortbeke at dawn, to help the ailing and aging Fr. Steffen, Fr. Kries had been wakened from a nightmare. One in which a strange creature hunted down people in the town he had been residing in now for three years. Yawning, he wiped his eyes and glanced at the ticking clock on the nightstand. The time read 12:15 AM. He hadn't planned on waking and heading back to Kortbeke until six and had been asleep for just slightly over three hours.

He thought back to the words seemingly whispered to him before being startled awake, *You will meet her and her kind, and you will do battle with them.*

Shaking his head, puzzled, he spoke aloud, "Lord, are you trying to tell me something? Or should I have passed on that second glass of wine after dinner earlier this evening?" He thought back to the wine, locally made, that was certainly stronger than what he was used to but glad that it had put him to sleep so quickly. Now, however, its effects had greatly diminished and the nightmare had left him wide awake. He placed his hand on his heart, feeling it thump hard inside his chest.

He whipped the bed covers off and sat on its edge, quickly lighting the lantern resting on the nightstand beside him. He stretched his thin frame. He was of normal height but had always been underweight, likely from the malnourishment he had experienced as a young child. He had filled out some as he got older and now would be considered rather handsome if not for his sad eyes. Even when he smiled, a deep sadness bubbled up from beneath his gentle exterior.

It was his reserved nature that endeared him to many people. He had a kind and loving heart, wanting to do good wherever, and whenever, he could. Almost as though he felt his life were one long atonement.

Shaking his head, he decided to splash his face with water to get rid of the quickly drying, sticky sweat. His undergarments were equally wet with perspiration. At the small wash basin on the other side of his bed, he dipped his hands in the cool water and splashed several handfuls onto his weary but alert face. Not bothering to dry it, he ran some of the water up through his hair.

"Well, if I wasn't before, I'm fully awake now. What was that dream about?" He tried to recall the last time a dream like that had terrified him as this one had and came up empty.

He stripped his wet shirt off and lay back down once more, this time choosing to keep the lantern lit. He hated to admit it, but he was still scared. The creature, or whatever it was in the dream, was stalking its prey down a narrow alley. He almost recognized the men it was pursuing. One had a beard, the other was balding, and the other was one he had seen before with these two.

"Did I dream about Chadwick and his two less-than-pleasant friends he runs around with? Jonathan and, hmm, what's the other one's name? Richard, maybe? Why would I dream about them? I don't even know them. They certainly don't attend Mass and they hang around Maximilian's often. I believe the bearded man has a wife and child…." Fr. Kries continued running the dream through his mind. So vivid he could nearly discern landmarks down the alleyway.

In the dream, he was the perpetrator. His eyes saw the horrors unfolding around him. Whatever body he inhabited inside the dream state was large and ferocious. Stalking its prey then quickly destroying their bodies, two of them, at least. Blood splayed out onto wet cobblestone. Gurgled pleas for help went unanswered. All ending with a sudden shift to a woman with yellow eyes looking up at him as she lay dying from a gunshot to the stomach. Those words she uttered; he shook with fear at the thought.

Picking up his rosary that lay beside the clock, he sat on the edge of his bed and began praying it. Focusing on it instead of the dream, in the hopes that it would calm him down and he could fall back asleep after all of the beads had been prayed. This was a typical ritual for Fr. Kries on many evenings when he wanted to lull himself to sleep in the sweet embrace of his Lord and Savior, Jesus Christ, and the blessed, loving Mother Mary.

Something else troubled him as he recited another Hail Mary. His dream had begun inside St. Raphael's, but it was fuzzy what had actually transpired there. He couldn't recall it, exactly. Brief glimpses of Fr. Steffen cleaning the church. Something in the shadow, maybe. Then the jump to the woman covered in blood, lying on the ground, *smiling* as she died. He felt as though he knew who the person was, but the image of her had faded upon stirring from his slumber.

Snapping out of it and realizing he was no longer praying, he set the rosary back on the nightstand. "Lord? What is thy will?" he said aloud.

As soon as the words were uttered, a feeling of dread fell over him. Not the feeling of waking from a night terror but one of utter and complete evil. *You shall be shown the means to defeat the evil that spawned her. You must be strong.* What did it all mean? Why were these dreams more like visions? It was as if someone or something was warning him. Preparing him for something that was coming. He jumped up once more. Without bothering to make the bed, he dressed in his clerical suit quickly, contemplating not putting on the white collar, but then feeling a strong desire to wear it, a premonition that something was very wrong pushing heavily on his psyche.

After dressing, he quickly grabbed a change of clothes and several personal hygiene items, hastily placing them in his knapsack and flinging it over his back. Lastly, he swiped his rosary off of the nightstand, clenching it tightly in his hand as he picked up the lantern. Satisfied he had enough oil to take him where he needed to go in the darkness of the midnight hour, he opened the cottage door and stepped out into the cold night.

Once outside, he considered asking the owner of the small cottage to run him back to Kortbeke, but Manuel

Kramer and his wife were old and waking him at this hour was out of the question. He couldn't bring himself to ask such a huge favor. Especially with the amount of time it would take to explain things and then hitch up the horse. No, he would go on foot and make haste doing so.

He looked up at the sky and was relieved to see the rain had ceased. He would walk fast to keep warm and, more importantly, get back to Kortbeke as quickly as possible. Glancing back at Salzben, he gave it the sign of the cross then, pulling his coat tight against his body, headed in the direction of his nightmare.

Thoughts of his seminary days raced through his mind, his ordination in Austria, and what a joyous occasion it had been. Especially considering his grim background. He was happy to receive his holy orders placing him in Kortbeke, and for the past three years he had made many friends and even a few unfortunate enemies—with the last name of Karlen.

He and the mayor hadn't exactly seen eye to eye on a great number of things that he guessed were issues Uma had taken up with him, demanding he put his foot down.

Like helping some of the less able-bodied in town with food and clothing. Supplying the Kortbeke Elementary School and its few teachers with better academic materials. Funds taken from the city's coffers which they felt would be better used for keeping the southside in tip-top shape with nicer buildings and up-to-date luxuries. The excuse, of course, was to bring in more monies to the town.

But Fr. Kries knew better. This was all to line the pockets of Uma and Nils Karlen. They wanted to be in charge of all things in Kortbeke, making it a town for only the most affluent. Something that flew in the face of everything Fr. Kries believed in and knew Fr. Steffen felt the same.

Fr. Steffen had warned him upon his arrival about the Karlens, but Kries wasn't a man to be pushed around, quickly standing up to the bully bar owners of Kortbeke and almost instantly making enemies. Especially with Uma, who seemed to particularly single him out and needle him every chance she got, constantly trying to trap him into a corner when it came to theology. He never backed down, in his own calm and loving way, and soon she saw he wouldn't be pushed around or bought out. So, she relented slightly, going around him and Fr. Steffen and taking matters to the town council. Especially when it came to matters of church upkeep and repairs, along with the distribution of food and clothing to, quite literally, anyone.

Something about the woman had struck him as odd ever since coming to Kortbeke. It wasn't just her mean-spiritedness. Something else. Like, she was either hiding something or she had gotten away with something that had likely molded her into the evil woman she was in the thirties. He kept a watchful eye on the Karlens and their exclusive bar for the elite of the town. Elites that hadn't existed before she came along.

While he quite liked serving the town of Salzben, he wished he could stay in Kortbeke to better serve under Fr. Steffen, a truly great man of the Lord. And a man who, as he aged, wasn't able to get around nearly as well, especially with his bad ankle.

After his dream, he feared something terrible had happened to his friend and mentor. Trying to push the thoughts out of his head, he hurried on down the dark road as the few lights from Salzben faded in the distance and he found himself in near darkness except for his small lantern.

The towns were close enough to each other that it wouldn't take long for Kortbeke to come into view after a few more miles of walking. Also nearby was the even smaller town of Granhal, which he would pass by on the road he travelled on this lonely Sunday night.

It was eerily quiet as he approached Granhal. He was moving fast enough that his body stayed warm, and he was thankful the rain had ceased. However, with no sound of rainfall, the utter silence began to trouble the priest. On any other night, he wouldn't have given it any thought, but he had clearly seen *something* take place in his nightmare vision, and while this was more or less a gut instinct, his were rarely wrong.

He peered over at Granhal as he passed the far edge of town, looking in at Florus Widmer's place. It was well past midnight, so it was no surprise that everything was dark in a town of only fifty people, but something seemed off. No pets or livestock could be heard, the only noise coming from his shoes on the dirt and gravel road. He wished the moon was out, but the night sky was cloudy after the rain, thus making it significantly more difficult to see.

He held out his lantern toward Widmer's small field where he kept his cattle. There were none to be seen. None standing up, that is. His lantern revealed large lumps laid out on the darkened field. Fr. Kries's eyes widened as he realized what he was looking at. He quickly moved toward the fence and saw that a portion of the top wood plank had been ripped off and lay on the ground several feet away.

"What in God's name happened here?" he uttered, confused as well as frightened.

He contemplated whether to investigate further or keep moving toward Kortbeke. Once more, he raised his lantern toward one of the large lumps lying still in the field, this time seeing blood and organs as though a cow had been turned almost inside out. He gasped and recoiled at the grisly sight.

Something nearby made a sound on the road. *The footstep of an animal!* With nothing to defend himself, he instinctively called out, "Who's there? Show yourself!"

The sound came again, this time closer, along with heavy breathing. Fr. Kries instantly filled with terror imagining what could be lurking out there in the dark that had perpetrated such butchery on the cows.

He held out his lantern as far as his shaking arm would extend to try to get a look at the animal. He saw a shape walking toward him.

"Those are horseshoes I hear!" Fr. Kries exclaimed, keeping his arm extended.

The sound of a horse's soft grunt rose from the darkness as Lambert's brown Swiss-bred Freiberger stepped out in front of him. He knew the horse well, as he was friendly with the chief of police in Kortbeke and had taken a liking to his large steed.

"Brutus! What are you doing out here, where's—" Fr. Kries stopped talking as events were connecting in his mind. The strangeness of the chief of police's horse in a town several miles away from where it should be at this time of night without its owner wasn't just strange, it was sinister.

The horse, recognizing the priest, came up to the young man and nuzzled his free hand, giving a slight neigh as it did so.

"Shh, shh, it's alright," Fr. Kries said in a whisper, holding up the lantern so he could inspect the horse for any injuries as he stroked its neck and nose. "Well, big fella, you don't look injured. But the mystery of you being out here in the middle of the night is troubling indeed."

He noticed the horse was saddled up and still had its bit and reins attached. Shaking his head in puzzlement, he took the reins gently in his free hand. "If you're here, so is Lambert. Looks like I'm not leaving Granhal just yet, but I can certainly make up time with you if we can't locate your owner. Come on."

He led the horse to the town's entrance and peered down the lonely single street at the homes that lined either side. He had been to the town on several occasions, a Protestant town with a Protestant church and pastor who lived beside his small church building. From his vantage point, he could see Church of the Risen Christ up the darkened street. All was quiet as expected.

Fr. Kries walked a bit farther on, toward old man Fritz's house that subbed as a police station. Everyone knew, though, that Lambert and his deputy Erni were the men really in charge of Granhal and because of that, hadn't pursued replacing Fritz, who was well past his prime.

His shoes and Lambert's horse made light crunching sounds on the dirt-covered road until something caught

Kries's eye. He held the oil lantern near to the ground and, to his horror, saw what looked like blood in front of Fritz's tiny house. The drizzling rain had surely washed some of it away, but it was clearly visible even in the darkened night.

He quickly stood to his feet. The nightmare, the slaughtered cows, and now this. Something was very wrong in the small town of Granhal and Fr. Kries had a sinking feeling it was tied to the horrible dream he had just had.

Holding the lantern out, he aimed it in the direction of old man Fritz's door, which, to his surprise, was opened. Leading Brutus up to the entrance of the old run-down shack, he tied the reins around the front porch post and gave him a gentle pat on the neck. "Don't run off on me, big fella, you hear?"

The horse gave a brief snort in response, as if it knew what was requested of him.

Turning to face the opened door, Kries went inside.

Chapter 10

†

The Blackest Night Arrives

12:30 AM

Once Davide left for Granhal, Nina, Ruppert, and Klaus were the only ones left in the church. With Davide out of the picture for the time being, they felt the return of chaos, confusion, and ongoing unrelenting fear pressing in on them.

The discovery that his nightmare the previous night wasn't just a random bad dream but something far more sinister had shaken Mayor Klaus to his core. *Great sacrifice would be needed to stop the evil.* The words uttered deep in subconscious haunted him.

He had never believed in the supernatural and was barely even a man of faith, relying on his good looks when he was younger to get by in life. Now in his mid-thirties, with no wife and no kids and having an affair with the most divisive person in town, he had begun to re-evaluate his life. He would certainly be voted out when it came to election time, unless Uma was able to work her devilish magic and win the mayor's seat for a second term. Highly unlikely even for her, at this point. Then what?

These thoughts had been plaguing him as of late, knowing that sex with Uma was just that, sex. Empty, loveless and at times, violent sex. Always from her. Biting, scratching, slapping, spitting, degrading. It would come to an end, eventually, and likely, with him disgraced.

He knew people talked in a small town like Kortbeke, and he saw the way they eyed him with utter contempt. He had done his best to side with the townsfolk on numerous issues but ultimately, Uma had him wrapped around her little finger. If her dufus husband Nils had half a brain, he would know she was fucking the mayor to service increasingly morbid desires she was certainly not getting from him. The power she craved seemed to grow stronger with age.

And Klaus was stuck with her. He had made his bed, so to speak, and now he was lying in it.

Then the dream happened. Not just to him but to Davide and Nina. Who else had had this same crazy dream of a woman with yellow eyes the previous night? And for what reason? *Why them? Why me?*

"Klaus! Hello?" Nina called out.

Blinking, he snapped out of his daze, looking over at Ruppert and Nina standing in the entrance to the church.

"You coming?" Nina said hastily.

He looked toward the altar in revulsion and disgust. Who could have done such a thing? Especially to a harmless old priest? *God doesn't give a shit about me, but that guy? He was one of the good ones.* He shook his head.

"I suppose we shouldn't just leave him there like that, right?" Klaus exclaimed.

Ruppert nodded slowly and joined Klaus. "Come on, Nina, you can wait up front."

"Not a chance. I'll help," she quickly fired back.

Ruppert turned to face her. "No, we need to watch each other's backs. Watch the front entrance for anything out of the ordinary, got it?"

"Alright. But then we go to Leonz."

"Then we go to Leonz," Ruppert repeated as he and Klaus headed up to the altar.

"Crazy old man, this could have likely been avoided regardless of what caused this. That geezer should have retired when he broke his ankle," Klaus blurted out, covering his mouth at having to see the massacre once more.

"Do you listen to the words that come out of your mouth? I'm no altar boy or saint, but a small bit of respect might be in order here, all things considered. Right, Mayor? Now come on, grab his legs," Ruppert said grimly, glaring at the mayor.

Klaus mumbled under his breath, "Look who's talking there, Mr. I-can't-keep-my-wife-and-kids," but Ruppert didn't have time for Klaus's shit, so it was ignored.

After the men removed Fr. Steffen's body from the altar, they placed him on the floor then took the blood-covered sheet that still lay on the stone slab and placed it over the corpse.

Ruppert looked down at the priest's head, still on the ground. He bent down and gently picked it up and carried it over to its body. He averted his eyes as he set the head down gently beside it then looked over at Klaus. "Whoever, or whatever did this, I hope to have the opportunity to shove that club up its ass."

"I just want to get the hell out of here, place gives me the creeps," Klaus retorted.

Ruppert was going to reprimand him once more but was interrupted.

"Guys, better get up here. Something's happening out here," Nina called out.

Klaus and Ruppert ran to the entrance of the church and peered out at what had caught her attention. The night sky had seemed to disappear above Kortbeke and a blackness that was indescribable had replaced it. Along with this, a thin blanket of fog was washing through town.

"What in God's name…" Klaus said in a hushed tone.

Ruppert replied, "God has nothing to do with any of this."

"We have to go, now!" Nina said, watching the fog begin to blanket the outskirts of Kortbeke.

Ruppert looked gravely out at the black emptiness blanketing the town and slowly started to shake his head. "Nina, we can't go out there in this. I don't know what's happening, but we won't be able to see in front of our faces! We'll be sitting ducks!"

"I don't care! I'm not leaving Leonz up there alone!" she exclaimed.

"Shh! Keep your voice down!" Ruppert added, watching the usual nighttime sky grow dimmer and dimmer.

She glared at him and realized he was, in fact, correct. They all had to keep their voices down in the hopes that the town of Kortbeke would simply sleep on through the night until dawn and be none the wiser. But then what?

"Fine," she whispered. "But we have lanterns. We can do this!" She looked back at the sky and quickly doubted herself. *Shit!*

They all stood in the doorway in silence, debating what their next move would be.

"That is the blackest night my eyes have ever seen," Ruppert exclaimed in a hoarse whisper.

Mayor Klaus, at a loss for words, wished he was as far from this town as his legs could carry him.

✝

Leonz finished up the cleaning duties required of him, lit his small lantern for the walk home, and left Maximilian's. He locked the door behind him and started his trek back to his place, making sure to avoid looking in the direction of Uma's house across the street.

He had several blocks to walk and, at times, this was the best part of his day if he wasn't planning on meeting up with Nina later. Tonight, however, they had planned on meeting back at his place.

He stopped, noticing an eerie silence had fallen through the street. No wind, no rain. It was as if the air itself had ceased to move.

His eyes were drawn to the mountains above Kortbeke. He shook his head in disbelief. Even on dreary nights like tonight, the mountains were usually visible from town. But they had all but vanished, replaced with mere outlines in the distance. Along with the darkness came a blanket of fog cover moving rapidly through the streets, as though it were alive.

"What the hell?" he said in astonishment, blinking hard to make sure he wasn't seeing things. He held up the lantern to see if that would be of any help. It wasn't.

"You there, something catch your fancy?" a voice from down the street called in his direction.

He quickly looked over to the sound but couldn't see anything. The street, what he could see of it, was empty. The only things visible were the two gas lanterns on the sign above the bar reading "Maximilian's Inn," lighting up their immediate surroundings. Directly across the street, even Uma's house was darker than usual at this time of night.

"Little colored boy wants to go home to see his lovely little lady-friend, that's what little boy wants to do!" the male voice called out once more.

Leonz narrowed his eyes, suddenly frightened and angry at the man's racist taunts.

Gathering his courage and extending the lantern in the direction of the voice, Leonz called out, "Show yourself, coward!"

From across the pitch-black street emerged a large shape. It moved out until it stood in the center of the street, a tall, imposing figure. Its arms hung at its sides and its back hunched over slightly.

Leonz squinted to get a better look, instantly becoming filled with terror. "Who are you?"

The figure walked forward and soon, even in the darkness, it became evident to Leonz who this was. It was Chadwick, but somehow, different. Stronger and taller, wider and more muscular in appearance. And he looked crazed, like a rabid dog. The closer he got to Leonz, the more apparent it became that something was seriously wrong with him. His eyes appeared to be almost solid black, and his hair was slicked back tightly against his large skull in a fashion Leonz had never seen before.

Instantly, Leonz began backing up toward Maximilian's as the imposing Chadwick grew nearer.

"Chadwick, I don't know what's gotten into you, but you need to get home, we both do! There's a dark fog bank coming through here any minute!" Leonz exclaimed.

But the man didn't stop. Saliva dripped from the grin wrapping across his face as his hands clenched into fists then released, then clenched back again.

He's huge! Why is he so massive? Leonz thought of his few options if the man attacked. Run back to Maximilian's and fiddle with the lock? Or, make a run for it and hope he could lose him on a side street and get back to his house by another route?

Before he had a chance to make a decision, someone else stepped out from behind Chadwick.

Long, blond hair flowed elegantly around a woman whose sheer beauty gave Leonz pause. Everything about this was completely off. Chadwick had grown in stature and appeared to have black eyes. And this woman, who was she and what was she doing in front of Maximilian's?

"S-stay back!" Leonz called out, more frightened at the sheer absurdity of this woman in a light-blue dress standing in front of him than he was of Chadwick.

Looking him over, she glanced back to Chadwick, "Tisk, tisk. I think I made the wrong choice. This dark-skinned one is quite…fetching. Oh, well." She turned and walked toward Uma's house, leaving Chadwick standing in the street facing Leonz.

The dig from Everly made an already ferocious Chadwick even more feral. He glared at his opponent, licking his lips in anticipation for the meal that was to come.

"Shit," Leonz muttered, seeing Chadwick breathing heavily and moving in toward him.

Instead of turning back to Maximilian's, he quickly cut over onto a side street. He knew the alleys and shortcuts well on this side of town that would take him further north. He was defenseless and had only a small lantern to light up his immediate surroundings in the dark alleyways.

Right on Seventh Street.

He heard footsteps behind him, slamming against the cobblestones. His mind raced, trying to remember which way to turn. The route he was on wouldn't take him past his own house but that wasn't an option, unless he wanted to go through the rock wall that was now Chadwick. *So, where do I go? What if Nina is waiting for me?*

He ran as fast as he could as the steps behind him grew louder, gaining on him.

"Keep running, little boy! I can see oh, so clearly in this darkness!" the deep voice called out.

Left at Fifth Street.

The lantern swung in his hand as he clung to it tightly. Without it, he was doomed.

Almost back to Main Street. Then where?

The voice called out again, but this time it was a snarl.

What the hell?

He kept running as fast as he was able on the wet stones from the rain earlier. He saw one more right turn coming up and something else. A stack of apple crates. He was near the Whitmer's produce store on the other side of the street, adjacent to St. Raphael's. Old man Whitmer had set his apples and cart out for the night to set up first thing Monday morning. The cold and rain would protect them and keep them fresh.

"Sorry, Whitmer!" Leonz exclaimed, approaching the crates. He slid to a halt, grabbing hold of one of the crates in the middle and pulling it out. It, along with the three crates above it, came crashing to the ground, busting open and spilling apples everywhere across the street.

Leonz took off, not looking back to see if the stall tactic would work. He heard a crashing noise from behind him and the thud of something large smashing to the ground. Along with it, another snarl rang out into the night.

What the hell is that?

He was now on the main street running through town. On the opposite side of the road was St. Raphael's. *Fr. Steffen, be inside, somewhere in that church, please!* Out of breath, he ran across the street and saw that the door was closed.

Behind him, Chadwick was back on his feet and moving toward him once more.

He glanced back for a second but could see nothing in the darkness other than a vague outline moving quickly in his direction. Leonz ran hard across the street, up the few steps leading to the front entrance of the church, grabbed the handle and twisted it.

It was locked. "No, no, no! Shit!" He began pounding on the door with his free hand, hearing the footsteps behind him landing on the street as they made their way toward him.

Leonz smashed his fist against the door once more. *Please, Fr. Steffen! Please wake up and open the door!*

Chadwick reached the steps and Leonz had no other options left. He turned to face his pursuer, pulling back his arm holding the lantern and, as hard as he could, throwing it in the face of what had once been Chadwick.

Leonz stared, horrified, at the grizzly figure in front of him. His facial structure had widened and what was once his nose appeared to be pushing out, forming a snout. His eyes narrowed, gleaming yellow. Human-shaped ears were replaced with pointed, fur-covered ones and his face sprouted black fur. The rest of his large, hulking body was also growing at an exponential rate, towering over seven feet tall with huge, muscular arms and hands sprouting thick, long claws hanging at his sides. His chest was bubbling and continually expanding under the skin as the tight shirt ripped from his body.

The glass from the lantern shattered against his mutating, continuously evolving face, spilling the small bit of remaining kerosine and open flames across his exposed flesh.

Chadwick instantly put his hands against his engulfed face as fire singed his thick, black hair. His snarls sounded like an animal in pain mixed with a man's voice attempting to cry out. The figure flailed around violently, lighting up his immediate surroundings as the flames had now caught his clothes on fire.

Behind Leonz, a latch clicked and the church door pushed open. Leonz, who was leaning against it, spilled inside and onto the floor. "Close the door, now!" he shouted, pointing at the being outside flailing around, trying to extinguish the flames.

"Leonz!" a woman's voice called out behind him.

"Nina!" Leonz shouted, seeing her run over to him. He immediately pulled himself up and saw Ruppert Sprenger and Klaus Kessler peering out the front door of the church at the flailing figure just outside.

"What the hell is that!" Klaus called out, holding the door open.

"Close the door, damnit! Do it, now!" Leonz shouted.

Ruppert, seeing the terror in his eyes, quickly grabbed hold of the door with Klaus and slammed it shut. "Lock it, Klaus!" he exclaimed.

Hastily, Klaus turned the lock, bolting the thick wooden door shut tight.

Leonz stood to his feet with Nina helping him up.

Ruppert and Klaus turned to look at their new guest, doubled over and gasping for breath.

"What in the hell was that?!" Ruppert asked.

"Oh, Leonz, are you hurt?" Nina asked.

Leonz looked around, his eyes falling on Nina. He leaned forward and kissed her on the lips, holding her in his arms. "Thank God you're okay. Thank God you all were here, or I would most assuredly be dead right now!"

Klaus inspected Leonz. "Well? What was that out there?"

"I'm not entirely sure. It used to be Chadwick Kern. But it isn't him anymore. He, or it, is something different. Much larger, huge. I don't know how to explain it but whatever it is, was over seven feet tall! And he was changing! Damnit, he was changing into something else! I saw hair pushing out of his face. His nose was, I don't know how to explain it." He paused. "It looked like it was pushing itself outward. And his teeth, Christ! His teeth were *huge!*"

The three of them watched him anxiously, waiting for more.

"Why was he burning? Should we be helping him?" Klaus replied, confused.

"I smashed my lantern on its face! Are you not hearing me? It wasn't Chadwick any longer. Whatever that thing is out there, it sure as hell is no longer human! That much I am certain of! Some kind of creature that could stand on its hind legs! It wasn't a bear, it had human attributes!"

"That's not possible! You're speaking nonsense!" Klaus shouted, not wanting to believe this morbid new bit of information.

Leonz shook his head at the mayor, "Feel free to go back out there and inspect it. Whatever it was, it was changing before I lit it on fire!"

Ruppert stared at Leonz, from the panic etched across his face, he guessed the young lad was telling the truth, or at least what he *thought* he saw.

Outside, in the pitch blackness, Chadwick had extinguished the flames at last. Most of his clothes were burned off, he was smoldering, and he felt the pain of what normally would have killed him. But, thanks to the woman's mysterious, supernatural, life-giving blood that now coursed through his veins, he was still alive. In his rage, he had begun transforming into what he truly was now before being lit on fire. The strength he felt as he changed was indescribable. Pure animalistic power and strength pumped through his massive body along with hate-fueled rage.

Lit on fire by that little bastard inside this church.

He stared at the door with blackened, hate-filled hungry eyes. His bones were caught in a state of limbo, as if he had been thwarted in his efforts to transform. Not quite human and not quite beast. All that mattered was feeding the craving in the pit of his stomach and sating the rage that filled his mind,

Shaking his sizzling head as bits of burnt flesh fell to the ground, he tried to think back to what he was like before this. *Who was I?* His fogged-over mind was becoming less human and more animalistic, with only one thought on its mind, getting inside that church and killing all who had evaded him.

Behind him, in a nearby house, a voice in the darkness called out. "Who's there? I heard shouting. Why is it so dark out there?"

The Chadwick beast slowly turned to face the voice coming from the house opposite the church. Saliva began dripping from his opened mouth onto his burnt body.

Chapter 11

✝

Nils Opens Up

1:00 AM

Davide rode Bertha as fast as he could toward Granhal, considering the late hour. On the way, he thought of Emila and Frida, knowing his wife would stay awake until he returned. His mind went to the last argument they had in which she had shared her growing concerns with his late nights at the bar, arguing that their daughter needed him home in the evening, not serving a room full of drunks with Nina as his only help.

The longer Hubschmid's was opened, the more Uma and her husband tried to throw a wrench into its gears. Sanitation notifications from the town council. Seemingly new permit notifications every year for any number of minor and quite ridiculous things. All of which made the job less and less enjoyable, which he admittedly took home with him. He understood her concerns, and, on many nights, he missed both his wife and little girl immensely.

But tonight was different, and his absence couldn't be avoided. He weighed out his options for help, of which none were very good. If he pushed any of this onto Mayor Klaus, things would certainly get worse, the man simply wasn't a leader. Waiting until morning to attempt to figure out what was going on was equally dangerous, as Davide had a strong hunch that whatever did this was likely not finished, especially in the cover of night. The town he left was without any law enforcement, which Davide had an even worse feeling about the closer he got to Granhal.

This bizarre night continued to get worse, and while he wished he was home protecting his family, he knew this was ultimately their best protection. He would get to the bottom of what was happening in their town and stop it before more people were killed. If not him, then who?

He feared the worst about Granhal. Lambert and Erni never, ever, let their horses loose. And they were always back from any and all assignments before now, no matter how involved the disputes and police duties might be.

What will I find there? Will either of our officers be alive? Or will their fate be similar to our beloved priest?

Bertha galloped onward in the darkness of night, the cold wind whipping against Davide's face as he flinched at the cold pain. His shotgun was holstered onto the horse's saddle and with both hands, he clasped the reins tightly, ensuring the horse never slowed down on its swift, three-mile journey.

He hoped Fr. Kries was safe and sound over in Salzben. He knew the priest would have his hands full with the death of Fr. Steffen. They had been close, as Steffen had been a mentor to the young twenty-six-year-old parochial vicar.

It wasn't long before Granhal came into view. He glanced at his watch, 1:00 AM. The last three hours had been a blur. One minute he had been cleaning up the bar and chatting with Ruppert, the next he was riding to a tiny town three miles away looking for what would likely be two injured, or worse, murdered police officers from Kortbeke while his wife and daughter were left alone.

Damnit. Damnit! He cursed the situation he and the rest of the town unwittingly found themselves in.

At last, the rain ended and the clouds dispersed, making it easier to see on the dirt road. The moon had even decided to peek out.

"Lord, I know I'm not as diligent as I should be in my faith. But I need you right now. The town of Kortbeke needs you right now!" he exclaimed, looking up to the sky while pushing away thoughts of the dream he had of the dying woman. She had been on the ground muttering about killing a priest, and now their own priest was murdered. He tried to push away the thought of Nina, and Klaus of all people, having the same dream as he had. On the same night. *What could it possibly mean?*

Swatting at the reins and giving a light kick to Bertha's ribs, Davide shouted out, "Come on Bertha, git!"

The horse obeyed and galloped at an even greater speed as Granhal grew closer.

✝

Uma and Nils slept soundly, both having climaxed in their own ways earlier. When Nils had left the bathroom after finishing his business, something he often did, he found Uma soundly asleep. He hated her, yet knew he needed her. Not just her wealth but *her*. She was his prize of sorts, a wealthy prize. One that had gained him a small fortune of luxuries along with what he and many other men knew was an admittedly beautiful woman. So, he was forced to turn a blind eye to her true manipulative and evil nature.

They both knew she was clearly in charge, although, at times she would ensure he took credit for some of their deeds in Kortbeke. And, unlike tonight, there were brief times when sex was offered. But those seemed to be fewer and farther between these days. It had been years since she had agreed to put his member in her mouth. Nils often wondered if she even remotely enjoyed their sex. He doubted it, as he had at one point noticed she had stopped attempting to orgasm during their intercourse. It had become quite utilitarian in every way. Especially when he began gaining weight.

But Nils wouldn't complain. He knew better than that. Even when rumors spread through Kortbeke that Uma was having an affair with the town's mayor, he chose not to believe it. The truth was, deep down, he was scared of her. Scared she would leave him and take her grandfather's inherited wealth with her. Or worse, he would end up like her parents and younger brother. He knew what really happened, he had figured it out early on in their marriage by the subtle hints she had thrown out and the almost joking nature of the comments about her poor, weak and burnt-to-a-crisp family and their unfortunate "accident."

So, it was advantageous for him to simply not believe such gossip and enjoy the wealth and luxury he had been gifted, even if it meant putting up with a crafty and most likely adulterous woman. If he didn't hear or think about her evening strolls or sudden council meetings at odd times of the day, then they didn't exist. Or if she returned home with her black hair looking hastily put up in a bun when she had left earlier with it perfectly styled. Or if her lipstick was smeared off. He would look the other way, changing the subject, more times than not, to Maximilian's. She would always smirk at him, as if she knew that he knew.

Nils had just fallen asleep after the quick and dirty jerk-off session, using Leonz's girlfriend as inspiration, when he was suddenly stirred awake. His eyelids fluttered open as he heard something rustling outside.

What the hell is that? An animal? Possibly a dog hanging around the bar, sniffing for food. He continued to listen, surmising they were likely footsteps on the cobblestone street.

Shaking his head, he sat up in bed then carefully crawled out of it, not wanting to wake up Uma, who no doubt would lash out at him for interrupting her precious eight hours of sleep. He slept naked, which Uma hadn't minded for a while after they had been married. She even liked it. But when the weight packed on and his appearance grew less and less favorable to her, she began nagging him to wear something to cover his fat stomach. This nagging had only made him crave food all the more. And so, the vicious cycle continued. But the battle of his bedtime attire was one fight she didn't win. And he liked that. A small victory for him in their otherwise ruler and servant relationship.

He peeked out their second-story bedroom window and was taken aback by the sheer darkness of the night. He was usually able to see Maximilian's easily, even with the gas lanterns turned off, but tonight they were barely visible. But the strange darkness wasn't what immediately bothered him. What troubled him was the fact that the lanterns were still on.

"Leonz, you fucking little twit. I'll have your ass for not putting out the lanterns on your way out," Nils muttered under his breath. He sighed, realizing he would have to do the deed.

Shaking his head, he walked over to the bed and grabbed his underwear and bathrobe. It was cold outside, but he was large and rarely got cold. This was ample attire to take care of a simple turning of the knobs that would take no more than a minute.

Nils put on his slippers and quietly made his way out of their bedroom. Carefully walking down their steps to the living room, he made his way to the front door and hesitated, thinking about how absolutely dark it was outside. He put his hand on the handle of their door, thinking back to the sound once more. Like the snarl of an animal.

Is that what I heard that stirred me awake?

Suddenly uneasy at the prospect of leaving the relative safety of his house in the middle of the night, he turned the handle and stepped outside. He was met with a blackness he had never experienced before. Looking up, he could see nothing. It was as if all the stars in the heavens had been swallowed up by an invisible monster covered in the deepest black imaginable.

"What the bloody hell is going on?" Nils muttered. He looked toward Maximilian's and was glad to see the two gas lamps lit, which would ensure he could find his way over to his place of business. It dawned on him then that the walk back to his front door would be in complete darkness. "Damnit all to hell. I don't want to have to get a lantern out!"

He decided instead of wasting time fidgeting with a lantern, he would simply take his box of matches over and upon extinguishing the gas lanterns above his bar, light one and make haste back to his house. He'd go back to bed and in the morning, all would be back to normal. All, that is, except for Leonz.

"You worthless little shit, I've half a notion to fire you. At the very least, you'll be heavily penalized in your wages for this fuck-up," he spat out as he made his way outside and into the street directly in front of their house, quickly walking across it to Maximilian's. It was only feet away, but in this odd blackness it seemed like a mile.

Once in front of the bar, he reached up to the gas lamp on the right and twisted the knob counterclockwise. The light went out. He blew out a heavy sigh, glancing back toward his house. Nothing. Only the thin outline of a structure.

He moved over to the left gas lamp and looked up at its precious light. One turn and he would be met with utter darkness. He hesitated, once more scanning his surroundings, prepared to light his match. "Come on, Nils, you're braver than this! It's just across the street. You're afraid of a little darkness?" He twisted the knob and was suddenly engulfed in black night.

He couldn't see his hands in front of his face, but felt them tremble as he held the match against the striker on the matchbox and flicked it outwards. The match lit up as he quickly held it in front of his face, thankful for the tiny bit of sight.

Get the hell back home, now.

Nils started across the street but halfway across, the match went out. "Shit!" he exclaimed, but continued on toward what he guessed was his front door.

He rushed forward until his outstretched hands hit a wall. The box of matches slipped out of his left hand and fell to the cold ground, spilling its contents and scattering the matches.

"Shit!" Nils cried out as his hands ran across the flat substance trying to find his door handle. But it wasn't there. *Where am I?* He had to be close to his door. *Keep searching, damn you!*

Growing more frantic and disoriented by the second, and not having any luck finding the door handle, he crouched down, feeling for one of the matches. His hands ran across cobblestone. Was he still on the street? Or the path to the front door? He thought he was closer to his house by now.

Where are those damn matches! "They must be here! I dropped them right at my feet! Where are they?" he muttered, though he couldn't feel anything except dirty stones embedded in the road.

Now in a full-on panic, he called for help. "Uma! Uma, wake up!" he shouted. It came out cracked and hoarse. He cleared his dried throat and tried again. "Uma, please, wake up!"

His house felt miles away. No air blew through town. It was as if he were no longer in Kortbeke at all. "This must be what hell is like," he muttered.

He began feeling along the wall directly in front of him again, at times pounding on it in growing desperation. *The door must be here somewhere, damnit!* His housecoat had come undone and his large, pale stomach hung out. He felt sweaty and suddenly nauseous. Bile formed in his mouth, which, for a brief second, was a reprieve from the dryness. Then his large stomach filled with Scotch and junk food gurgled and flipped, sending it all back up.

Nils didn't even have a chance to bend over, the alcohol-laden vomit spewed out of his mouth, covering his belly and landing with a splat on the ground.

"Tisk, tisk, shouldn't be outside at this hour," a gentle voice said in his ear.

"Who said that?" Nils cried out, turning around and meeting with more darkness.

He felt something like a pinch on his wide stomach, starting on his left side and following all the way to the right, running across his navel. He froze in place, confused as to what had just happened.

Someone, or something, was standing close to him. He felt its breath. A match was lit and held up in front of his face, revealing a beautiful woman standing directly in front of him. Long, flowing golden hair, blue eyes, full lips. The match gave him enough of a glimpse to see in her blue eyes a quick flash of yellow. He held his breath, unable to move or cry out, as his eyes went from her face to the burning match.

"You must be Nils. I am in need of your wife," Everly said softly as the match went out.

"What? Who are you? Ouch!" he cried out as the pinching in his stomach worsened.

Another match lit from his spilled box. His eyes went from the match to his immediate surroundings. His front door was mere feet away. *I knew it was just there! But I couldn't find the door!*

"Listen, you are going to die now. Painfully. But know that I will take good care of her, until her usefulness expires, then she will join you," the woman whispered, lowering the match to his vomit-smeared stomach.

He instantly felt dread wash over him as his legs became weak. She was so calm, so elegant. His eyes followed the lit match down to his stomach. The pinching he had felt wasn't a pinch at all. It was a thin line running from one end of his belly to the other. And blood had begun trickling out of the line.

"What's going on?" Nils exclaimed, suddenly hyperventilating. His heavy breathing opened the perfect slice wider. As the match burned down and started to extinguish, Nils saw the entirety of his stomach spill out of the deep cut, landing with a *splat* onto the cobblestone road. He attempted to grab the spilling guts and stuff them back to their rightful place, but his hands had given out, as had his legs. He crumpled over, unable to do anything but fall face-first onto the stones below, splitting his nose open.

As his mind went black forever, he tried to utter a prayer, but no words escaped his lips before death consumed him.

The street was silent. Nils lay atop his spilled intestines while Everly, satisfied at her clean and efficient butchery, silently and gracefully walked to the Karlens' front door, left unlocked by the obese dead man.

She entered the house and closed the door behind her. With yellow wolf's eyes, she scanned the living quarters. "These look like Bürgermeister Hartjenstein's quarters," she mused, thinking back to the beginnings of her new life. Extravagant furnishings decorated the place. Likely purchased from money that didn't belong to the black-haired woman and her fat husband to begin with. Or were nefariously obtained somehow.

"I'm liking this woman more and more," Everly said coolly, looking up toward the stairs leading to the bedroom above.

Delicately, she moved toward the staircase and began ascending.

†

Davide entered Granhal and pulled back on Bertha's reins. The horse came to a halt in front of Fritz's place where he immediately saw Brutus tied to a post right outside the house.

Davide dismounted and grabbed his shotgun. Holding onto Bertha's reins and tying them to the post next to Brutus, he called out in a loud whisper, "Lambert! Erni! You guys in there?"

He heard steps and instantly took a firing pose with his gun raised to his shoulder. "I've got a double barrel pointed at the door. So, whoever the hell is in there had best be stepping out with their hands pointed to the heavens or you'll be met with two slugs to the chest!" Davide said.

"I'm coming out! Don't shoot!" came a frightened voice.

I recognize that voice. Davide kept his gun pointed at the door, his finger on the trigger. As wracked as his nerves were, a part of him felt deadly calm, ready to take out anyone that wasn't the least bit friendly or following his orders.

A man stepped outside into the moonlight with his hands as instructed, pointing to the heavens.

"Fr. Kries!" Davide exclaimed, glancing past his still raised shotgun at the nervous young man standing before him.

"Davide? Davide Hubschmid? That you?" Fr. Kries spoke, keeping his hands held high.

Davide motioned for him to lower his hands as he lowered his shotgun. "Sorry, Father, I had to be sure."

"Don't apologize. I'm just glad you're here. Bad things, Davide. Bad things have happened in this town. Horrible and evil things," Fr. Kries uttered.

"Horrible and evil things are happening right now in Kortbeke, too, Fr. Kries," Davide replied gravely.

Fr Kries's eyes widened as he motioned for Davide to come inside Fritz's house.

Chapter 12

✝

Burning Revenge

1:15 AM

Chadwick hadn't been able to change completely into the beast he was now cursed to become before the fire had stopped the transformation. He was now half-man, half-beast. Hair began to sprout on his morphing body and his bones extended. Large claws protruded out of his hands and feet. His face, most of which was covered in burns, had some remaining human attributes but with an extended snout and pointed ears. One of his eyes was now lost in the fire that engulfed his face minutes earlier.

He turned away from the church entrance to face the man that had called out in the night. If he had ever recognized the voice, he could no longer recall who it was. His rage consumed him. Rage at the witch that had done this to him and the man that had later burned him. Rage at the wife who escaped his wrath with his child. Rage at a God that would not have him. Not anymore.

His remaining good eye could see well, even in this pitch-black darkness. It saw the man standing by his spilled apples.

"Who's out there? Why the hell is it so damn dark?" old man Whitmer exclaimed, holding out a candle from his doorway.

Chadwick lunged forward, claws outstretched. Whitmer only saw the man's charred face for a split second before it crashed into him, knocking him to the ground and landing on top of him.

Whitmer never knew what hit him, or bit into his face, with such ferocity his neck snapped, killing him instantly while the beast gnawed on its fresh kill.

†

Inside St. Raphael's, Leonz was doubled over, breathing heavily while Nina tried getting information out of her young lover.

Ruppert shook his head. "I know that voice. That was Whitmer calling out."

Klaus remained quiet, playing out the events of the past hour. And now Leonz claimed a wolf standing on its rear legs was loose in his town. "Son of a *bitch*, why is it so damn dark out there!"

"I don't know but if anyone else starts waking up and going outside, and that thing hears them, they're dead. I can't believe I made it this far with that thing chasing me in that darkness!" Leonz said, raising his head to look at the three standing near the entrance.

"Fr. Steffen is dead," Nina blurted out.

Leonz looked at her, stunned, and replied, "What? Fr. Steffen, he's, he's...dead?"

Nina pointed to the front of the church and handed him her lantern. He took it and made his way up, stopping at the large puddle of blood halfway to the altar. Grimacing, he stepped around it and moved forward, stopping at the bloody sheet that lay atop the dead priest.

Leonz quickly made a sign of the cross and hung his head in sorrow after taking a peek at the carnage underneath and headed back to the front.

"I know you told us what was chasing you, but start from the beginning," Ruppert said to Leonz.

"What can you tell us?" Nina asked softly.

Shaking his head, he told his tale. Of being stuck at Maximilian's past closing and the three men being expelled from the establishment, only to have one of them return, changed, and this time, with a woman. "She stepped out from behind him before he was ready to attack me. Said something along the lines of making the wrong choice with Chadwick and that I was *fetching*." He shuddered at the thought.

This instantly caught the attention of Nina. "Who is this woman?"

"I only saw her for a second before that beast of a man took after me. But she was beautiful," he paused, looking sideways at Nina.

"What do you mean?" Klaus asked.

Shaking his head, he said, "I don't mean that as a compliment. She was, *unnaturally* beautiful. She hardly looked human. I mean, she was, I suppose. But it was unnatural, she looked too perfect. No blemishes, hair perfect even in this cold, dreary weather. In fact, her blue dress was something you would expect someone to wear in the middle of the summer, not now. It was just…odd. And her eyes, they were blue, but almost seemed to glow, as if they were another color entirely, masked by blue paint. I know this all sounds crazy, but I know what I saw, and that woman was not any normal woman."

Nina gently put her hand on his cheek, turning his face to meet hers, and gave him a gentle kiss on his lips. She was fiercely protective of her love and trusted him implicitly. But others she did not. Especially one that called her man fetching. *Try saying that to my face, you bitch.*

"Klaus, Nina, you both spoke of a woman in your dreams. Same with Davide. Could this be her?" Ruppert asked.

"I was thinking the exact same thing," Klaus answered, then added, "Surely not. I mean, what are the odds?"

Nina piped up, "The way this night has been going, I would say there is a better chance than not they are connected. Especially considering we all had the same dream, about the same woman."

Leonz asked, "Dreams? What do you mean, dreams?"

Nina answered, "I haven't had a chance to tell you yet. Several of us dreamed of a woman being murdered. Her dying words were—"

"'Don't bother sending for the priest, I killed him,'" Klaus finished.

Leonz's eyes widened as he asked, "And Davide had that same dream? Where's the police? Shouldn't they be involved here? And this damn darkness! What's that about?"

"No clue. That's where Davide headed before you got here, to find Lambert and Erni, who went to Granhal earlier yesterday to investigate some of Florus Widmer's cattle being slaughtered. They never came back. Later, he found Erni's horse roaming the streets. Before things got so dark," Ruppert replied.

Leonz turned to look back at the dead priest. "Whatever killed him, it likely wasn't Chadwick."

"Why not?" Nina asked.

"Because, until fairly recently, he was sitting in Maximilian's. I'm no doctor but the blood on the floor is dry. There's no way it was Chadwick," Leonz answered.

They all fell silent.

"Why their dreams? Why not ours, Ruppert?" Leonz asked.

Shrugging, Ruppert replied, "Beats the shit out of me. I'm not sure whether those of us that didn't dream of this crazy woman should be more or less nervous than those that did."

"Why is that?" Nina asked.

"Well, perhaps more may be required of them, if we're going down the supernatural route. And it appears we are, all things considered. Not that I believe such things…" Ruppert trailed off, looking in the direction of the dead priest before adding, "Strange things are afoot in Kortbeke, and we best get prepared for what is coming. The night's not over."

An ominous silence fell over the four of them. Klaus had never seen Ruppert this serious since knowing the man. He was a loser and a drunk, chasing his wife and kids into the arms of another man. Spending his days at the butcher shop and drinking his nights away, drowning out his sorrows. This sudden threat to their town had sobered him up quickly, making Klaus himself begin to question everything, including his own distinct lack of faith and the merits of the lonely man named Ruppert.

"What's the plan, people?" Leonz said, breaking the silence, eager to turn the tables on this evil presence stalking their town.

They looked to Klaus who sadly shook his head and shrugged, in his usual uncertain and noncommittal fashion.

This wasn't good enough for Leonz. "The people of this town are not safe. Not with that *thing* out there! Chadwick was with two others earlier. Jonathan and Richard. I can only wonder what became of them. There's a dead body lying on the floor up there," he said, pointing. "And that's not even taking into account Lambert and Erni. We have a serious problem, but with that blanket of blackness outside, we can't see in front of our faces, much less let the townsfolk know what's going on. We have to do better than this!" he exclaimed.

"The plan is, we stay put until Davide gets back," Ruppert said firmly, feeling like the voice of reason in this group, a strange turn for him.

"And what if he doesn't come back? I mean, two police officers went out to Granhal and are still missing. What makes you think he's going to be safe?" Klaus replied angrily.

"If you've got any better ideas, I'm all ears!" Ruppert replied sharply. "You want to take off toward Maximilian's in that darkness, with that thing out there when we know so little of what we're dealing with?" He was about to add that they should all be armed in some fashion but fell silent when he heard a noise coming from the right side of the building.

St. Raphael's was built of solid stone and featured numerous stained-glass windows about ten feet up from the ground floor. When the church was built, it was determined this would be the best location for sunlight to shine through, illuminating the church and its parishioners. The windows were six feet in height by three feet wide. There were four on either side of the church, with one large half-circle behind the altar further up the wall to shine on the cross that hung from the ceiling. They featured a mixture of scenes from Jesus's passion, recounted through the various glass arrangements in different colors, an extraordinary, elegant display of artistry in an otherwise rather modest town.

Now, however, the group of four suddenly realized these windows offered a way in for what lurked in the darkness. A sound similar to fingernails scraped against glass but didn't break it open. They listened in rapt attention to the sounds coming from outside, slowly forming a tight semi-circle as a protective measure against what was likely right outside the church walls.

The scurrying continued, making its way further along the outside wall. Each stained-glass window rattled in place as whatever was outside leapt from windowsill to windowsill. Four sets of eyes travelled with the sound until it came to the last stained-glass window, where the movement outside ceased.

Ruppert, the only one with any sort of weapon, gripped Davide's small club and pushed it out in front of him, holding it with both hands.

The church grew quiet once more until Nina broke the silence, whispering, "I think it's behind the stained-glass window above the alt—"

She was cut off by the shattering of glass exploding inward. The entirety of the half-circle stained-glass window shattered, sending shards of beautifully colored glass everywhere near the altar.

With the exploding window came a beastly and severely burnt figure, jumping through and landing on the large cross hanging from the ceiling.

The weight was too much for the cross to withstand and the old chains that had held it up for many years buckled under the pressure and snapped, sending the chiseled-out wooden Jesus figure, the cross, and the beast flying down to the ground together. The thick wooden cross hit first and instantly burst into fragments, the Jesus figure smashing on top of some of them.

The beast stood to its feet, further mutated from its original form, looking less human and more like a huge wolf with muscular arms standing on its long, bony, and equally muscular hind legs.

"Chadwick, that's Chadwick!" Leonz screamed.

"Oh shit, not good! Not good at all, people!" Klaus shouted.

Without taking her eyes off the creature, Nina bent down and picked up a large wooden shard from the destroyed cross laying some twenty feet away. Its tip was sharp, and it was roughly two feet long.

Ruppert continued holding out his club while surveying the destroyed cross and carved, wooden Jesus that had hung above the altar since the church's creation one-hundred years prior. He trembled with fear, but also fury. He had hated God for years. Hated the mere thought of what God was and what He represented. But this hellish abomination that had just destroyed this sacred cross, while a truly good man named Fr. Steffen lay near the desecrated altar, felt as wrong as anything possibly could feel. Whatever had come to their town on this dark night was winning.

The Chadwick creature peered at his prey with its one remaining good eye. It snarled through a half-burnt snout filled with sharp teeth that almost looked as if it were smiling. Legs extended further, arms grew longer, muscles bulged. The short snout protracted out while the bones around it shifted, looking less and less like anything human. What little clothing it wore had torn off and fallen to its feet that now were covered in black fur. The ball of its foot was large and round, making the creature stand even higher at over seven feet tall.

Its full transformation was complete. And with glowing yellow eyes, it roared at its prey.

"Grab something and fight!" Leonz shouted, grabbing a long piece of broken cross from the ground.

The wolf mutation ran forward at full speed toward Nina and Leonz, the closest to it, but they ducked out of its way, protecting themselves with their new weapons out-stretched.

The huge beast, focusing on the man who had caused him harm, came to a stop, turning to face Leonz, who was backing up through a row of pews nearby.

Klaus, the only one without a weapon, quickly backed away from the chaos altogether.

Ruppert moved in stealthily behind the wolf beast, holding his club with both hands. Seeing Klaus retreat, he called out angrily, "Klaus, you bastard, find something to help us fight this thing with!"

Klaus stared at the creature towering in front of them, shaking his head while feebly attempting to find something that could be of use. Beside him, near the old pipe organ, against the wall of the church, was one of the two blessed holy water fonts. He picked up the large bowl designed for dipping fingers in to bless oneself, the water splashing around as he crept toward the creature.

Meanwhile, the werewolf continued stalking Leonz as Nina came up behind it. Sensing the woman's presence, it spun around, letting out another roar of anger and bending over slightly toward the petite figure in front of it, swatted its large, clawed hand at her, smashing the piece of wood out of her hand while just missing her face and causing her to fall backwards, crashing into the pew, then to the floor.

Ruppert ran toward it and with all his might, cracked the creature over its head. The force was powerful enough against the hardened facial bones of the wolf beast to crack the club and break it in two.

It let out a howl of pain and anger, turning its attention to Ruppert who now had only a shard of the club remaining in his hands. The creature lunged at him, grabbing Ruppert around the neck and lifting him up, off the ground. It opened its large mouth, drool dripping from its jaws.

Ruppert began choking at the immense pressure from the werewolf's thick hands wrapped around his throat. His feet dangled off the floor as he tried desperately to find footing that wasn't there.

The creature was about to sink its fangs into his face when out of the corner of its yellow eyes, it saw Leonz moving in with his pointed piece of wood. It dropped Ruppert to a crumpled heap on the floor and swatted Leonz away just before he was able to make contact with the wolf.

After filling his lungs with much-needed air, Ruppert took the brief few seconds the wolf was focused on Leonz to drive the sharp splinter of the club he had busted over the creature's head directly into the side of its leg. The creature howled in pain and stumbled backwards away from his prey.

Klaus moved forward and awkwardly tossed the holy water onto the creature's face, which had no effect other than angering the creature all the more.

The huge beast swatted Klaus away, causing him to fall backwards, crashing against a lantern and knocking it to the floor. Blood oozed from the fresh wound in the creature's leg as it stood over Klaus who tried to slide away from it. The creature reached down, pulling the splinter out of its leg with ease, tossing it away.

Grabbing the lantern on the floor, Klaus haphazardly threw it at the Chadwick creature. Missing its mark and falling just short of it, the lantern broke open, spilling its flammable contents onto the floor and igniting stacks of altar server albs awaiting being returned to the sacristy from Mass earlier. The fire spread quickly across other flammable materials nearby, including hymnals and pillowed kneelers.

Swatting at the fire, the Chadwick creature tripped over a nearby pew with the freshly wounded leg, falling backward and crashing to the floor, letting out a bellowing howl as it fell.

Nina backed away from the flames, bumping against Leonz, both of them watching the creature begin to crawl back up to its feet behind the rapidly fanning out flames, backing away from it as it spread.

Ruppert joined them, along with Klaus, shaking himself off from his own spill.

From their vantage point, they could no longer see the creature behind the immense wall of fire and smoke wafting into the air, blocking it from reaching them. Fire had begun taking hold of the back row of old wooden pews and was spreading to the church walls draped with cloth.

They all stood, mouths agape, watching the flames spreading. All knew, at this point, it would be a lost cause trying to extinguish it.

Shaking his head in despair, Klaus uttered, "What have we done? I need to get the hell out of here."

Chapter 13

✝

House of Horror

1:30 AM

Davide entered Fritz's small house at the entrance of Granhal with Fr. Kries holding his lantern up to guide their way. It was dark inside, but the nighttime sky lit enough of its interior to illuminate the scene.

Two bodies lay inside. One was clearly deputy Erni, his body twisted into a gruesome pretzel form, eyes wide open in perpetual terror.

Davide put his hand to his mouth, shocked at the violent murder of the town's deputy.

"Over here, there's another one," Fr. Kries pointed toward the corner of the house.

"Sonofabitch," Davide whispered to himself, looking over the gruesome remains of old man Fritz atop his bed, eyes also opened in lifeless terror.

"Something terrible is happening, Davide. I awoke to-night from my sleep from a nightmare that–" Fr. Kries started.

"Sorry to interrupt you, Father, but I had a dream too. A lady, evil. Muttering—"

"'Don't bother sending for the priest, I killed him' fol-lowed by, 'You will meet her and her kind, and you will do battle with them.' Me too! But how could this be? I had that dream several nights ago, and hadn't given it much thought until these latest series of dreams several hours ago. I'm at a loss for words," Fr. Kries whispered gravely.

They stared at each other in stunned silence until Davide asked, "How did these latest dreams end?"

"With a voice in my head telling me that l will be shown the means to defeat the evil that spawned her and that I must be strong," Fr. Kries answered.

Davide thought on this different message than the one he had received. "Our mayor and Nina Gesser had the same dream, they're back at the church now. At least, that's where they were, along with Ruppert Sprenger, when I took off for Granhal to find our missing cops on Erni's horse that just showed up."

"Who could have done this?" Fr. Kries asked.

Davide shrugged and shook his head in dismay. "Father, there's something else. It's Fr. Steffen."

Quickly looking over from the murdered Fritz to Davide, he asked, "What of Fr. Steffen? Is he well?"

"He's dead," Davide replied gravely.

Fr. Kries took a step back, away from Davide. "What? No. No, no, no, that can't be!"

"It is. I'll spare you the gruesome details, but now that I'm seeing what happened here, I'm sure we are under attack, and we must move now!" Davide paused, looking around the room. "Wait, Brutus is outside. Where's Chief Lambert?"

Both men stared around the small room that appeared empty. Fr. Kries went to pick up his lantern sitting on old man Fritz's small wooden table. Reaching for it, he saw what appeared to be saliva dripping down from above, then heard a low snarl. Immediately looking up, his gaze was met with a pair of bright yellow eyes staring intently at him.

"Father! Look out!" Davide shouted as the shape in the small loft above dropped down toward the priest. Davide pushed Fr. Kries out of the way and the shape crashed atop him instead, driving both Davide and the assailant to the floor.

Fr. Kries, startled and knocked off-balance, also slipped to the floor in a pool of blood near the unfolding struggle.

Davide and his assaulter wrestled in a struggle for dominance as two hands gripped Davide's throat tightly, pinning him to the floor. Davide frantically groped for the shotgun he had dropped when he fell, but his weapon was out of reach, having slid into the corner.

He instantly recognized the attacker by the grizzled facial features and slightly large nose. It was none other than Chief of Police, Gabriel Lambert himself. His face was covered in blood and his clothes appeared to be in tatters, but it was unmistakably him.

Davide focused on keeping Lambert's snapping jaws away from his exposed face, while driving his knee into his attacker's groin. With the sudden momentum, he pushed harder with his knee, sending the aggressive Lambert up and over his own body.

Unable to keep his hold on Davide's neck, Lambert released it and came crashing to the ground after flipping over Davide's head.

Davide, meanwhile, slid away from him, and over to his shotgun resting in the corner.

Fr. Kries scrambled back to his feet and got his first look at their aggressor, thanks to the lantern that remained lit on the table against the wall. He clearly saw, from the man's attire and facial features, that it was Kortbeke's law and his personal friend, Gabriel Lambert. But this person appeared to be either possessed or infected with some sort of rabies, judging from the drool dripping from his mouth and wild, yellow eyes.

Lambert's eyes fell on Fr. Kries, watching him intently. A distant part of him remembered this kind priest and all he had done for the town he himself had sworn to uphold and protect as the law. Lambert then stopped his aggression, taking in the priest standing in front of him with his palms up, as if showing Lambert he meant no harm.

Davide jumped up with the shotgun, pulled the hammer back, aimed, then paused. Fr. Kries had his hand up, motioning for Davide to stop. With his finger already half pulled back on the trigger, Davide released it slightly, glancing over at the priest, wondering what he had in mind.

"Davide, wait!" Fr. Kries paused, staring at the blood-covered man. "Lambert, can you hear me?" he asked in as calm a voice as he could muster.

Staring at the priest with glowing yellow eyes, the man breathed heavily, hands clenched into fists. Then he charged toward him.

Instantly, Davide ran forward as he spun the shotgun around until he was holding the barrel end and smashed the long wooden handle onto the back of Lambert's head, bringing him face-first to the ground.

"Rope, over there!" Davide called out, pointing to some baler twine laying amongst Fritz's odds and ends in the corner of the house.

Nodding, Fr. Kries ran over to the twine, scooped it up and came back to Davide who had dropped on top of Lambert and pinned him to the ground. Davide was larger and stronger than Lambert, but the police officer was showing more strength and resilience than expected.

Fr. Kreis quicky unwound the twine and began wrapping it around Lambert's wrists as fast as he could.

Once they were securely fastened, Davide hoisted the bound man up and threw him onto an old wooden chair by Fritz's table, all while Lambert continued to fight his restraints. With Fr. Kries's help, Davide wrapped more twine around Lambert and the chair until the man was not only bound around the wrists but around the chair as well.

Lambert fought his restraints fiercely, gaining his strength back after the hard knock to the back of his head. He kept his piercing yellow eyes focused on the priest as thick drool rolled off of his open mouth.

Davide, seeing Lambert wasn't going anywhere, picked up his shotgun and stood back, raising it to his shoulder and looking down its barrels at the bound man at his feet.

Silence fell over the room.

"If he breaks loose and comes after either of us, I'm going to blow his head off," Davide said, keeping his gun trained on the seemingly possessed man.

"He understands," Fr. Kries exclaimed, holding his hand up to Davide to remain calm. "Easy there, Lambert, just stay calm. What has happened to you?"

Lambert looked from Davide to Fr. Kries, his mouth still open, blood and drool spilling from it. In a guttural voice, he spoke slowly, as if every word hurt coming out of his mouth. "She did this. Forced me to drink from her. Said she would take care of me. But I must catch anyone attempting to flee Kortbeke. Said she was here for the priest."

He paused, gritting his teeth. "Ahh, oh God, it hurts!" he screamed in pain, trying to double over but the tight twine held him to the chair securely so instead he lowered his head to his chest that was covered in the continuous flow of blood and drool.

Glancing at Fr. Kries, Davide continued aiming his shotgun at Lambert's head with his finger resting on the trigger.

Fr. Kries looked into Lambert's eyes. "Drink from her?"

"She was going to kill me like the rest of this town. Bit her wrist, forced me to…" he trailed off.

"She's here for a priest?" Fr. Kries said.

"For you. Aims to kill everything in sight until she gets you. She changes from a wolf to something…more. Then back to human," he sputtered, raising his head to meet his captors. His eyes had turned back to their normal color.

"Look!" Fr. Kries said to Davide, peering into the man's now brown eyes.

Davide spoke to the bound man. "Lambert, listen to me. Steffen has been murdered. His head was severed inside St. Raphael's and his body was left on the altar."

Fr. Kries quickly looked over at Davide, shocked to hear the gruesome details.

Behind the chair, Lambert slowly worked his wrists back and forth, the twine cutting into his flesh, drawing blood that dripped over and soon covered his hands.

"Father, listen, I'm not entirely sure what's going on here," Davide whispered so Lambert couldn't hear him, "but we need to stop whatever is out there right now! The others in the church, they planned on heading to Maximilian's before I left, but God knows what's happened since then. I saw the wolf he speaks of, in the shadows. It's still in our town! This man, our friend, he's changed! We need to make haste."

The twine began to slide down Lambert's bloody wrists and hands.

"If what you say is true, and these dreams we're having are playing into it, she's likely killed others in town. We must go now!" Fr. Kries whispered back urgently to Davide.

Shifting their attention to the bound man, they both had the same thought: *What do we do with him?*

"Davide, listen…to, to…me," Lambert paused, struggling to form sentences now. Grimacing at the pain in his bones and blood that felt as though it were boiling as it travelled through his veins. "I-I don't have long now. I can't fight off this…disease! Woman, infected…me!

Davide was about to speak but Lambert shook his head violently back and forth, motioning him to remain silent. "Last order of business before I," he trailed off, gritting his teeth as tears of pain and rage began streaming down his face. "My last order of…business, you're in charge…of Kortbeke. You're the law…now!" He paused once more, breathing heavily, forcing his final words out. "Now, take care of that filthy bitch demon…and take care…of me…as well."

His eyes had shifted back to yellow. His pupils no longer resembled a human's. Drool continued spilling out of his mouth in long strings. Behind him, the twine had been pulled away from his bloody hands.

Everly's blood pumped through his veins, and while he had been fighting valiantly against what she had infected him with, he could no longer contain the urge that had been lying in wait, fighting for dominance within him. His muscles bulged, stretching the twine to its very limits as his clothes ripped from his body. Hair pushed through his skin while bones grew, ripping muscle from them.

Lambert cried out in agony as the twine so tightly bound around him snapped off. Blood spurted out of his nose, mouth, and ears as his facial bone structure painfully shifted, pressing against his cranium. He immediately jumped to his feet and put his hands to his head, shaking it violently.

Davide gasped at the grisly sight, knowing it was up to him to end this man's life. A friend for years. A good man.

Fr. Kries grabbed the lantern off the table with his left hand and in his right, he clutched his rosary, holding out the small cross attached to it toward the mutation in front of him as his mind wrestled to make sense of what he saw.

"Father! Stand back!" Davide exclaimed, realizing Fr. Kries was too close to his blast radius in the small house and would likely be hit by projectile if he pulled the trigger on his shotgun now.

Lambert's head changed. Pointy ears sprouted from his human ones. His nose stretched as the skin around it burst open to make way for a long snout. Large fangs pushed away Lambert's teeth and his tongue swelled to nearly four times its normal size.

Fr. Kries moved back as far as he could, giving Davide the shot he needed right as Lambert, the wolf mutation, completed its transformation, towering above both men.

Slugs from the shotgun erupted in the small house, blasting the creature in its head, instantly disintegrating its newly formed snout and half its face.

Wolf blood and pieces of its furry face splattered against the rear wall as the creature grabbed at its destroyed face and fell backwards.

Davide opened the action release, quickly pulling out both used slugs and dug into his jacket pocket for another two. Slamming them into the empty chambers, he swiftly closed it and pulled back on the hammer once more, aiming it toward the fallen creature.

What was once Lambert was now thrashing on the ground with half its face missing. Fr. Kries frantically prayed while focusing on the man this awful, wild beast had once been and not what it was now.

As the priest recited prayers, Davide moved in, looking down the barrel of his gun. He hesitated, looking at his old friend whose face was a mess that was continually shifting. Fragments of bone appeared to be reforming where the shotgun blast had seemingly disintegrated minutes earlier.

"Father, look! I think he's regenerating! Look at his face!" Davide exclaimed, lowering his shotgun slightly, pointing to the damaged face starting to reconstruct itself.

"This can only be the workings of the fallen angel, Satan. This man…" Fr. Kries paused, hardly believing what he was about to say. "He is a lycanthrope! A werewolf!"

Lambert's yellow eyes peered up at him and blinked. A slight bit of recognition remained as the large beast raised its fur-covered clawed hand, pointing at the lantern now in Fr. Kries's hand.

"What does it want?" Davide asked, puzzled.

It opened its partially regenerated mouth and uttered, "Burn me, please. Then burn *her*."

Davide looked over at Fr. Kries. "Hand me the lantern. I'll do it."

"No. I will do this deed." Fr. Kries hung his head before the mutation in front of him that continued healing itself. His mouth moved silently, his eyes closed.

The beast continued to writhe on the floor while its body was regenerating. Soon its face would be completely healed.

"Father, now," Davide urged.

The beast sat up, its face nearly restored, bared fangs, snarling. Drool dripped from its mouth onto the floor while the patches of hair that had been blown off sprouted new fur.

"In the name of the Father, the Son, and the Holy Spirit, amen," Fr. Kries said, turning the lantern upside down, spilling its flammable contents onto the Lambert werewolf's shaking legs and floor surrounding it. He dropped the lit lantern onto the kerosine soaked floor, instantly igniting it into flames.

What was once Lambert howled in agony as fire engulfed it, travelling up the wolf's legs and torso, all the way up to its freshly healed head.

Fr. Kries stood firm, looking at the flames and making a sign of the cross. He recited a Catholic rite he had learned back in his seminary years. "Lord God, Almighty Father, inextinguishable light, Who hast created all light, bless this light sanctified and blessed by Thee, Who hast enlightened the whole world: make us enlightened by that light and inflamed with the fire of Thy brightness…Amen."

"Amen," Davide muttered, also making a sign of the cross as he and Fr. Kries backed away from the rapidly spreading flames toward the door. "This fire is going to consume the whole house. We've got to get out of here, now! Careful of scaring those horses off. We need them to get back quickly to Kortbeke!"

Nodding, Fr. Kries took one more look at the carnage spread throughout old man Fritz's house. It was a nightmare of violence. Three dead bodies, all done in by this mysterious woman. He shuddered at the thought of what she wanted with him, of all people, and of what horrors the rest of the town of Granhal had been through.

Outside, Davide and Fr. Kries saw that the horses, while agitated, had remained fastened to the front porch railing.

"Shh…easy, girl," Davide said, gently taking the reins and pulling them slightly for Bertha to remain calm.

Brutus shook his head back and forth, trying to break free. The horse knew Fr. Kries and seeing the young man calmed the large beast down enough for the priest to take hold of the reins.

Smoke poured out of the windows of Fritz's house as the non-human howls of pain slowly subsided until no sounds were heard but the crackling of burning wood that filled the dead silence that was now Granhal.

Both men quickly mounted their respective horses, Davide once more slinging his shotgun into the rifle slot on Bertha's saddle. Seeing a pair of steel handcuffs in the saddle bag, he pocketed them in case they came in handy later.

Pulling back on their reins, with Davide in the lead, they made haste out of the dead town.

In the distance lay Kortbeke, and surrounding it was a near impenetrable darkness. Davide grit his teeth, his mind going once again to Emila and Frida, then to the rest of the town, hoping all had slept quietly while a hideous evil had arrived with murder in its blood and on its mind.

Whoever or whatever you are, you're not going to win. Not in Kortbeke and not while I'm alive.

Everly stood near the spot where she had murdered Nils earlier, looking up in anticipation at what awaited her inside the house where the alluring woman with black hair lay.

She suddenly grimaced at what felt like flames engulfing her, the sensation strong enough that it caused her to double over in pain, dropping to one knee until the feeling passed and she was able to regain her composure.

Standing back up and brushing herself off, she shook her head at the realization of what had happened. The police officer in Granhal was no more. Her connection with the man she had turned early was gone.

"So, I have an adversary. Good. I welcome you to try to stop me. You will fail. They all do."

She turned her attention back to the darkened house where her sleeping beauty awaited.

Chapter 14

✝

Visions of Evil

3:15 AM

Emila rested on her couch with little Frida fast asleep on her lap. She hadn't been able to fall back asleep in bed, so her mother granted her wish: to sleep in the living room while they waited for Papa to return.

Softly stroking her little girl's hair, a cross between her red and her husband's brown, Emila watched as Frida's chest slowly rose then fell with each breath. She could feel her little heart pattering away inside her chest. She loved this child and her husband more than life itself and would gladly give hers if it meant saving either one of them. She shivered at the thought that their lives had suddenly taken a summersault into madness in the course of a single evening.

She closed the blinds of their house once the deep darkness had fallen. The knife from her kitchen lay beside her on the end table atop several books Davide was working through when he had the time to read. Periodically, she looked over at the knife, just to make sure her weapon of choice still lay nearby in case she needed it. She wondered what was out there that could have killed the kind old priest.

Her mind drifted to her husband. It had been a stressful year, with Frida needing her papa in the evenings, right when he needed to take care of Hubschmid's. On top of that, the tension surrounding the silly rivalry between the dueling bars in town had, at times, brought her to tears. She hated that her husband had to deal with the likes of Uma and Nils Karlen and, to a lesser extent but still annoying, Mayor Kessler.

For the two years Kessler had been in charge of Kortbeke, Uma had pushed through numerous initiatives, all of which benefitted her and her husband. Her husband in name only, it seemed, if the rumors were true. She knew they were. She knew if Klaus stood up to Uma his career as well as his life in Kortbeke would be over. She would likely accuse him of improper conduct with a married woman and that would be the end of it. He would move on to another town and she would notch another win on her belt.

That bitch somehow always gets her way. And if she doesn't, hell hath no fury, Emila thought darkly, then said aloud, "Come on, quit thinking the worst. You have much to be thankful for, and in the morning, all will be well. Please, God, please, let all be well."

She doubted her own words as she looked toward the window then her door, longing for her husband to come through it, throw his arms around her and Frida, kiss them both, and tell them everything was going to be okay.

But everything was not okay.

Emila's eyelids grew heavy. The warm glow of the lantern on the table in front of her cast an orange and yellow hue throughout the dark living space. Her daughter's warm body on her lap, covered in blankets, and the hour of night made her weary. The crackling fire was nearly extinguished; all that remained were glowing embers, causing further drowsiness.

The excitement from earlier in the evening was subsiding. Not that she wasn't worried, she was beside herself with fright, but the adrenaline was fading, and in its wake, sleep was beckoning her. She would just close her eyes for a minute to rest. Just a minute...

Emila found herself in a dark room. It was quiet except for the soft breathing of something in the corner, out of sight. "Who's there? Show yourself!" she said with as much confidence as she could muster.

She was met with silence. Whatever was breathing earlier was likely still in the room with her, as she felt its eerie presence. Holding the knife out in front of her, she called out again, "Whatever you are, show yourself, you coward! I know you're there!"

"Your precious little daughter, so tasty, so young. Truly delectable!" a woman's voice called out.

Emila's eyes widened at the very real threat now lurking in the darkness of her dream.

A lantern flickered on. She was in Frida's bedroom, but Frida wasn't in bed. Blood was splashed across the walls of the tiny room.

Gasping at the grisly spectacle, Emila shouted out in revulsion, "Frida! Where are you! Please honey, come to Mama!"

"She's no longer here, but I am," the woman's voice uttered.

I know that voice, I know who that is! *Emila thought.*

There was no bedroom door in the room. Just four walls, her daughter's bed and a small table where the lantern rested, all of which were covered in blood.

The lantern went out. "Soon…" the woman's voice uttered.

"You stay away from my daughter, you bitch!" Emila shouted, once more waving her knife around in the darkness.

"You're talking in your sleep, Mama. Mama!" a little voice said, shaking her mother gently.

Blinking her eyes and quickly sitting upright on the couch, Emila looked around, still feeling as though she were in the dream until her eyes fell on her daughter looking up at her.

"Mama? Are you okay? You were shouting about someone to stay away from me! Who were you talking to? I'm scared!" Frida exclaimed, her soft, childish voice confused.

Catching her breath and quickly composing herself, Emila shifted nervously on the couch, trying not to scare the child further. She wiped her sweaty, tired face with her hands and glanced over. The knife was still there. Good. She wrapped her arms around Frida, pulling her in tightly against her warm body. "It's okay. Mama just had a bad dream, is all. Everything is fine now," Emila said.

Looking down at her yawning daughter, she forced a nervous smile and looked at the time. "Well after three o'clock in the morning. Oh, Davide, where are you, my dear?"

"Where's Papa?" Frida asked.

Emila's mind went to the dream. Everything in it seemed intensified. No door, she was trapped by an unseen assailant. Someone had breached the safety of her home, threatening her and her daughter. The blood on the wall scared Emila the most. So much blood, so much blood, from her daughter!

"Frida, I think Papa is going to be home soon. I have a good feeling. We just have to wait a bit longer, okay, sweetie? Try to go back to sleep now."

The little girl nodded as Emila gently lifted her up, carrying the exhausted child to her bed.

"Wake me up when Papa gets home, okay?" Frida asked meekly.

Emila smiled at her daughter and nodded.

She laid Frida down, kissed her forehead, and told her she loved her before leaving her room, making sure to keep the door cracked open.

She walked back over to the couch, picked up the knife, and walked to the window, peering out into the blackness.

"What evil has descended on our town this night, able to enter our dreams?" she uttered.

Chapter 15

✝

House of Lust

3:00 AM

On the opposite end of town, Uma slept soundly in her well-appointed bed with soft, white sheets and the fluffiest pillows money could buy. These were imported from Italy specifically for her after calling in a favor with the local owner of Weingart's Fine Linens, something she loved to do. The more people who were indebted to her, the better. *You never know when you'll need to make a withdrawal on those favors,* she would tell those that would listen, typically the upper crust on the southside who appreciated her flair for the dramatic.

Since she was a young girl, she had thrived on drama in some form or another. After her family's unfortunate accident and she had moved in with her grandfather, she bloomed in ways she never would have living with her pathetic parents.

Jügen Stoller had taught her how to use her charm to con, lie, cheat, steal and get her way in nearly all situations.

"You've got one life, Uma. Use it while you can. Take what you can get because one day, you'll be dead, and this will all be over. Seize every moment and make it yours. Why live in poverty when you can live luxuriously? That is what sets the wolves apart from the sheep. We, Uma, are the wolves. That's been my motto my whole life and that's what I expect of my granddaughter as well!" He would say this numerous times in various ways throughout her childhood.

She had watched him swindle people out of money, out of their homes and livelihoods, all to further line his pockets, along with deriving a sadistic joy in dominating other people. He was a puppet master, happy to pull their strings. She ate it up. The way she saw it, if people were stronger willed, they would have pushed back! But most were *weak*, and weak people could be exploited, manipulated, and taken advantage of.

She and her grandfather were like two peas in a pod, and he was the only person on earth she looked up to and respected. But he was dead, and now it was just her.

When he was still alive, she also witnessed him take advantage of people's religious beliefs, using them to control and take from them. This is something even Uma could not accomplish. She was the furthest thing from religious and, in fact, hated religious folk, but her strong will, and the fact that she was a woman in a man's world, made it impossible for her to fit into religious society. So, she focused on her aggressive nature and her looks, which worked nearly as well.

And now, in Kortbeke, she was its silent leader, pull-ing the puppet strings as much as the mayor allowed, even when Lambert pushed back. Most of the money in town passed through her hands in one way or another. And if not, she knew about it. Hubschmid's pub was a great source of contention with her. She hated Davide and his red-headed bitch wife and dreamed of the day when she would ruin his business and drive them out of town.

Once Hubschmid's was closed, its patrons, an unsavory lot, would need a place to wet their whistles and would look to Maximilian's, but they'd be swiftly turned away. Especially that loser, Ruppert Sprenger. An upstanding bar like Max-imilian's had no room for his kind. Dead-enders. The same applied to people of other ethnicities. No one of color was welcome at her establishment, except for her lovely, young and handsome bartender.

After Nils had brought her to orgasm while she thought of Leonz's tongue working its magic instead, she had fallen into a deep sleep. If Uma had dreams, she never remembered them in the morning, nor did she want to. A part of her sub-conscious knew, deep down, buried under all of the hurtful, mean-spirited and evil things she had done in her life, murder included, that what she was doing was leading her soul to damnation, and there was nothing she could do to stop it.

Dreams were the spirit's way of informing the mind that not all was well and to course correct, or else prepare to fall into the abyss. Therefore, she had learned early on to try and suppress them. Upon waking, she made herself believe she was a clear slate, rested and ready for the next day, never once giving thought to the horrors that had visited her the previous night. Dreams of her killing her family over and over and over. Dreams of a large, beastly figure, shrouded in darkness, having its way with her violently. Screaming in agony at the pain in her stomach as the seed that was spilled immediately grew. Her barren womb no longer barren and filled with an evil spawn.

Part of Uma's identity in her adult years was her barren womb. Early in their marriage, she had indeed become pregnant, but only for a short time, as the baby in her womb only lasted three months before perishing. Her doctor had informed her that not only was the child dead, but she would never be able to have children of her own.

This news affected Nils more than it did her. He turned to eating and drinking far more than his normal daily allowance while Uma doubled down on her cruelty and need for power, along with keeping her appearance as perfect as she could the older she got. She couldn't pass on her legacy to the next generation, so she would make the current generation suffer all the more. How could she, such a beautiful and alluring woman, so strong and powerful, *not* be able to bear children? It was something she had to push from her mind.

Wake up.

Uma opened her eyes in her darkened bedroom which appeared extra black as she tried to focus her eyes. *Did someone just whisper in my ear to wake up?*

Not one to feel scared for any reason, she found herself tense, especially in the utter darkness. "Why the hell is it so dark outside?" she muttered as she sat up in bed and felt around her nightstand for a lantern. She picked up a match lying beside it, struck it, and quickly touched the match to the wick, bringing much needed light to her surroundings.

She turned to look at Nils, who she assumed was fast asleep beside her. He was gone.

"Nils?" she asked with growing unease. She leaned over the bed and saw that his bathrobe and slippers were not in their usual place.

She looked toward their window. It was closed but something wasn't right. It was the middle of the night but, even so, it was too dark.

Sitting in bed, truly unnerved, she glanced at her bedroom doorway leading out to the upstairs hallway. It was cracked open slightly, likely from Nils getting out of bed. Uma rarely heard him and even more rarely woke up like this. Her breathing was growing heavier the longer she was awake and alone. She would never admit that she needed Nils and that she was more than able to handle most any issue. But she suddenly felt very much alone and vulnerable. A feeling she wasn't used to and didn't like at all.

"Is someone there?" she called out in the room, which was much too quiet. Her heart raced in the utter silence, her lantern casting soft light across the room that was empty but didn't feel empty.

Fuck! Come on Uma, get a hold of yourself, damnit!

She contemplated crawling out of bed but that would make her even more vulnerable. She had been groggy upon waking up, but she was wide awake and quite alert now. She looked around the room for any sort of weapon to defend herself with.

Defend myself against what?

A creak in the floorboards sounded right outside her bedroom door in the hall.

She froze, terrified. "Nils? Is that you? Nils, say something, damn you!"

Another creak, this one closer. Whatever it was, it was right outside the bedroom door.

Uma wore a short white nightgown, loose fitting and comfortable. It also exposed quite a bit of her curvy body. She liked the freedom it gave her in sleep, even when it was colder outside, but in this instance, she felt unprotected. On a chair by the window lay her substantially thicker bathrobe. While she didn't want to get out of bed, she needed to feel safer, and her bathrobe was a start.

Quickly ripping the covers back, she slid out of bed and rushed over to the chair, putting the bathrobe on hastily and tying it tightly around her trim waist. She looked back toward the bedroom door once more, holding out the lantern in front of her. "Hello? Who's there?"

A hand from right outside the door reached onto the cracked door's edge and slowly began pushing it open.

Uma, now overtaken with fear, frantically looked around the room for anything at all that could be used as a defense against the intruder that was most assuredly not her husband.

On her nightstand lay a hairpin. She used it often upon waking up, to keep her long hair out of her face, pinning and holding it in place before she cleaned up. It wasn't much, but it was better than nothing. Gripping the lantern in her right hand, she scooped up the seven-inch hairpin and pointed its tip toward the door.

"Whoever you are, get out of my house! Or, so help me, I will scream! I have a weapon!" Uma exclaimed, trying to mask her terror.

The door pushed open further until Uma could see the dark outline of a figure standing in the doorway.

Uma's breathing became frantic. *What the hell am I going to do? Who would dare break into my house? Nils, you pathetic excuse for a protector, where the hell are you!*

"Shh, no need to shout. No need to shout at all, my dear," a soft, alluring female voice spoke from the shape in her bedroom door.

"Wh-who are you?" Uma stuttered, her mouth dry, making it difficult to speak.

The figure didn't answer, instead moving forward into her room. "I saw you earlier. Walking to the building on the opposite side of the street. I watched how you carried yourself. And now you're a timid little rabbit. Do I scare you, little rabbit?"

Normally, a comment like this would invoke Uma's full wrath, but here, those same words shook her to her very core. The voice was so calm, almost alluring. "I-I'm not scared," she lied.

"Oh, you should be," the voice came back.

Shit! I'm going to die in this fucking bedroom! Uma kept her mouth shut, for fear the words she uttered would be her last.

The figure was coming into view. Though Uma thought herself attractive, this figure was on a whole other level of beautiful, catching Uma by surprise. She was typically not attracted to the same sex, but she did appreciate an attractive woman. The woman that stood before her had hair so golden blond it appeared almost white. Her dress fit snugly, revealing perfectly proportioned breasts and her lips were parted in a whisper. Uma's lantern revealed piercing bright blue eyes staring back at her seductively.

The woman continued forward, not phased in the slightest by the hairpin pointed in her direction. "Put that thing down, silly woman."

"You…stay back! Where is my husband?" Uma demanded.

"Ahh, the fat man. I assumed that was your spouse," the woman said nonchalantly.

"Was?"

"You won't need him any longer. You've never needed him. I knew when I saw you earlier, you need no man. All you need is," she paused, "me."

The mysteriously alluring woman was now close enough to Uma as to be within striking range.

What is this woman saying? Is my husband dead?

"You get away from me! Get out of my house, I'll scream!" Uma cried out.

"Oh, you'll scream all right," the woman's blue eyes flashed yellow, her smile grew large.

Uma plunged the hair needle at her just as the woman lifted her hand. The needle drove through the center of her palm and came out the other side, blood instantly trickling out of the wound.

The woman held her gaze and continued smiling, not flinching at the needle sticking in her hand. She gently reached up and pulled it out, inspecting the weapon that had pierced her. Looking at the terrified Uma, she opened her mouth and licked the blood from it, dropping it to the floor uselessly when it had been cleaned.

"What are you?" Uma said, shaking with terror.

"I, my dear Uma, am your future. I can use you to hasten my purpose here. You are destined for something greater than what you are now, all you need is to be…willing." She moved in closer until Uma was tightly backed against the corner with nowhere to turn. Her lantern was shaking in her hand.

The blond woman raised her hand, taking the lantern from her. As she did, the soft touch of this mysterious and frightening woman made Uma quiver. For a second her fear was replaced by instant arousal.

Carefully, the woman sat the lantern down then brought her focus back to Uma.

"My name is Everly. And I am here to change your life," she said, now so close to Uma's face she could feel the woman's breath on her lips.

"Your eyes turned yellow! And, my husband, where is he?" Uma said, fear, anger and arousal now mixing together.

"You will soon understand. But first," Everly said softly, moving even closer until her lips touched Uma's.

Unable to resist and feeling her body instantly going limp from the tension, Uma leaned in, opening her mouth, letting the woman called Everly inside. The kiss was instantly passionate and one Uma couldn't resist even if she tried.

She felt a hand against the knot of her bathrobe, loosening it. Then two hands pulling the bathrobe off of her shoulders, falling to the floor. She felt the same hands run across her thin nightgown, every touch more sensual than the last.

What am I doing? What is happening? How does this woman have such control over me!

Everly's hands wrapped around the back of Uma's head, pulling her in tightly, their bodies smashed together. To her surprise, Uma found herself running her hands down the woman's back, trying to find the zipper to loosen her aggressor's tight, blue dress.

Everly, meanwhile, with her bloodied hand, grabbed hold of Uma's nightgown and ripped it off with ease.

Uma felt herself lifted up off the floor of her bedroom and dropped onto her bed. Everly stood at her bedposts, looking down at the naked woman. Her own blue dress was hanging from her shoulders, ready to spill off.

In all her years, Uma had never been aroused in such a way, not by the mayor of this town nor the men she had seduced and bedded in her teens and early twenties. And most certainly not by her husband. She desperately wanted the woman standing over her to take her own clothes off and have her way with her.

"Please," Uma muttered, looking lustfully at Everly.

Everly's dress fell to the floor as she bit into her lip, instantly drawing blood.

Crawling on top of Uma, she opened her mouth, the blood mixed with spit falling from her lips into Uma's open mouth. Uma couldn't resist, accepting the blood that ran down her tongue and into her throat before being completely swallowed.

Everly lowered herself atop Uma, placing her bloody lips against her prey once more. With her pierced hand, she rubbed Uma's chest as Uma moaned in ecstasy into Everly's mouth.

Releasing her lips from Uma's, Everly looked down at the writhing woman with eyes glowing yellow. Uma's eyes closed tightly as Everly worked her hands down to her sex, immediately drawing louder moans from Uma.

Everly whispered in her ear, "I have chosen you, my lovely. I saw in your eyes the hunger for power and I like that. Not many humans I have met in my travels have that look. You have drive and cunning. I can grant you more once I have completed what I came here for." She paused, staring down at the squirming woman on the bed before continuing. "But first, you will do what I say. I am your master now. Your new life is a gift, but not a free one. It belongs to me, and I expect you to mind me and my orders, do you understand?"

"Yes," Uma whispered in rapturous pleasure, feeling Everly's bloody fingers penetrate her.

Smiling and satisfied with her latest trophy, Everly opened her mouth. Sharp fangs pushed forth. "You must drink and die and then you shall be reborn, my black-haired princess." A small snarl escaped her throat as she lowered herself once more atop the writhing Uma, now lost in the throes of lust, reaching the height of her climax. Everly sunk her fangs into the woman's neck and in that instant, sealed her fate.

†

Chapter 16

The Fire Spreads

4:00 AM

St. Raphael's was on fire. Ruppert, Klaus, Nina and Leonz knew it was a lost cause. The meager fire department of Kortbeke could in no way handle something like this. Furthermore, the fire department was little more than several appointed officials with large drums of water, stored in barns behind their properties on the outskirts of town, which would have to be loaded up and hauled to the fire.

There had never been a substantial fire of this sort in Kortbeke. Plus, Uma had seen to it that something she considered as frivolous as better firefighting equipment was a waste of the town's money. Lambert had pressed the issue further until Klaus tabled it for a later date. That was over a year ago and it hadn't been brought up since.

Klaus thought back to Lambert slamming the door on his way out of that council meeting. He thought of the shame he felt, knowing the right thing to do for the people of Kortbeke was channeling the funds for the town's safety, and that it was only a matter of time before a fire did occur. But safety wasn't on Uma's agenda, so it was squelched. And now, the church of Kortbeke, the oldest building in town and its very landmark, was burning.

"I started this!" Klaus said grimly, watching the flames rise, thinking not only of his clumsiness earlier, but also his weakness in the town council meeting a year ago.

"Not now, Klaus! What's done is done! Let's hope that thing in there won't survive the fire!" Nina shouted, pointing to the area where it had fallen.

Ruppert, still rubbing his neck from the tight grip the creature had on him minutes earlier, glanced at the flames from the church and shouted to the rest, "We've got to get out of here!"

"And go where?" Nina retorted.

"If we can just make it back to Maximilian's. It's built strong. In case *she* comes back," Leonz exclaimed.

"Great, so back to the original plan of getting to Maximilian's. Out in the open, damnit!" Klaus exclaimed, watching the flames rise higher and higher up the sides of the church.

"Hey, if you've got any better ideas, I'm all ears!" Ruppert shouted back.

"I've got the key, we can make it, but what of the rest of the town?" Leonz said.

Shaking her head, Nina watched the flames. "He's right, the town is going to wake up to this. Soon, there will surely be chaos on the streets!"

"Well, at least this will light things up a bit. What time is it?" Ruppert said.

Klaus glanced at his wristwatch. "Little past four. Sun won't start rising for another few hours."

"We can't warn everyone! What do we do?" Klaus asked frantically.

"Davide will be back, hopefully with Lambert and Erni. But we can't wait on them. He knows we were headed to Maximilian's. Right now, we must get there. But before we go, let's make some torches. If anyone comes out along the way, we tell them to get inside and lock their doors," Ruppert said, then added, "Let's move!"

The smoke was taking over inside the church. Quickly, each of them grabbed another large splinter of the broken cross from earlier and then grabbed nearby albs, tearing large portions of the cloth and wrapping the ends of the wood with it. With Nina's lantern they soaked the ends of the cloth and held them into nearby flames, instantly igniting them.

Armed with torches, the four ran to the door and out into the black night.

✝

Davide and Fr. Kries made haste on Bertha and Brutus back toward Kortbeke. Soon they saw, where the town should have been, a haze of darkness hanging over and around it, appearing to have swallowed it whole.

Fr. Kries pulled back on Brutus's reins, bringing the large beast to a halt as he stared in horror at the dark haze.

Up ahead a few yards, Davide pulled back on Bertha's reins and circled back. "What is it, Father?" he asked hurriedly.

Pausing for a second, Fr. Kries looked gravely at Davide before speaking. "Davide, evil is at play here. Where it comes from, I do not know. But I am just one man, and this town was Fr. Steffen's. I don't know if I have what it takes to fight it."

Nodding his understanding, Davide replied, "Fr. Kries, I've known you now for the full three years you've been in our town. And you've proven yourself well in that time. Whatever plagues our town is pure evil, straight from hell, and we need you now, more than ever. I have a wife and daughter back there, waiting for me. And there are many other families that are, right now, in serious danger unless we do something. What it is, I'm not sure, but if there are more of what Lambert became then it's up to us to take care of them. We dealt with him and we can deal with what lies beyond that wall of black up ahead."

"Lambert didn't put up a fight. At least not much of one, from what I saw. He was fighting whatever infected him. What's in that town likely will not be as accommodating," Fr. Kries said.

"Be that as it may, we ride. Come on, Father, Kortbeke needs you. I need you!" Davide said, then gave a hard crack on Bertha's reins, taking off once more for Kortbeke.

Grimacing, Fr. Kries snapped his reins and Brutus galloped forward, following Bertha toward a black fog, where behind it lay a town under siege.

✝

Ruppert, Klaus, Nina and Leonz ran out of the church with torches held high. Smoke billowed out from the windows and up into the night sky, the air outside smelling of smoke.

Immediately, Klaus held out his torch, shining light ahead and onto the body of the elderly produce stand vendor, Whitmer, lying dead in the street, murdered earlier by Chadwick.

The man had been ravaged to the point of being barely recognizable. His skull looked as though it had been pummeled into the cobblestone street until it ended the old man's life. Intestines were strewn about, extracted from a large gash in his stomach.

Nina turned away in revulsion, leaning into Leonz's chest, gasping.

Ruppert grimaced at the ghastly sight and glanced at Klaus, asking, "I wonder if he will turn into what Chadwick became?"

"Don't know," the mayor replied numbly, still shaken by the terrible turn of events in Kortbeke, all on his watch.

"So, we can't be sure that thing is dead, but it seems as though fire hurts it. What else might be of use in case it's still alive?" Leonz asked.

Quickly thinking, Ruppert pointed out, "My mom told me stories as a kid of a big, bad wolfman, and the only way to stop it was with something silver. Usually, a silver bullet. Anyone bit was infected and had to be killed with silver. Scared the shit out of me when I was a kid. Obviously, they were just fairy tales. But, hell…I'd try about anything to stop whatever is inside that church, let's just hope the fire took care of it."

Voices sounded from down the street.

"What's going on here? Is the church on fire?" a man shrouded in darkness exclaimed.

Several more voices rose from the black night.

"What is this darkness?"

"What's happening?"

"Look! Up there! Flames!"

Klaus recognized several of the growing number of voices and turned to Ruppert. "This could get bad. We have torches and the church is on fire, and here lies Whitmer with his brains bashed out and his guts ripped from his body."

Before Ruppert could respond, a voice rang out near him. "Hey, you there! Ruppert Sprenger, is that you? What are you doing out here with the mayor at this time of night, and why do you two have torches?" It was Erwin Brahms, a local farmer and a large man standing at slightly over six feet tall.

"Erwin, hang on here, you've got to get back to your house, it's not safe out here!" Ruppert exclaimed.

"Is that Whitmer? Oh, my Lord! Is he, is he *dead?*" exclaimed Esther Klee, the town's schoolteacher, seeing the fallen produce vendor lying lifeless in the street.

"Look! That Leonz kid and his bar maiden girlfriend are with them!" Pascal Blattner, the local ironsmith bellowed.

More people were now joining, all looking at the murdered body in the street then over to the burning church.

"What have you done!" a voice from the growing crowd shouted out, this time panic replaced with anger.

"Listen! All of you! Get back to your homes! There's something out here in our town that's already killed tonight, and it will continue!" Ruppert called out.

Klaus backed away from the growing crowd just as the fire inside the church belched and flames exploded out of all the stained-glass windows, jetting out into the street and causing the small crowd nearby to fall to the ground or run in terror.

"It was an accident!" Klaus wailed, more to himself than those around him.

Ruppert grabbed him by the shoulder and spun him around so they were face to face. "Listen to me! You're the mayor of this town, so lead, damn you!"

Klaus shook his head, puzzled, then turned back to watch the flames shooting out of the front door that had fallen in. Smoke billowed from the church building into the sky while the flames lit up the immediate area even more as they got higher.

"Look! Up there!" Nina exclaimed.

Ruppert looked up along with several of the townsfolk.

The smoke and light from the flames had revealed what appeared to be a dome shape above them. Beyond it, normal night skies spread out in space. But in the town of Kortbeke, a blanket of black was now visible to those with a keen eye.

Taking his eyes off the smoke-filled sky, Erwin Brahms shouted out, "I don't know what the hell is up there, but I know what my eyes see here! I see a dead man lying on the street and you lot with torches standing outside our church that's burning to the ground! Where is Fr. Steffen?"

Ruppert looked uneasily at Nina and Leonz as the situation seemed to get worse with more people arriving to inspect the strange goings-ons. The murmurs of the crowd were intensifying.

"We need to get to Maximilian's, our safety is in jeopardy here," Ruppert said to Klaus, Nina and Leonz.

"I asked you a question! Where is Fr. Steffen?" Erwin called out.

"He's dead, damnit! You hear me? He's dead and we're all going to be dead too!" Klaus shouted out.

Ruppert stared wide-eyed at the man who was clearly losing it and unable to lead, as well as compromising their current situation to an even greater degree.

"Klaus, you will *shut up*, you understand me? You're making things worse!" Nina hissed.

"The priest is dead? Is what he says true?" Pascal Blattner asked sternly.

Ruppert looked warily toward him and the crowd of now roughly twenty people and growing. He slowly nodded yes. "We didn't kill him. There is something evil loose in this town! Please, people, you need to get to your homes, lock your doors!"

"You expect us to believe that!? Where's Lambert and where the hell is Erni? We need our chief of police here!" a woman called out.

"We can't stand here! We must take cover!" Ruppert pleaded with the growing crowd.

The shouting grew louder, to the point that none of them could understand the other.

The church, engulfed in flames, continued shooting smoke and burning debris up into the sky, higher and higher.

"They don't believe us! What the hell is wrong with you all!?" Klaus shouted out angrily.

Fighting back the immense urge to punch the mayor in the face, Ruppert shot back, "Klaus, damnit! You're doing nothing but riling the crowd up. Can't you see that?"

Realizing he was right, Klaus finally fell silent, his eyes darting from person to person in the crowd. Many he knew well and wouldn't so much as hurt a fly, let alone suddenly become raging mad men, out for mob justice. But with their church burning to the ground and a mysterious darkness ever present throughout the entire town, who knew what they would do?

The eeriness of the smoke and flames lighting up an invisible dome was proof enough that this wasn't just a fire taking place in town. Something far more sinister and supernatural was at play.

Leonz leaned into Nina and whispered, "We have to get out of here. This crowd is turning into a mob. And with a mob comes mob justice."

Nina nodded her understanding and looked toward the side street Leonz had taken previously to get down to the church.

Someone hollered out, "I think it's that colored fella that works over at Maximillian's! Figures someone like that would do something like this! We should have never trusted him!"

"What have you done, Mayor? You're supposed to be in charge of this town yet you come out of the burning building? Of *course* Uma Karlen's puppet would be involved in something like this!" another person shouted.

The faces of the townsfolk grew angrier by the second. Not helping matters was Whitmer's mangled, dead body on the street for all to see.

Klaus looked around in terror at the now hostile crowd, many of which shot accusatory looks at him, forming their own theories as to the strange occurrences. All of this, he knew, could be explained away easily if these people were being rational, but they were no longer rational.

A bottle flew from the crowd, tumbling end over end as it sailed forward toward Klaus but narrowly missing him, instead making direct contact with the side of Leonz's head, shattering as soon as it connected.

He immediately fell to one knee, raising his hand to the injured spot where the bottle connected and feeling it wet with blood.

"No!" shouted Nina furiously at the crowd.

But the floodgates had opened. "Get them! If Lambert won't come to take care of this, we'll take these four to him!"

"Lambert's not here! I heard him and Erni left town earlier, saw them myself!" an old man who had just joined the growing crowd shouted out.

Nina looked at Leonz's bloody face. "Time to go, now." She pulled him to his feet and saw Ruppert had made his way to them.

"You all, stay the hell back, you hear me!" Ruppert shouted out, waving his torch out in front of his face.

"What are you going to do? Burn us all like you burned our church? Murderer!" Pascal Blattner exclaimed.

A figure ran forward, his fist raised. It was Erwin Brahms, his face a mixture of rage and fright. Seeing the approaching man, Klaus took off running up the main street toward Maximilian's, leaving Ruppert to fend for himself.

To Nina and Leonz, Ruppert shouted, "Get the hell out of here, go! Now!"

Nina gave a brief nod and, with Leonz, took off down the side alley. Instantly, several men took chase at what they perceived were fleeing arsonists and likely murders.

Running behind Nina, Leonz struggled to keep up, feeling woozy from the blow to his head.

"You keep running, Leonz! You hear me?" Nina exclaimed, glancing back worriedly.

Behind them, the sounds of angry townsfolk began to subside, lost in the darkness.

Ruppert, meanwhile, the last remaining arsonist suspect with neither the time nor strength to defend himself, took the brunt of Erwin's fist across the side of his face. He fell backwards onto the ground with Erwin standing over him, ready to deliver another blow to the face.

"What is wrong with you people!?" Ruppert exclaimed.

A loud howl sounded from the smoke shrouded entrance of the church, causing the angry townsfolk to freeze. Erwin, too, stopped and looked in the direction of the sound.

In the doorway of the church stood what had once been Chadwick, its injured leg apparently healed, its fur and skin heavily burnt. The beastly form raised its arms and stretched them out completely on either side, then opened its thick, saliva-covered mouth and roared at the onlookers. Its lone black eye scanning over them.

"It's not dead," Ruppert muttered, shaking his dazed head and scooting away from Erwin who was now focused on the wolf standing on its hind legs towering over them all.

Its jaws opened and, with fangs exposed, it snarled in rage at the onlookers.

Chapter 17

✝

Kortbeke Falls

4:30 AM

Uma opened her eyes. She was still in bed, but the covers had been ripped off. It was dark but her eyesight was more than capable of seeing in the darkness. She sat up in bed and looked around the room, suddenly realizing her nakedness.

She looked over her body. Her beautiful, smooth-skinned body. She felt infinitely stronger, sexually charged and animalistic, thanks to her beautiful female lover that had visited her earlier with a most precious gift. But she was gone, and Uma was left alone. She felt her throat where small traces of puncture marks remained, now miraculously healing up.

She thought back to the incredible experience. "Where are you, my lover? My life is yours now." She slid from her bed. A bed she would no longer need. She was now destined for far more than even her grandfather could have imagined for her. Thanks to the woman she had given herself to, body and soul. The woman that had almost instantaneously seduced her and changed her. Made her something *more.*

Uma went to her closet, pulled out a long black slip, and slid it over her body, looking at herself in the mirror beside it. "Ravishing," she said coolly.

She had the sudden urge to eat. And she knew just who would make the tastiest morsel at this hour of the night.

†

Mayor Klaus ran as fast as he could down the main street of Kortbeke—the destination, his house. If he could just get to his house, lock the door, and pack his bags, at first light he would get the hell out of this town! He heard a howl in the distance and froze, listening to the awful sound. Then he heard something even more chilling, people screaming.

He had abandoned the others, once more the coward he knew, deep down, he was and always would be. If he survived this night of horrors, his tenure in Kortbeke was certainly over. Between his ongoing affair with Uma becoming common knowledge and now the church's destruction, the dead bodies, and the way the townsfolk were reacting, he would be lucky to make it out of Kortbeke in one piece.

He thought of his dream. Of the woman on the ground with a shotgun blast to her stomach. *Why me? Why Nina and Davide? Why us?* Whatever the reason, he wasn't sticking around to find out.

He had heard footsteps behind him as he tossed his torch and took off for home, and while the church fire had lit up the immediate surroundings, the further from it he got, the darker the streets became. *Good, they won't find me.*

The footsteps gradually faded, and he was left by himself. In the distance, flames rose above the buildings, continuing to illuminate the invisible black dome over Kortbeke. An ominous silence fell over the street as he neared his home.

After what felt like an eternity, he got to his now barely visible doorway and burst inside, slamming the door behind him and locking it. Once confident it was secure, he leaned against it, breathing heavily and wiping his sweat-covered face. Even with the cool wind blowing outside, he found himself perspiring profusely.

"Damn, I need a cigarette," he mumbled.

He looked around the room, it was empty. Lighting a lantern, he made his way to the washroom and quickly cleaned himself up, splashing water on his face. He looked at himself in the mirror and hated what he saw, quickly looking away in shame.

"Sonofabitch," Klaus muttered. "I didn't want this! I never wanted the damn mayor job in the first place! I've got to get out of here!"

✝

The wolf beast leapt out of the church doorway and lashed out at the first person it reached. Gertie Geraldine never knew what hit her. One second, the elderly woman stared in wonder at an impossible looking creature, and the next, her head was ripped from her body and tossed uselessly to the side of the road, the rest of her body left bleeding out onto the street.

The townspeople that had gathered erupted into screams.

Ruppert, meanwhile, moved back, away from the unfolding chaos. *Get to Maximilian's!* he thought as he tried evading the running and panicking citizens of Kortbeke.

The wolf beast saw the man it knew was Erwin running toward it in an attempt to tackle it to the ground. It grabbed him, stopping him in his tracks, lifted him off the ground with ease, and threw him through the doorway of the burning church, into the flames that quickly engulfed the screaming man whose cries for help went unanswered.

Numerous people were now attempting to run away from the monster that had emerged from the burning church mere seconds earlier. Anyone in its way was instantly killed.

Esther Klee attempted to run down the nearest side street, but the wolf stopped her in her tracks with a line of deep scratches down the length of her back.

In the escalating confusion, a teenage boy named Elias Stöcker absently ran right into the creature that grabbed the boy by the sides of his head, raised him up till he was eye level with it, and squeezed.

Pascal Blattner, the ironsmith, had picked up one of the dropped torches and attempted to light the beast on fire, but it had learned quickly, swatting the burning stake out of his hand and jumping on top of him, sinking its fangs into his waiting neck, tearing it open with ease before moving on.

Ruppert was on his feet, watching in horror at the unfolding turmoil outside the decimated church building. Most of the town had been awakened by the screams or the smell of smoke wafting through town by now. The more people that came out to see what was happening, the more the carnage piled up.

The fire spread to the bank next to the church, the side wall igniting as it moved up and onto the ceiling inside, quickly burning through to the roof, at which point the building was completely lost. The owner of the bank looked on in horror as his business was decimated by the flames. He didn't even notice the creature that ran past him, until it was knocking him to the ground and slashing his stomach open, removing its contents. All in the timespan of several painful seconds.

The wolf beast was killing anything that got in its path. Ruppert watched in helpless horror as Nina's elderly mother and father, shouting her name, looking for their missing daughter, became its next victims. The massive black wolf took her mother first, raising her off the ground and biting the back of her neck out. Nina's father, in a feeble attempt to help his already dead wife, grabbed hold of the wolf's large, muscular arm while pleading for the release of his wife. The woman was dropped to the ground, collapsing into a bloody heap as the wolf easily slammed its clawed fist through the man's chest, ripping his still beating heart from his body.

Ruppert grimaced, closing his eyes tight against the unholy evil ravaging the town and killing at will. "Run! Get out of here!" he yelled at the confused and panicked people scattering in all directions, clearing away from the creature that had lifted a small child by its leg into the air, howling.

Seeing no other options, Ruppert took off running down the same side street Nina and Leonz had taken back to Maximilian's minutes earlier.

Behind him, the chaos continued as one of the sides of St. Raphael's roof collapsed in on itself, causing the ground to shake at its impact. He didn't turn around again, focusing instead on getting to Maximilian's.

✝

Back at Emila and Davide's house near the edge of town, Emila stepped outside, staring up at the flames shooting above buildings, smoke exposing the dome-shaped darkness above. She heard the screams of the townspeople and something else in the ensuing chaos from what she guessed was St. Raphael's parish. The roar of something not human.

Eyes wide with terror, she quickly ran back inside her house, quietly closing the door and locking it. Feeling utterly alone, her thoughts went to her nightmare earlier. Shaking her head and wiping fresh tears away, she hastily went to check on her daughter, keeping her butcher knife with her at all times.

Seeing her exhausted daughter sleeping through the noise, she breathed a sigh of relief, then tiptoed back to the living room, once more hearing the distant sounds of screams and destruction from the center of Kortbeke. She looked at the clock. Slightly past four o'clock in the morning

"Maybe we've all died, and this is hell," Emila uttered gravely.

✝

Nina and Leonz made it to Maximilian's in near darkness, the haze from the fire their only source of light after dropping their torches earlier. Nina was thankful it was enough to light their way to safety, a painful twist of irony, as those same flames engulfed the church around which numerous people were being slaughtered.

Behind them, several townsfolk continued their pursuit, but this route was one Nina and Leonz travelled often in their late-night meet ups. The only thing slowing them down was Leonz's injured head, which was of growing concern for Nina.

"Up ahead! We're almost there!" Nina said, pointing to Maximilian's now in view roughly two hundred yards away.

Leonz grunted his response as he slowed his step.

Nina knew instantly there was trouble and grabbed hold of him just as he collapsed to the ground.

"No, not now! Leonz, get up, come on!" Nina cried out.

"There they are! Get them!" two approaching men shouted out.

"*Sonofabitch!*" Nina muttered, glancing around for something to use to defend herself and an ailing Leonz.

A piece of wood in a nearby trash bin was the best she could muster in short order. Pulling it out, she spun around to greet her pursuers who both came to a stop.

She was certain they were from the southside and Maximilian patrons.

The first one, a scrawny, middle-aged man with a lisp, spoke, "You're coming with us, the both of you!"

The second one, slightly taller but an equally ugly specimen with teeth too large for his narrow mouth and thin face, catching his breath, pointed at them. "You're both in a heap of trouble, you hear me!"

Raising the wooden board like a bat, Nina exclaimed, "You want us, you can damn well come and try!"

"Feisty one! I see why that colored orphan fella likes you, missy!" the first man sneered.

What is wrong with these people? It was as if the darkness had turned them disoriented and aggressive, making Nina terrified at the crazed look in the men's eyes.

Indeed, the black cloud had brought with it confusion and chaos, making the more susceptible of Kortbeke to somehow lose their rational thinking and fall into fear and confusion.

The second man made an attempt at grabbing the wooden board Nina was clenching tightly in her hands. Without hesitating, Nina swung, striking the man across the face and sending him flying backwards onto the street.

Leonz had groggily stood back to his feet with Nina at his side just as the other man moved in. With a hard right hand, Leonz connected with his nose.

Blood instantly spilled out onto the man's chest as he fell over backwards, stunned at the hard blow the seemingly incapacitated young man had just delivered.

"No one attacks my woman, got that? Come on, Nina, let's go," Leonz said coolly, staring down at the pathetic Maximilian patrons he immediately recognized as Lutz and Reiner Ullrich. Sketchy cousins in Kortbeke's southside and friends to Chadwick and his small gang.

Neither man made any further attempts in apprehending them as the two lovers, hand in hand, moved past them to the doorway of Maximilian's.

"Shit, someone else is heading this way!" Leonz said, pointing at a figure heading up the main street.

"Get the door unlocked, hurry!" Nina said, keeping her eyes on the approaching figure while watching the flames in the distance continue to burn.

Leonz fumbled through his pockets until he found the key, easy to pick out from his own rusted key for the tiny room he called home, as this one was made of pure silver. "Got it! Wait, what is that?"

Nina looked in the direction he was pointing. Near the Karlen household, on the ground, lay the eviscerated remains of Nils Karlen. "Leonz, hurry, get that door unlocked, now," she urged, turning away from this latest atrocity.

Leonz was about the put the key into the door's lock when they both heard a familiar voice.

"Leonz, Nina!"

They turned to see the figure quickly approaching was Ruppert.

"Ruppert! Sorry to have left you," Nina began but Ruppert shook his head and raised his hand.

"I understand, just get that door unlocked. We need to regroup!" Ruppert said with a nod, out of breath and wiping a bit of blood from his nose from the hard punch he had received from Erwin earlier.

"Good to see you, Ruppert," Leonz said just as two screams suddenly rang out from the alley they'd come from.

Ruppert and Nina froze while Leonz, now shaking, fumbled with the key in the lock. "Got it!" The latch clicked. As he pushed it open, they glanced back toward the alley to see a shadowed figure walking toward them. Tall, slender, long hair. Uma.

"Well, hello there," she uttered, now close enough that she was recognizable.

"Uma, uh," Leonz said, surprised to see his boss out at this hour.

She looked slowly toward her murdered husband and smiled nonchalantly then back to the three attempting to gain access into her establishment. "Where do you think you're going? At this time of night?"

"We could ask you the same thing, Uma," Nina retorted instantly.

Uma smiled and tilted her head. "Ahh, the pretty little girlfriend of *my* employee actually speaks."

At this, an instant wave of rage coursed through Nina. Seeing her begin to step forward, Ruppert shook his head and muttered, "Something's wrong with her, apart from just being the normal bitch that she is."

Ignoring him, Uma's eyes locked onto Leonz who was staring back at her as though mesmerized. She looked beautiful, seductive, entrancing.

He shook his head and grimacing, pushed the door open.

"I wouldn't do that if I were you, my dreamy young man," Uma said calmly, continuing to move forward. Her eyes flashed yellow.

"Her eyes!" Leonz exclaimed to Nina and Ruppert. He felt mesmerized and confused by her otherworldly stare that seemed focused on him alone.

"Get inside!" Nina replied, pushing Leonz forward with Ruppert quickly following, slamming the door shut behind them.

Once inside, Leonz quicky locked the door behind him and leaned against the door, breathing heavily.

"Whatever has infested this town must have gotten to her, of all people," Nina said coldly. "As if that wretched woman couldn't possibly get any worse." Thinking, she turned to Leonz. "Is there another entrance into Maximilian's?" she asked urgently.

Rubbing his injured head, he nodded and pointed to the back. "Yes, back where we keep the extra liquor there's a side door where the trash is stored. It should be locked, but it's not as solid or thick as this one. No one would dare break into Maximilian's, so Uma and Nils never reenforced it."

"We've got to make sure that door is barred up," Ruppert said as Nina nodded her agreement.

"I need to sit down. My head," Leonz said as he felt his knees buckle.

Once more, Nina grabbed hold of him, this time with Ruppert's help.

"That bottle hit to your head must have been harder than I thought," Nina said anxiously.

They sat him down in a nearby chair and lit a lantern, inspecting his head. Fresh blood ran from the wound onto his shirt.

"Oh, no!" Nina cried out.

"He needs stiches. That glass cut him pretty bad," Ruppert said, glancing at Nina.

"Hang on, let me get a wet cloth," Nina said, hurriedly running back to the bar.

"Steady, there, Leonz. We'll get a makeshift bandage wrapped around your head until we get the doctor to look at it," Ruppert said, not believing himself. He was pretty sure he saw the town doctor getting torn apart by the wolf in the town square massacre likely still taking place.

"Ruppert, take care of Nina, alright? I mean, if I don't make it, you make sure she lives," Leonz said as blood continued seeping from his temple.

"Don't talk like that, Leonz, you hang in there," Ruppert replied urgently as Nina came back with a cold, wet towel.

Ruppert quickly took it and placed it against the bleeding man's head. Leonz grimaced as Ruppert then took the belt from his pants and hastily strapped it around Leonz's head to secure the wet towel in place. Satisfied it was tight enough, he nodded.

"It's bad, I feel it. But don't worry about me. Take care of that door back there," Leonz said woozily.

"He's right, Nina, I'll go back and reenforce it," Ruppert said quietly, heading to the rear of the bar, leaving Nina to tend to an increasingly incoherent Leonz.

Wiping tears from her eyes, she turned to Leonz. "You hang in there." She leaned forward, kissing him gently on his forehead.

Leonz nodded and closed his eyes as Nina stood to her feet and headed back to the bar to see what else she could find that could be of help to her love.

Back in the stock room, Ruppert found the door Leonz had spoken of and saw that it was indeed cheaply made and could easily be broken down. Thinking quickly, he muttered to himself, "I'll just push these crates against the door, they're heavy enough to do the trick, I suppose. That'll give us enough time to make a run for it out the front."

As Ruppert began to reenforce the door and Nina searched cabinets under the bar for anything useful, Leonz sat quietly in the chair, his mind growing increasingly woozy with the continued loss of blood.

"Help me! Please, open the door, help me!" a soft child's voice said outside the door.

Leonz, confused, stared at the door and felt the key in his pocket.

✝

Chapter 18

The Priest

and

his Secrets

4:45 AM

Davide and Fr. Kries were nearing the edge of town and could see flames rising from the town's center. "What has happened here?" Fr. Kries exclaimed as he ran his hands through his hair, pushing it back against his skull, a nervous quirk.

"Father, it's been going on since last evening. Even I didn't think it could get this bad. The fire, it looks like…"

"Yes, I know, the church! Come, hurry!" Fr. Kries exclaimed.

"Father, I must check on my wife first. She is likely worried sick, and I need to make sure she and Frida are safe," Davide said as they were about to pass his house.

Fr. Kries looked worriedly at his travelling companion. "I don't think we have time, Davide."

"We have to make time. She needs to know I'm safe," Davide said firmly.

"Maybe I should ride ahead and meet you there," Fr. Kries relied.

"I'm sorry, Father, but we need to stay together. I'll make it quick."

Fr. Kries nodded and pulled up on Brutus's reins, following Davide up the hazy, darkened street to his house.

Once at the small cottage situated on the northside of town, Fr. Kries remained on his horse while Davide jumped off Bertha and ran to his front door and knocked quietly.

In seconds, the door cracked several inches, and Emila's worried face peeked out. Her eyes instantly widened at the sight of Davide, and she pushed the door open further, falling into his arms.

"Oh, Davide! I've been so worried! This town…" Emila exclaimed, then stopped, seeing who was with him. "Fr. Kries, thank God you are here!"

"Emila, honey, we must get to the town square, the church!" Davide said hurriedly. "I stopped to make sure you and Frida were safe and to let you know I was as well."

"I am. Frida is asleep now, finally. But Davide," Emila began.

He kissed her cheek. "I will be back as soon as we get things under control, I promise."

Davide turned to leave as Emila said to Fr. Kries, "Father, what do you make of this? Why is this happening to us?"

Fr. Kries had been wrestling not just with this immediate question, but also with whether to tell Davide everything about who he was, who he really was. He suddenly felt a deep desire to let these people know the truth.

"These dreams we've been having are of my mother. The town I grew up in, I'd pushed it out of my mind for many years, but I recognized it from the dream. I am more and more certain that she was the woman shot outside the doctor's house there. Her name is Everly Seiler. I am her son, Christoph Seiler, originally from the town of Burnmere, in the Carpathian Mountain region of Romania. I left many years ago, vowing to never return, and took my vows, becoming a priest, ordained in Austria, as you know. I thought it was all behind me, but it seems my past has caught up with me."

Digesting this new information, Davide said sternly, "And the woman taking a shotgun blast to the stomach? Eyes that flashed yellow, you're sure that is your mother?" If this is true, it seems your past has indeed caught up with us all, Father."

Shaking his head, Fr. Kries replied, "That I do not know. If we dreamed of the same woman, she didn't look like the mother I remember years ago. But everything about the past six hours isn't normal."

"You left this town, Burnmere, why? What was so bad that you had to change your identity?" Emila pressed.

"If I had stayed, I fear my mother would have killed me. She hated me like she hated the man she was married to. She would talk to herself on numerous occasions, saying she wanted to smother me as an infant and wished she had the opportunity once more. She knew I could hear her. Seeing no other option, I left, vowing never to return. Barely giving my father notice," Fr. Kries said sadly.

Davide and his wife stared at the shamed priest, all three falling silent. In the distance, the sounds of a building crumbling echoed from the center of town, jarring them back to their immediate situation.

"We need to get to the church. This will have to wait for now," Davide said urgently, turning his attention to the inferno that raged above all other buildings in Kortbeke, continuing to cast an ominous glow over the invisible dome of darkness that enshrouded the town.

He quickly kissed his wife on the cheek. "Lambert is dead. So is Erni. Both killed back in Granhal by whatever is here. Listen to me, Emila, Lambert's last order of business was putting me in charge. So, I must do what I can, while I can, to save this town."

Wiping away her tears and dumbfounded at this sudden news, Emilia had no words as both men hopped back up onto their horses. Fr. Kries glanced at Emila briefly, giving a quick nod, before kicking the side of Brutus and taking off with Davide into the early morning hours toward what seemed to be certain chaos and quite possibly, their own death.

"'Some are born great, some achieve greatness, and some have greatness thrust upon them.' Be careful, my love," Emila said, watching them ride off into the haze of darkness and smoke as she went back inside her home, quickly closing and locking the door behind her.

†

Nina decided to check on Ruppert's progress in the stock room and headed back, taking one final quick glance at Leonz sitting quietly with his eyes half-closed before he fell out of her sight.

She found Ruppert busily stacking crates in the small room and wiping sweat from his brow. "It's rough and won't keep us safe for very long, but it's better than nothing," he said.

"And if anything comes through the front door, this could be a problem if we have to make haste out of here."

"No matter how you slice it, we're all in a world of shit here. Just doing the best I can," Ruppert said as he lifted the last crate, putting it atop another. "How's Leonz?"

Nina attempted to sound positive. "The cut is deep; however, I am believing that he can pull through until we can get him to the doctor."

Ruppert glanced at Nina, seeing the doubt in her eyes after hearing it in her voice. He had gotten a close look at the wound and, if left untreated, the man would likely die. The cut was too deep and was a direct hit to the temple, a dangerous place for such an injury.

Sighing heavily, Ruppert said, "Nina, we don't have the tools to fix him up. He's becoming delirious and that blood flow isn't stopping."

"We are not going to let him die, damnit!" Nina retorted, instantly angry.

"I know, I know. We are going to do what we can. But I need you to prepare for the worst and hope for the best."

"Fine. You've prepared me. But he's strong, so let's just get this done. God, I hope my parents are safe. They're already old and frail. I can't imagine how frightened they are right now."

Ruppert thought back to seeing them fall at the hands of the Chadwick beast.

"Nina, there is no good time to tell you this, but you must know now, rather than seeing the aftermath later…"

Nina, glancing around the stockroom for something to better wrap Leonz's wound, stopped and looked at him, sensing from his tone he had more bad news. She raised her hands in the air. "Well?"

"It's your parents. I-I saw them right after you and Leonz left. They showed up to see what the commotion was all about." Ruppert stopped, looking down at the floor.

An awful feeling in the pit of Nina's stomach overtook her. "Tell me they're safe, tell me!"

Looking at the distraught young lady, Ruppert shook his head solemnly.

"No! No!" Nina wailed, putting her hands over her face, tears instantly springing forth.

"I'm sorry. I'm sorry for all of this," was all Ruppert could say.

Nina continued sobbing, unaware of the malevolent force right outside the front door of Maximilian's.

†

Leonz heard it again, the young girl's voice asking for help and to be let in.

"Help me, mister! They're coming to get me! They killed my parents! I know someone is in there! Please, let me in, I'm begging you!"

Leonz looked toward the bar but Nina was gone. It was just him in the dimly lit room. His mind was foggy, but he was sure a small child was begging for entry.

Carefully, he stood to his feet, and holding the silver key in his hand, unsteadily made his way to the front door. After carefully inserting the key, he once more turned it. The door unlocked and Leonz opened it.

Standing in the doorway barefooted was Uma, her long black slip fitting her curvy body perfectly. The cold temperature outside no longer affected her. Her dark eyes seemed even darker, nearly black. Her skin had taken a slightly paler tone, but her lips were bright red.

You tricked me! You bitch, you tricked me! Leonz tried to pull back, but her piercing gaze locked onto him. He stared back at her in both revulsion and a new sensation, arousal.

Seeing the object of her desire, she smiled slyly and spoke in the small child's voice once more. "You opened for me, my love. I see you're injured, poor boy." She raised her hand, sliding a finger over the slow trickle of blood down the side of his face and put it to her nose, smelling it. She watched him as she placed her finger in her mouth, sucking the blood off of it, smiling. Then, she squeezed her bottom lip with her teeth until it punctured.

Licking her lips of his blood and tasting her own from the thin stream her bite had produced, she moved in one step.

"I-I can't let you in, Uma," Leonz said, feeling about to pass out from the blood continuing to slowly trickle out of the side of his head.

She leaned in, her lips only an inch from his, this time speaking in her own voice, "Oh, I don't need to come in, I have what I came for right here."

"Sorry, Uma, but I can't go with…" He trailed off, no longer feeling pain from the deep cut on the side of his head.

"I have a gift for you, my sweet morsel, a gift that will make you so much more powerful and virile, it will even take care of that pesky little cut on the side of your head that tastes oh, so good! Close your eyes, now," Uma commanded in a whisper.

Unable to resist her voice and her deep, hypnotizing stare, Leonz closed his eyes. He felt her wet tongue running up the side of his face, through his blood. He felt a soft but cold hand wrapping around his neck. He felt her breath on his face as she removed the makeshift bandage, releasing a fresh stream of blood into her waiting mouth, mixing with her own. She moaned with pleasure.

"I've wanted you inside of me of years, and now it is I who will be inside you, my boy," Uma muttered.

Her lips pressed against his, her tongue sliding into his mouth. Warm liquid spilling into him.

Must…resist…this!

Leonz tried to push Uma away but was unable to move her. She was incredibly strong for such a thin, petite woman, and he was too weak from the loss of blood to be any match for her.

She pulled back from his lips, a long strand of saliva and blood still connecting them. Her eyes fell to his wound, seeing it pushing out blood. Leaning in, she bit down onto it, sucking in with her teeth, deeper and deeper into the skin on the side of his head. The warm blood flowed freely into her waiting mouth and down her eager throat.

This is better than sex! she thought, indulging in the man's lifeblood. Greedily, she pushed her tongue into his wound, her saliva mixing with his blood as she continued to drink.

Her hands stayed tight around Leonz's throat as she drank from him. In her ecstasy, she was unaware she was choking the life out of him. Leonz's eyes rolled back into his head. Unable to break free from her tight grasp, along with the heavy loss of blood, his breathing slowed until he went limp.

"You dirty rat-bitch!" a voice cried out from the back of Maximilian's. A furious Nina, fresh from learning of her parent's murder, ran toward the invading woman.

Uma released Leonz, who fell to the floor, unconscious, and stared down her approaching aggressor.

"Nina! No, wait!" Ruppert called out from behind her.

In her rage, Nina hadn't prepared for the new Uma. Blood covered her lips and chin, dripping down onto her exposed upper chest and black silk slip.

Uma jumped over an unmoving Leonz and grabbed Nina by the throat, easily lifting her up off the ground.

"Oh Lord, she must have been turned!" Ruppert shouted out, seeing the woman's strength and recalling how a short time ago it was he that was lifted up into the air by the Chadwick creature.

Uma, squeezing Nina's neck tightly, glanced over at Ruppert. "Smart man. Now both of you die. But not my tasty morsel, here. I shall be enjoying his company for as long as I see fit."

Nina tried to gasp for breath but was unable to get any air and already feeling dizzy. With her free hand, she tried to pry Uma's death grip from her throat to no avail.

Grabbing a nearby whisky bottle from behind the bar, Ruppert ran toward the black-haired woman. "Let her down, you *bitch!*"

"Or what?" Uma spat out, pulling back and throwing Nina hard against a nearby table.

Nina broke the wooden structure and chair beside it on impact and fell to a bruised, unconscious heap on the floor.

Ruppert was left speechless at the vile, evil woman of Kortbeke being given even more power. He stood in front of her, fully expecting this would be his end, armed only with a whisky bottle.

Uma smiled wide, looking down at Leonz who lay still on the floor in front of her. She raised her bare foot, running her toes through his wound then pressing against it harshly, down his face and into the puddle of blood spreading on the floor.

Leonz felt nothing, but his body was working hard to reject the new substance churning in his blood after his life was sucked from him by Uma's cruel hands around his throat. The blood and saliva from the infected, disease-spreading woman was slowly beginning to work its way through his bloodstream.

"Who would have thought a worthless, washed-up drunken loser whose wife and bastard kid left town would be standing here, of all places?" Uma spat out. "I would have been furious about that at one point, but my priorities have changed. I'm so much more than a lousy bar in a town that will never recover from my master's arrival. But enough talk, now you die. And Leonz here…"

Leonz opened his eyes, he saw bare feet near his head. *Uma, you bitch.*

A sharp pain pierced Uma's bare foot. She cried out at the sudden sting and looked down to see the key to Maximilian's, the pure silver key she had made specially for her establishment, jammed deep into the top of her foot.

A burning sensation ripped through her foot and up her ankle and lower leg. The blood pumping inside her turned hot and smoke hissed out of the cut on the top of her foot where the sharp edged key was stuck.

She opened her mouth, blood pouring out of it, and let out an ear-splitting shriek of pain, stumbling backwards, out through the open door. Leonz held onto the key and pulled it out as she fell.

Ruppert, seeing his opportunity, rushed forward, preparing to slam the door. He glanced down to see her writhing in pain on the ground, her foot and lower leg charred black. The ugly hole on top of her foot bubbled with blood, black and steaming.

Uma continued to shriek at the pain she was clearly not expecting. Her arms flailed and slashed in every direction, as if to get revenge but not quite sure how. Her eyes went from near black to bright yellow and her teeth were replaced with fangs.

As Ruppert began closing the door to Maximilian's, he took one last glance at the woman who leapt out of sight into the darkness. He quickly slammed the door shut, picked up the blood-covered key on the floor that Leonz had dropped, and placed it in the lock.

Once he was certain the door was secure, he looked down at both Leonz and Nina.

Nina appeared to be coming to groggily. "What happened?" she mumbled, pushing herself to a sitting position on the floor.

"Thank your boyfriend here for saving our asses," Ruppert said, glancing down at the young man lying in a pool of his own blood at the foot of the front door.

"What? How?" Nina scrambled to her feet and rubbed her aching head and sore neck as the skirmish was now coming back to her.

"With this." Ruppert held up the silver key. The silver key he was already forming a plan for later. *We might just survive this and send these things to hell where they belong. Maybe.*

Leonz shuddered, feeling a cold sweat wash over his whole body. Something foreign had seemingly entered him by way of Uma's blood and saliva sliding down his throat into his stomach. It began to slowly heat up once it was inside of him. The pain, at first manageable as a bout of stomach flu, increased in intensity, little by little.

Nina and Ruppert noticed his discomfort as he became more restless, tiny beads of sweat forming on his forehead and soaking through his shirt as they knelt down beside him.

Ruppert looked at the wound on the side of his head and grimaced at the bloody sight. Around the wound there appeared to be fresh cuts that were clearly not from the broken bottle. Teeth marks.

"Oh shit," he muttered.

Chapter 19

†

Mayor Klaus Meets His Destiny

5:00 AM

The mighty werewolf that had once been Chadwick had laid waste to the town square. Countless people lay dead, murdered by its hands. It peered out at the destruction it had brought to the town, all in the service of its master, the beautiful blue-eyed woman named Everly.

Now, it was being summoned to perform other tasks, unable to fully act of its own free will any longer. That had ended when Chadwick was reborn earlier that night.

As it surveyed the dead bodies lying on streets that were now drenched in their blood, and those that remained attempting to tend to their loved ones' lifeless bodies, it fell back to the shadows, past the still burning church that was now little more than a hollowed-out shell of itself.

Several townspeople had arrived with horse-drawn wagons carrying large drums of water, attempting to stop the fire from further spreading. This was of no concern to the beast. Its focus was now on those that had harmed it earlier in the church.

Sniffing the air, it bounded down the darkened alleys of Kortbeke to its next prey.

✝

While Davide and Fr. Kries made their way through town to face whatever awaited them at St. Raphael's, Mayor Klaus was devising an escape plan. He peered out his window at the chaos that was once, mere hours ago, his town. Several buildings had caught fire since the church and bank. People's homes and livelihoods were destroyed, if they were even alive at this point.

Better you than me, he thought, then wondered if he had done the right thing by fleeing the scene.

He mumbled aloud, rationalizing with himself. "I'd be dead if I had stuck around. I mean, who in their right mind would willfully wait around for that thing to have its way with them? Not me! If I could just get out of this town, I'd keep riding and never look back. They don't deserve me. At this point, it's best just to cut losses and make haste elsewhere."

Contemplating this, he reasoned that he would need a horse and thought of Erwin Brahms' barn. He had horses and was, quite possibly, dead by now if he was still down by the church. Brahms' place was out on the west end and shouldn't take him more than ten minutes if he hurried. He could get there unnoticed through the back alleys, take a horse, and ride out of there, forever.

He hastily threw several changes of clothes into a small carrying case, the remainder of his money, a bit of food and, finally, his loaded but never fired, single-shot pistol and some ammunition for it. Closing it up, he took one last look at his house. It was five AM. *Go in the cover of night, now.* He nodded and exited his small house, taking off toward Erwin Brahms' property.

No sooner had be begun his quick walk, turning on the first street that would lead him to Erwin's horse stables and then further on to freedom, than he heard faint screams and shouting in the near distance. He tried to push the cries and pleas for help out of his head. He knew he was the cause of the fire—even if it was an accident, the blame would surely rest on his shoulders—and he would pay for it with what was sure to be a very public humiliation.

But I won't let that happen, will I? You all got along just fine without me and you surely can figure this out when I'm gone.

As he slipped along through the dark side streets, he thought of the people still hunkered down, frightened, in their homes. *Fools.* They should be doing the same thing he was, saving themselves! Their demise wasn't on his head. *Uma can run the show for all I care anymore.* Hell, she was running it while he was still mayor, now let the easily swayed people of this town contend with her.

A thought pierced his conscience momentarily: *I was the mayor.* Now he was abandoning the people he had once sworn to protect. Walking silently toward Erwin's barn, he looked toward the glow of the fire, not believing that he had come from there and was still alive and in one piece.

From the direction of Maximilian's, he heard a sickening shriek. His eyes grew wide, instantly knowing from the otherworldly tone that whatever made it wasn't human. At least not anymore.

His mind went to Ruppert, Nina, and Leonz, wondering if they were still alive and why he had a shared dream with Nina and Davide. Pushing not only the dream from his mind but his one-time, short-term companions as well, he whispered to himself, "Look out for yourself, Klaus. You can survive this, keep moving. Sacrifice, my ass. I'm going to live, damnit!"

Nearing the old barn, he breathed a sigh of relief seeing several horses in the field out by Erwin's stables, continuing to survey his surroundings for any trouble. In this part of town things were quiet, and he still had roughly an hour before any sign of daylight, *if* it appeared at all. He looked up into the still black sky and could see the edge of the black invisible dome, viewable due to the smoke that floated hazily above all of Kortbeke.

"Damnit, I didn't grab my cigarettes," he said, checking his pockets. He looked at the horses in the field, four in total. He would have to saddle up quickly. "Let's get this done." He climbed over the fence into the field.

Light footsteps sounded nearby.

He spun around to see where the noise came from, but no one was there. "Is anyone out there?"

Silence.

"To hell with this," he grumbled, walking to the first horse, hoping it would be led easily to the stables to be saddled up quickly.

A low snarl.

Klaus stopped again. *Oh shit.* He glanced behind him into the darkness. Tall grass blew in the wind but something else was there. The horses, sensing something wasn't right, all took off running, leaving him completely alone in the middle of the field. In the far distance, he heard faint cries of anguish coming from the church. *Where I should have stayed.*

He weighed out his options, of which there were precious few. Run in the opposite direction as fast as he could toward the heavily wooded mountains, or face whatever was out there in the darkness with his single-shot pistol.

Choosing to not look back again, Klaus bolted away from the noise as fast as his legs would take him. If he could get to the edge of the field and jump the fence, he would just keep going, running until he got to the next town. *Screw the horses, this was a bad idea.*

He neared the fence and didn't hear anything directly behind him, so he slowed down slightly to better grab the top wooden plank and climb over the fence.

Tossing his small travel bag over the fence as he came to a stop, he couldn't resist the urge to glance back. All was quiet behind him. He faced the fence again and quickly began climbing but got no further than his right leg on the bottom wooden plank.

If he had looked over to his immediate left-hand side, he would have seen, standing next to him in the darkness, a huge fur-covered beast with glowing eyes, waiting for him. *Playing with its food.*

Sharp claws reached out, grabbing him by the back of his neck, slamming him to the grassy, cold ground. Klaus turned to look up at his aggressor, the enormous creature from the church. Still clenching his single-fire pistol, he raised it to the creature's face as it peered down at him.

"Fuck you," he murmured as the beast placed its large foot against his face, pushing down. He had precious few seconds to process what was happening to him, as his last act before perishing was aiming at the beast's chest and squeezing the trigger of a gun he had never fired before. The bullet exploded out of the barrel, driving up through its organs before hitting its target, the large, beating black heart of the wolf.

He had a fleeting second to think one last time about his shared dream of the evil woman. *Maybe this was my destiny, why I had the dream. Maybe I was chosen for this moment. Killing this beast is my great sacrifice, now I understand.*

The pressure was devastating as skull gave way to the immense pressure of the beast's huge, clawed foot and popped, spilling its contents out on the field. Then, the cowardly Mayor Klaus Kessler was met with eternal darkness.

The black fur-covered werewolf lifted its foot from the crushed head of Klaus. It had little time to relish in its victory. Raising its head to the sky, it let out a howl of pain, causing the horses in the stables nearby to run in the opposite direction.

The Chadwick beast had no way of knowing that the single bullet from the mayor's shiny gun was solid silver, a small gift from Uma upon his ascension to mayor. She had told him jokingly after a quick and lust-filled sex break while Nils had been busy at the bar, "Here you go. Payment for services rendered. You'll never have need of it, or any other bullets for that silly gun of yours, but it sure is pretty, isn't it?"

The beast raised its massive, clawed hands to its chest. Streaming blood from the pure silver slug poured out of its stomach and down into the tall grass. The howl quickly turned to snarling and gnashing as it struggled to breath with lungs that were burning through. The silver bullet had a similar effect as acid on a human body, quickly eating away through its punctured organs and heart while spreading its death throughout the rest of the wolf's body.

Within seconds, the werewolf dropped to its knees beside the lifeless body of Mayor Klaus. Bones shifted inside as its snout shrunk back into its head. Its one remaining eye turned from yellow to black then back to its original brown. Grasping at its throat in a vain attempt to breathe with lungs that had collapsed, the beast's hands no longer had claws. The fur on its body pulled back into the skin while the wolf-like facial features were erased, replaced with that of the stunned human face of Chadwick.

At last, unable to prop himself up on his knees and buckling under his own weight, he fell beside what was left of Mayor Klaus, naked and very much human in appearance, though barely recognizable from the numerous burns and injuries he had sustained.

With his remaining good eye, he stared up into the sky, into the blackness that was his immediate future. For a split second, as he took his final short breaths, the mind of what was once a man named Chadwick thought of his abused wife and their child, and of the evil he had perpetrated against her and against the town of Kortbeke. Then he, too, fell into eternal darkness.

†

As Klaus shot his first and last silver bullet in Erwin's field near the edge of town, Fr. Kries and Davide reached the center of town, surveying the destruction.

Davide jumped off his horse immediately, shotgun drawn, looking down at victims too numerous to count just yet.

Crawling off his own horse, Fr. Kries had to compose himself and try to stay strong as he looked at the destroyed church. Efforts to extinguish the fire had been largely unsuccessful, and while not as intense as it had been, it was subsiding on its own. The bank beside it was destroyed as were several surrounding houses.

No one remained on the streets, having retreated back to their homes until the morning sunlight soon showed its face.

"I feel like the world ended, and we're witness to its destruction," Davide said coldly, looking around at the dead bodies lying haphazardly in the street.

Shaking his head in despair, Fr. Kries replied, "Surely, my actions have brought this on these poor people."

"Father, listen to me. That wouldn't have made a damn bit of difference. We still would have hired you," Davide began.

"That's just it, Davide! I didn't want to be a priest, at least not at first. It was a way to hide in plain sight. Then, once in seminary, learning more about our Lord, about priesthood, I saw it really was God's will. It was my calling. And my parents were my cross to bear, heavy as it was. So, I changed my name, became a priest, received my holy orders and settled down somewhere quiet, serving the people."

Shaking his head at the destruction, Davide turned to the priest. "What has happened here tonight was out of our control, but it's up to us to deal with it. Lord knows, I'm not prepared but I need your help, damnit! We need to find whatever did this and take care of it. We can't change what happened tonight, but we can do something about it moving forward. Is there anything you can tell me about your mother that might lead us to her?"

Fr. Kries thought back to his childhood as he stared up at the desecrated and burnt church, transported to a time he had long wished to forget. "She was awful. She would lock me in small rooms with no source of light, no bathroom and no food. She did this for the most basic, minor infractions when I was a child. Things like eating too loudly, not thanking her for any of the small things she did for me, claiming they were her motherly duty."

"I'm sorry, Father, truly, I am," David said, empathetic to the man's pain but anxious for more information. "But is there anything about her that we might be able to use now? If indeed she is responsible for this?"

Fr. Kries thought long before answering, "It has been a great number of years, but when I became a young man, she started seeing me as an object to conquer. As though she wanted to destroy my spirit, once and for all. And one way she went about that was trying to make me…" he hesitated, feeling the shame of it, "lay with her. That was the final act that got me out of there, for good. And what pushed me into the priesthood, I suppose. If such a vile and evil person exists in the world, then having come from her, I have to try and do something good in it. And I think she knew it. She knew I was destined to do something that was fundamentally opposed to the evil she perpetrated. And she hated me all the more for it. Now she's finally found me, and I think her blind hatred may be her downfall."

Davide let out a heavy sigh. "If she is indeed here for you, I feel as though you will be instrumental in stopping her. You, Christoph, must be the good that God has brought forth from that evil to vanquish it! So, whatever crisis of faith you may be having, take care of that with God, because we need you! This town needs you now, more than any other time in its history! Northside, southside, the only real sides in this fight are good versus evil. All of Kortbeke needs a shepherd, so you must take care of its lambs and vanquish the wolf!"

Fr. Kries stared at the lowly bar owner, a man who also appeared to be stepping into his own this night, and nodded his understanding.

Davide nodded back, satisfied. He glanced at a nearby deceased child, no more than six years old judging by her remains laying lifelessly on the ground, and instantly thought of Frida, saying, "And that wolf is going to pay with its life, mark my words."

✝

Standing in the shadows of a nearby alley, Everly watched the priest talking with the man she had seen earlier after the murder of Fr. Steffen. The man was of little concern, another nameless, useless human piece of meat that would likely be dealt with by her newest recruit, the black-haired woman. The priest, however, she instantly knew.

Watching the robed young man intently, she licked her lips and grinned. "There you are, my boy. Mommy has finally found you. So very naughty of you to leave home all those years ago. You, ungrateful boy, will be heading back to the town I raised you in. Not while you're alive, once I have my way with you, but you shall return."

Everly fell silent as the young priest made signs of the cross to fallen victims of Chadwick's massacre. Her smile faded and turned to a scowl as she watched him hugging lost ones' family members. Crying with them, *loving them. How dare this town think they could have him?*

With all of the chaos, death, and destruction she had wrought on Kortbeke, how could there be so much love and selflessness emanating from *her* son? Love of fellow man, not of self. Her hatred for him grew as she continued witnessing not a broken cowardly offspring of Marco Seiler but a strong man of faith. *My darkness and the darkness of my master will quelch your light soon enough, boy.*

She thought of those she had turned thus far, starting with the police officer, whom she suspected was now dead as she had felt a hot flash ripple through her body earlier.

Suddenly, she grabbed her chest which, again, felt hot to her touch. Grimacing, she closed her eyes at the pain that was so intense she had to catch herself on a nearby wall so as not to fall over. She closed her eyes tightly and waited for the pain to subside.

Gaining control of herself once more, she stood back up and shook her head at the realization of what had just occurred. "The wife beater is gone, so be it. That scum served his purpose and spread panic throughout Kortbeke. I have no need of him any longer, anyway. I should have gone with my instincts earlier and taken the handsome young Black man. No bother, my sweet, tasty, black-haired princess will help me complete my task here in this town."

Even as Everly uttered the words, for the first time in years, she felt the slightest tinge of doubt trickle into her mind, wondering how the burly man had met his fate. Whatever it was, it was a painful death and one specific to her kind. She knew of only a few ways she and those she had infected could be killed. One was by fire and the other was... *No, they can't know that.*

At the sound of a building collapsing in on itself, she opened her eyes, peering out once more at the destruction her actions had caused. Her son and the other man were gone. She gnashed her teeth angrily as her eyes flashed yellow and looked up at the slightest hint of dawn coming. Even she had no control over that. The black darkness would soon be lifted, and with it, her powers, accentuated primarily at night, would be diminished.

"I have found you, my son, and soon, very soon, I will end you and this miserable excuse for a town, mark my words. You won't slip through my fingers again. You will die by my hands and your body will be brought back to Burn-mere. And then, my master, the prince of darkness, will see just how resilient I am. I shall sit by his side, and I shall help rule this land. No...I shall help rule this *world*," she hissed.

✝

Chapter 20

The Internal Battle of Leonz

5:20 AM

"We need to get to Maximilian's," Davide said to Fr. Kries. "Ruppert, Nina, Leonz, and Klaus are likely there. That was the game plan when I left for Granhal earlier. We need to speak with them and ensure their safety, along with gathering any more pertinent information that could be helpful in vanquishing the evil that now plagues this town."

Fr. Kries hung his head. "I feel it is wrong leaving this place right now; look at the death and destruction around us!" His eyes fell on a mother holding a child in her arms, its lifeless body being cradled. Instant hot tears sprung to his eyes. His parish, the one he had been entrusted with, had crumbled. Righteous anger welled up in him as he bent down and prayed for the fallen child and offered loving words of encouragement and shared sadness with the mother who was nearly inconsolable.

Davide watched him intently, not wanting to interrupt such holy work, even though time was not on their side, seeing the young priest helping others as well as grieving in his own way.

Once Fr. Kries returned to his side, Davide spoke quietly, so none of the townspeople around them could hear. "Father, listen, I'm not letting you out of my sight. We need to stay together. We will mourn the dead later, but right now, we need to ensure more do not perish at the hands of this evil! Look, dawn is approaching."

"What is the next move?" Fr. Kries said, understanding the importance and urgency of their situation.

Davide answered, "Maximilian's. Our friends are waiting for us there. Together we will find a way to defeat this evil. I am confident of that."

A look of solemn determination and anger fell across the priest's face. "It looks as though you are indeed taking on the mantle of leadership in this town, Davide."

"We both are, Father. Come, time to go," Davide said, giving Fr. Kries a quick reassuring pat on the shoulder.

Fr. Kries nodded, once more scanning the immediate area covered in debris and dead bodies. Above them, the smoke continued to reveal a thin black veil of darkness surrounding the town.

Davide went to get Bertha, scanning for a lantern that could help them on their way. "A bit of light would help."

Looking up at the night sky with a hint of dawn approaching and sighing heavily, Fr. Kries once more made a sign of the cross. He glanced over at the hollowed-out opening to the decimated church where the front entrance had once been, the door blown outward along with some of the contents inside. Something caught his eye in the rubble near a completely destroyed pipe organ. It was one of the two holy water fonts located directly inside the church, overturned, its contents spilled out. It appeared to have either been taken from the stone pedestal deliberately or knocked over from the massive destruction.

He quickly walked over and kicked a bit of debris away, staring down at the empty font to reveal one of the crucifixes found right inside the entrance of the church. It was the oldest at St. Raphael's and had been one of the first items place within its walls when the church was erected over one hundred years earlier.

He bent down, carefully touching it, figuring it would be hot. But the wooden crucifix, with its tarnished and faded Jesus figure that was once shiny and vibrant, had miraculously survived the damage. Fr. Kries marveled at how the holy water must have spilled out onto it, soaking it and keeping it from burning. Or, at least, that was the rational explanation.

This particular crucifix was one he had looked at nearly every time he left the parish and had grown quite fond of, even more than the far nicer, more elegant ones spread throughout the church in later years. He picked it up and inspected it. It was warm to the touch, but not hot in his bare hands, and still a bit damp.

Fr. Kries held it out in front of his face, brought it to his lips and gently kissed the statue of Jesus. "This was saved for a purpose. Lord, give me the strength I need to rid this town of the unholy darkness that has come here. Please, my Lord, not my will, but yours be done."

Glancing over to his right, he saw the frail body of Oskar Bryner, the parish caretaker. His hand was moving slowly as he lay face down on the blood-covered street.

"He's still alive!" Fr. Kries uttered as he quickly ran to the man and gently turned him over, sensing he had serious wounds. He was right.

Oskar Bryner's throat had been ripped apart, with large chunks of flesh and muscle hanging out, flayed open. Blood spilled from the wound onto the ground, too much blood for even the slightest chance of the man's survival.

"Father, please, give me my last rites before I die," the man garbled from his ripped open throat.

Fr. Kries hung his head, making a sign of the cross and nodding before beginning. "I commend you, Oskar Bryner, to Almighty God, and entrust you to your Creator. May you return to him who formed you from the dust of the earth. May holy Mary, the angels, and all the saints come to meet you as you go forth from this life. May Christ who was crucified for you bring you freedom and peace. Amen."

The priest opened his eyes and saw that Oskar was no longer moving, but lying still with eyes wide open and mouth slightly agape. Blood trickled out onto the larger puddle of blood from his throat wound.

Sighing heavily, Fr. Kries made another sign of the cross over the deceased man then with his hand, closed Oskar's eyes for the final time before standing to his feet.

Davide, meanwhile, had made his way over to the rubble of a nearby wood framed house that was ablaze. Shielding his face from the heat and burning embers, he found a piece of wood with its tip on fire that he was able to pick up and use as a makeshift torch.

Climbing back onto Brutus and Bertha, Davide with his shotgun and wooden torch, Fr. Kries with his crucifix tightly in his hand, the two made haste toward Maximilian's.

Once they were out of the town's square, behind them another section of the roof of St. Raphael's fell, smashing onto the destroyed rubble of the chapel underneath it. Debris kicked out, along with a large chunk of rock that smashed through the overturned holy water font.

The noise reverberated through the darkened streets as both men galloped south, quickly making it to Maximilian's with Davide's broken splinter of wood burning dimly, shining enough light for them on their route.

As they passed through the street, the light from the torch and the sound of hooves hitting the cobblestone caused Uma to peer out from her shadowed spot near the town's shoe repair shop where she was attempting to track down Everly.

Her eyes turned yellow as her predator instincts kicked in. In the early morning hours, as dawn continued to emerge slowly, revealing small bits of light throughout the town, she could see well. She sniffed the air as human flesh approached.

As the two riders passed, she got a fleeting glimpse of who was on the back of each steed and her eyes widened at the sight of Davide and Fr. Kries. So, the priest had returned, Hubschmid along with him.

"I know how I shall help my master out now," she muttered quietly, still reeling from then damage done to her foot earlier. Uma continued watching them pass as they made their way to Maximilian's.

†

Inside Maximilian's, Leonz's head injury was still bleeding profusely as the strange sensations going on inside his body were intensifying.

"My blood, it feels like it's burning inside of me!" he managed to blurt out in his pain.

Hearing this, Nina and Ruppert looked gravely at each other then carefully moved him from the floor near the front door to back near the bar on top of a white tablecloth Nina had found in a nearby cupboard.

Gently tilting a beer stein filled with water gently into Leonz's mouth, Nina saw he could barely take the water in and swallow, most of it dripping onto the sheet. Determined to stay strong, she forced herself yet again to hold her tears back.

The blood from his head wound had slowed to a trickle, but most troubling now was what Uma had done to him. Her lips had been on his when Nina caught her, and the blood on both of their lips worried her. *How the hell did that happen?* Uma had likely mixed her blood with his. Was the same thing that became of Chadwick going to happen to Leonz? She shuddered at the thought, looking down lovingly at her man. So much sadness, death, and destruction in Kortbeke in such a short amount of time. She was still reeling from the news that her own parents had been murdered earlier near the church.

Ruppert put his hand on her shoulder, seeing how troubled the young woman was. She shook it off and quickly wiped her eyes of tears that threatened to burst forth.

"It's going to be alright," Ruppert said, not believing his own words.

Shaking her head slightly while wiping her eyes, Nina replied, "No, no it's not."

Leonz had slipped back into unconsciousness, but his mind was active with thoughts of the woman with the black hair, her alluring lips and smooth, cold flesh. Her seductive eyes, the way her thick, warm blood felt inside his mouth before running down his throat, how she had bit into and then drunk from his wound while choking the life out of him. Her tainted blood was now inside him. Was it hurting him or healing his injury? He couldn't tell.

Somewhere in the dark recesses of his mind, he saw another beautiful woman. This one, he loved. She was helping him, or at least attempting to help him. With her was the town drunk, a good man that had been dealt a bad hand. Why did he suddenly feel anger toward them? He was so confused.

Anger began turning to rage inside Leonz. Whatever was happening inside of him was seeming to make him nearly rabid. His teeth continually ground together as he fought through the pain. He closed his eyes, trying to relax, but this act simply made his muscles tense up more. His DNA was fighting a losing battle and he could feel it.

Leonz shook his head, trying in vain to resist the agony of the foreign blood invading his own, changing it and taking over his body.

Please, no. Make this pain stop! he tried to cry out, but his thoughts felt trapped inside his head.

His veins began to burn like acid as the blood pumped through his organs and up into his heart. Any noise in the bar seemed to be amplified, causing incredible stress to his mind. Even the dim lights seemed far too bright, hurting his eyes. Cold sweat was replaced with hot sweat pouring out of him.

Nina looked at Ruppert, seeing Leonz shifting around as if in pain. His eyes were closed tight, and he was moving his lips, as if trying to speak. "Something's wrong with him, not just his head wound, something isn't right, Ruppert! He said his blood feels like it's burning! What the hell does that mean?"

Ruppert looked worriedly down at the man lying on the floor, fearing what he was becoming and, in his mind, preparing for what would likely have to be done. In his hand, he clenched the silver key with sharp, pointed edges tightly. Hearing something outside, he looked up at the entrance to Maximilian's.

✝

When Davide and Fr. Kries arrived at Maximilian's, they immediately saw the body of Nils lying near the entrance of his home.

Davide, holding his burning wood shard out in front of him, inspected the gruesome remains and shuddered. Even someone as despicable as Nils didn't deserve to have his insides strewn about in this gory display of barbarity.

Fr. Kries ran his hands through his hair and whispered a prayer for the mutilated man while making a sign of the cross. Certainly, many more that had fallen back at the church were more deserving than this man, but Fr. Kries took particular pity on the man whose soul he was certain was in a place very far from God.

They both looked up at Uma's house as Davide muttered, "Where are you, Uma? What has become of the most hated woman in Kortbeke? Did you suffer a similar fate as your husband here?" He looked away from the darkened window above.

He turned from Uma's house and the mutilated body of Nils, shining his makeshift torch in the direction of Maximilian's, a place he vowed to never set foot in once Uma wrapped her claws around it and made it what it was. But he had to see if Klaus and the others were inside.

He tried the door handle and, as expected, it was locked. Knocking on the door, Davide leaned forward and called, "Is anyone in there?"

Silence.

He knocked again and heard movement inside. "Hello? Open up if you're in there, it's Davide. I'm here with Fr. Kries!"

"Davide? Is that really you?" a muffled voice from behind the door exclaimed.

There was a clicking noise and within seconds the door cracked open slightly. Davide and Fr. Kries saw half of Ruppert's face looking back at them through the glow of his burning stick.

Ruppert, seeing who it was, opened the door further, motioning for them to come inside.

Davide lay the burning piece of wood down on the ground as the fire subsided.

Both men slipped inside before Ruppert quickly closed and shut the door behind them, locking it back up. He put his hands on Davide's shoulders and looked him in the eyes. "Good to see you again, my friend. Fr. Kries, good to see you."

The priest nodded, looking past him to Nina who was tending to Leonz. "What happened to him?" Fr. Kries asked.

Nina said, "He was hit with a bottle in town after we were accused of starting the fire that destroyed the church. And then—"

"We have much to discuss, and likely not much time to do it," Ruppert cut in.

"Where's Klaus?" Davide asked, glancing around the room.

Shaking his head, Ruppert replied, "He took off as soon as things went to hell outside the church, as you likely saw on your way here. We were going to head out as well, but before we were able to leave, some of the villagers showed up and attacked us, accusing us of starting the fire."

He then told them of the gruesome murders committed by Chadwick, who had been turned by *her*, and how they thought they had gotten rid of him but hadn't. "It seems as though these things can regenerate their wounds," Ruppert finished, shaking his head in dismay.

Davide and Fr. Kries listened in rapt attention, eyes wide.

"After he burst out of the burning church, that's when the killing really started. We have no idea where he, or it, is now!" Nina exclaimed.

"What happened to him?" Davide asked, looking at Leonz who was still squirming on the ground.

Fr. Kries went to tend to him.

Nina watched as the priest knelt at her side and inspected him.

Ruppert said, "Another thing, Uma has turned. She's one of these creatures that have invaded this town now. Leonz opened the door for her, and well, we found her choking him and," he paused, not believing this madness was happening.

"And?" Davide pressed.

"And she was gnawing at the wound on his head. It was as if she were drinking from him," Ruppert finished, disgusted at his words.

Hearing this, Nina closed her eyes in anger.

"Sonofabitch, this keeps getting worse," Davide said, thinking back to what Lambert had told him and Fr. Kries earlier back in Granhal.

"I think it was some sort of transference. Her blood and her saliva, it's tainted. I don't know, I'm just guessing here, but infected might be a better word. Chadwick's as well. All from her," Ruppert said grimly.

"Well, if that's the case," Davide began.

"We are not tossing him out like garbage!" Nina exclaimed, glaring up at Davide.

"No one said that, Nina," Fr. Kries said softly.

His soft voice calmed her as she glanced from him back down to Leonz.

"Lambert and Erni are dead; in fact, the entire town of Granhal has likely been wiped out," Davide said to Ruppert.

"Oh, shit," Ruppert said sadly. "What the hell are we dealing with here?"

Davide looked to Fr. Kries. "Tell them the truth, Father."

The humbled priest looked up and, sighing, told Ruppert and Nina about his checkered past and the woman that had apparently been hunting him down.

✝

Leonz attempted to fight against the alien host now pumping through his veins and taking him over completely. He could soon tell that the mysterious woman's blood was too powerful to resist. He felt his mind slipping further and further away from humanity into something far darker and animalistic. Even Nina's smiling face became more distant, the dilemma they all faced becoming dim.

All that mattered was his allegiance to this new darkness that was rapidly taking over him completely. That's what it wanted, and his curse would be his undying allegiance to this evil and its creator.

His eyes fluttered. Dim light flooded them as he opened them further, gaining his consciousness back slowly. Shifting his eyes around while lying still, he saw hazy figures standing over him and listened to what they were saying. Something about the priest and his past. Of the mother that wanted him dead. Of him escaping and becoming a priest.

A profession built on a lie, because he was weak. The woman the priest spoke of, Leonz knew, was not weak. In his rage, he saw why she wanted this man dead. He wasn't worthy of her and the power she now wielded. She was strong and this man that professed his allegiance to God was no match for her.

A small part of Leonz's mind continued fighting back. *No! The woman is evil, she has caused this, all of it! Must... fight...this! Be strong for Nina.*

Leonz slowly shook his head as the two sides fought with each other inside of him. His own blood weakening at the powerful surge of evil from Uma's tainted blood.

Leonz opened his eyes wide, the lights in the bar no longer hurting his eyes as they had before. The pounding on the side of his head had subsided to the point that he wasn't sure if he was even injured at all. His eyes fell to the priest who appeared to be holding a crucifix with an old, corroded Jesus on it.

The liar and the fake. The coward. He is right there! Take him! Don't fight what you are, Leonz!

"No! No, I won't!" Leonz whispered to himself as he clenched his fists into balls and grimaced.

"What? Leonz?" Nina said, hearing his faint whisper as she quickly bent down to inspect him. "He's awake again!" she said, seeing his eyes open, looking into hers.

"Nina, wait!" Ruppert said, glancing down at the wound on the side of his head that had had ceased spilling blood and now looked more like an old scar.

Gritting his teeth, Leonz tried in vain to fight the urges coursing through his body. He grabbed hold of Nina, pulling her in close.

Ruppert and Davide instantly lunged forward in an attempt to help her.

"You all are in danger. They are coming. She knows the priest is here. Whatever is happening inside of me...I can't fight it off any longer!" Leonz exclaimed before screaming in pain.

Nina's eyes widened, staring into his, as she saw them shift to bright yellow. Like a predatorial cat at night, hunting its prey.

Leonz released her and pushed her back to the floor, shouting, "Go! Get away from me!" His voice came out like a growl, followed by a low snarl that grew in volume.

He jumped to his feet, swinging his fist at the approaching Davide, connecting with his jaw. The blow sent him careening backwards against a nearby table, causing him to drop his shotgun.

"Leonz! No!" Nina cried out.

Ruppert attempted to grab Leonz but was swatted away easily, falling to the ground. Still clenched tightly in his hands was the jagged silver key.

Fr. Kries stared down at the young man with eyes flashing yellow. Saliva dripped from Leonz's open mouth as the priest raised the crucifix to eye level in front of the infected, crazed man.

"No! Get that away from me! Please! It hurts my eyes!" he shouted at the priest, quickly averting his eyes from the small statue of Jesus atop the crucifix.

"Leonz, fight it! *Fight it!*" Nina shrieked, standing to her feet.

He shook his head, trying to avoid the sight of Fr. Kries and his crucifix.

Shaking to keep himself under control, Fr Kries exclaimed, "My son, fight this, you must fight this!"

With his hands on his face, he cried out, bellowing, "No, no! I can't, she's here!"

Outside, the sound of something smashing against the door reverberated through Maximilian's.

Chapter 21

Dawn Arrives in Kortbeke

6:00 AM

Uma longed to be with her master once more since their intimate interaction in her bedroom. She hadn't seen the woman for several hours and desperately wanted to be back in her presence, doing the woman's bidding.

Her foot had been injured worse than she had first suspected. How could her sweet young man do such a thing? She knew her master would find a way to fix it. Then, she would make his friends, especially the bitch, whore Nina, suffer for this indiscretion while he watched. *He will kiss my foot, thanking me for my mercy on him.*

She looked down at her blackened foot. The wound was still there, unable to heal. She now knew well what her kind were vulnerable to.

"I must be careful of Ruppert; he appears to have found a bit of courage in his otherwise pathetic persona. No bother, he won't be around much longer."

Uma had taken off since the incident in the doorway of Maximilian's, passing the two men she had murdered earlier in the alleyway without giving their lifeless bodies a second glance.

Seeing the two men riding atop horses had stirred up a devious plan. One minor, last little detail before she and her master would leave this town for good. Leaving in its wake chaos, death, and destruction.

This had been significantly more fun than the cold-blooded murder of her family when she was a young girl and still learning about her true nature. Now, her destiny had come to Kortbeke, and with it, immortality. And she intended to use it.

Walking past the destruction of the church for the first time, she smiled. She watched as townspeople attempted to put out the remaining flames, but the damage was done. The church was little more than several block walls still erected. Those would surely be brought down eventually, if the town itself could recover from the atrocities that had occurred.

Uma looked at the sky. The nearly impenetrable darkness of the night was passing. Even Everly and her master couldn't control all things weather related. And so, with dawn, the black cloud that had descended onto Kortbeke evaporated.

As dreary as the evening before it was, this morning was shaping up to be a cloudless and possibly sunny day, which Uma sensed was going to be more difficult than the night had been. The immense power she had felt mere hours ago seemed to be dwindling. She knew what rested inside of her hadn't been fully unleashed…yet.

People were already coming out of their houses, weary from the previous night. Many were in tears and seemed disoriented. Others had weapons and were quite obviously on a mission.

They will never catch my queen. Never. She will tear through them all once the priest is destroyed. Then, we will leave this place for good.

It was still relatively dark at six o'clock in the morning so Uma could travel unnoticed. No one knew of her new condition except those still inside Maximilian's. Still, it would be a good idea for her to keep to the shadows and stay hidden until this bit of fun was complete. She had longed for years to see Hubschmid's Pub close its doors. But now, she had an even better idea.

She walked past Hubschmid's with a slight limp from her still injured foot. The lights were out inside the bar as she peered into the front window. "Soon this place would be a distant memory like the rest of this pathetic town."

✝

Emila had tried to stay awake after her terrible dream hours earlier and figured she was done with sleep for the remainder of the night. But she was wrong.

Sleep washed over her weary body again while she sat on the couch waiting for Davide's return once more. Thankfully, this sleep was dreamless and sound. So sound, in fact, that she hadn't awakened when the door handle slowly turned. It was locked.

In the other room, Frida slept soundly as well. A normal night's sleep for the little girl was roughly nine hours and she was significantly behind tonight.

The window in her room was located against the wall facing her bed and was small, but wide enough for a body to slip through.

Uma peered into the window and watched the little girl sleeping soundly. She knew she could enter the house with ease if she wanted to, but an opportunity like this was too good to pass up.

Lying on her back, Frida's little chest rose and fell with her heavy breathing, her lips slightly open as she exhaled.

Suddenly hungry, Uma wiped her salivating mouth as her eyes flashed yellow. "The Hubschmid child looks tasty. Maybe I should indulge. Yes, yes. Maybe I should indulge indeed," she muttered.

✝

While the smashing continued on the door to Maximilian's in the early morning hours, the intruder sounding more and more like a snarling, gnashing wolf to those inside, Leonz was becoming more non-communicative and aggressive.

Ruppert and Davide glanced at the front door then to each other nervously while Fr. Kries continued holding the cross out in front of him. Davide's eyes went from Ruppert's down to the pair of steel handcuffs in his right hand, the one not carrying the shotgun.

Ruppert nodded his understanding and focused on Leonz, then lunged forward, wrapping his arms around the surprised man who began fighting back.

Fr. Kries quickly set his crucifix down and ran forward to help.

Nina shouted out in surprise, "What are you doing to him!?"

Davide dropped his shotgun onto a nearby table and helped the two men wrestle with Leonz who was turning out to be nearly more than all three of them could handle.

Leonz dropped to the ground as both Ruppert and Fr. Kries attempted to pull his arms behind his back so Davide could get the restraints locked. The first handcuff clicked into place around Leonz's right wrist.

"Come on, Leonz, it's for your own good! Try to understand!" Fr. Kries exclaimed.

"Hot damn, he is strong!" Ruppert said, trying to hold the man's left arm behind his back.

Nina was suddenly in front of them, kneeling beside Leonz as he snarled and saliva dripped from his gnashing mouth. Blocking out the pounding on the door and the otherworldly sounds her boyfriend was making, she said calmly, "Leonz, look at me. It's me, Nina. Come on, look."

He looked up at her, his eyes bright yellow, his teeth gritting in anger and rage.

"Listen to my voice, my love, just listen to me. Please?"

Leonz relaxed slightly, his yellow eyes turning back to their human color, and his snarls subsiding. "Nina," he uttered.

Click.

Davide sat back as all three men holding Leonz breathed a sigh of relief.

Leonz's eyes remained fixed on Nina's. His true love. Not the black-haired evil woman. "Don't let me become one of them. Please, if you must, take care of me before I turn!" he pleaded.

"Leonz, don't say that!" Nina answered, shaking her head.

Looking at the three men, Leonz, in a moment of clarity said, "All of you know what must be done."

"We aren't killing anyone except what's on the opposite side of that door!" Davide exclaimed, continuing to hear snarls and frantic scratching against the thick wood.

"Whatever's out there is toying with us!" Ruppert exclaimed, looking at Davide.

The pounding had stopped, and Everly's voice called out, "The priest! I want him. Send him out and I may spare your lives. Don't do as I command, and you are all assured a slow, agonizing death. What you saw around the church is only the beginning of what my kind is capable of. You would be wise not to doubt me!"

They all remained quiet, looking at the priest.

Davide said to the group, "He's not going anywhere."

Leonz, who had been helped up to a sitting position, stared blankly around the room. *Uma.* He could sense her presence, somehow, as though inside his head.

He closed his eyes, trying to fight the black-haired woman off. *The Hubschmid child looks tasty.* The words echoed inside his head. Opening his eyes wide, he stared at Davide who was watching the door intently.

"Davide," Leonz mumbled but everyone seemed to be focusing on the front door to the bar. He continued fighting off the animal urges inside of him, a task that felt impossible the longer he tried.

Come on, open the door, the woman's voice called out in the dark recesses of his mind.

"Davide," Leonz said again. This time getting the attention of Nina who looked at him puzzlingly.

"Maybe I should go out. It's me she wants. I need to face this head-on. I can buy you some time," Fr. Kries said sadly, seeing no other option.

"No. We have to figure out how to stop her. We put an end to Lambert, and we can put an end to her as well!" Davide said sharply.

Ruppert held up the silver key. "Leonz slammed this into Uma's foot earlier. It seemed to have quite an adverse effect, instantaneously."

Davide and Fr. Kries inspected the key. Fr. Kries shook his head, confused.

"This is a silver key. Could it be that silver can stop these things?" Davide asked.

"Well, that's what I assumed as well. Werewolves and silver went hand in hand with the stories our parents used to tell us. Maybe it's all true. Those stories had to originate from somewhere, right? All I know is, this thing stuck into her foot had Uma shrieking and running away!" Ruppert said, adding, "It's worth a shot."

"What do you have in mind?" Davide asked urgently.

"Davide Hubschmid! You need to hear this!" Leonz shouted.

The room fell silent. The weary, struggling Leonz leaned his head back against the bar, his eyes closed. "'The Hubschmid child looks tasty,'" Leonz uttered, in Uma's cool and conniving voice, surprised himself at the sound of it.

Davide's eyes widened. "What did you say?"

"And that voice! That was Uma Karlen's voice!" Fr. Kries said, astounded at this supernatural occurrence.

"I think your wife and child are in danger. I think Uma may be there now!" Leonz replied shakily, as though it took every ounce of his strength to help Davide. He closed his eyes, seeing a flash of Uma standing over Davide's little girl. He shook his head, trying to force the horrible image out of it. Once he opened his eyes, it was gone.

Ruppert grabbed Davide by his shoulders. "Get to your house, Davide. We'll take care of this one!"

Davide, strong and maintaining control even as this entire night had tested him to his very limits, felt his knees go weak and his mouth instantly dry up.

Fr. Kries was in front of him now. "Ruppert is right. The woman outside must be dealt with. But she must be dealt with by me. It is time I faced my past like a man and not the scared child I once was." He gripped the crucifix tightly in his hand.

Everly had given up breaking through the thick exterior front door to Maximilian's and had made her way around to the rear of the bar, inspecting the building.

With the sun rising, her ability to change into her true wolf-beast form wasn't an option, not without much coaxing and serious duress. This was a sad fact she had learned a long ago after being turned. Only during the night was she and her kind able to become the beasts on their own accord. She had found that over time, with much practice, she was able to become a wolf during the daytime, but she was much more susceptible to harm from humans.

She found what she was looking for. A back entrance. It, too, was locked. This door, however, seemed to be less reinforced that the thick, solid front door.

She glanced up at the sky and noticed dawn had arrived in Kortbeke. She would need to see this through; she couldn't wait until nightfall for fear of losing the priest. There would assuredly be people out looking for her soon, she had to act now. Then, she and the black-haired woman would be on their way.

She looked at the door, her eyes glowing yellow, and ran forward.

A loud crashing sound came from the rear of the bar.

"The back room! She's in the back room!" Nina shouted out.

Ruppert ran to the front door and hastily unlocked it with the silver key, swinging it open and pointing to Davide. "Go, now! Save your wife and daughter!"

He grabbed Davide's free hand and placed in it the silver key that had pierced Uma's foot earlier. "Stab her with this. One way or another, use it against her. Silver is the key. Perhaps these things that have invaded our town aren't as powerful during the daylight hours, if any of the stories about these infernal beasts are remotely true."

Davide nodded his understanding then glanced over to Fr. Kries. "I have faith in you, Father. Take care of this evil that has come to Kortbeke."

The priest nodded solemnly to his friend, thinking back to Davide pressing him to vanquish the evil from his past, then turned to face what was coming from the rear of the bar.

Davide ran out the front door and saw that the horses were not there. Scanning the area, he saw them both nearby, a block up from the bar, surprised they hadn't taken off with the woman's arrival but thankful, nonetheless.

Running over to Bertha, he pocketed the silver key he had been given by Ruppert and patted the horse's neck. "Thanks for sticking around, our tasks aren't over yet." He holstered the shotgun and climbed up onto his saddle, then, with a quick jerk on the reins, took off toward his home on the northside.

Back inside the bar, all heads turned to face the rear as a shadowed figured walked out. Nina and Ruppert stood on either side of Fr. Kries who held the cross out in front of him. Ruppert gripped a broken wooden leg of a chair he had crashed into earlier, its end splintered and sharp. Nina clenched one similar to it as her own means of defense.

On the floor, Leonz sensed one of his own had entered. A growl rose up from deep in his throat, his eyes flashed yellow. Behind his back, his hands remained shackled. Tainted blood coursed stronger than ever through his veins as he began wrestling with the restraints, slowly twisting them.

He felt his strength coming back in a rush. The infected blood had healed his wound and was making him stronger, infinitely more powerful than any mere human. His teeth ground together as a thin strand of saliva dripped from his hungry lips. He continued to wrestle with the steel restraints until he could feel them starting to buckle.

Chapter 22

†

Inside the
Hubschmid House

6:30 AM

Frida lay sound asleep. Her dreams were troubling, with visions of furry creatures, not the kind you pet, running freely in Kortbeke.

She was running from one of them but was unable to get away. It was far too big and fast for her. No matter where her little legs carried her, the creature remained in pursuit. She called for Mama, but she wasn't around. Neither was Papa. She was all alone.

The animal looked like a big dog. A big, black dog with funny-looking yellow eyes and big, scary teeth. It was making noises that weren't dog barks, though. These noises sounded much scarier and she was terrified of the animal pursuing her.

The streets all seemed the same. The houses all looked the same. Everywhere she looked, she was met with closed doors and windows. She turned down a street and was met with a dead end.

Turning quickly where she stood in her pajamas, the thing pursuing her was no longer a furry animal. It was the mean lady that Mama and Papa didn't like.

The black-haired woman peered down at her and licked her lips. "Well, well…if you aren't the prettiest little dish I've ever laid eyes on. If you were any cuter, I might just have to gobble you up." She smiled widely, revealing two rows of pointed teeth. Her eyes turned into the eyes of the big black dog chasing her earlier.

Frida opened her eyes from her dream, and sat bolt upright, about to scream but only releasing a gasp as she felt a breeze blowing through her room. A small bit of morning light shone through the window. Why was it open? It was closed tightly the night before.

Her eyes grew wide as she scanned the room. "Mama? Are you in here?"

Her little heart raced inside her chest. She didn't feel alone. In the early morning hours in her room facing west, it always remained darkest the longest. In one corner of her room in particular, it remained almost completely dark. Nervously, she pulled the sheets back slightly, rolled onto the side of her bed and taking a deep breath, quickly looked under her bed for any large black dogs.

Once she saw the coast was clear, under the bed at least, she breathed a sigh of relief. Then she looked back to the corner of her room that remained hidden in darkness, as if it fought with the morning light for dominance as long as it could.

She tilted her head and rubbed her eyes tiredly. *Did that shadow just move?*

She felt suddenly cold, even with the covers around her. The breeze from the opened window certainly was chilly, but something else. A flash of blinking yellow eyes from the blackened corner, followed by a soft voice.

"Why if you aren't the prettiest little dish I've ever laid eyes on. If you'd were any cuter—"

Frida screamed as loud as she could, jumping out of bed and running for the door to her room.

From out of the darkness, a woman in a long, flowing black nightgown lunged out, her hands opened and grasping for her. Yellow, unblinking eyes filled with evil stared at her hungrily.

Frida made it to the door just as the woman's claws grabbed hold of her right arm, yanking her backwards. She screamed in terror.

Emila slept soundly, continuing her dreamless slumber. In the darkness that was her sleep, she heard a scream.

Opening her eyes, suddenly very much awake, she was aware that the sound she heard was no dream, but Frida in her bedroom. The knife lying beside her at all times was quickly grabbed as she leapt from the couch, cursing herself for inadvertently falling asleep.

Emila sprinted to the bedroom in long steps, bursting the door open and peering into the dim morning light.

Uma stood in her daughter's bedroom. Tall, slender, and beautiful. Unnaturally beautiful with skin too pale and lips far too bright red. Eyes wide, blazing yellow, she looked at the frantic mother of the child she held up by the back of its pajamas and smiled wide.

Sliding to a halt, Emila gasped at the sight of her precious daughter lifted so easily in the air by one hand, as if she were no heavier than a small sack of grain from the local market. The presence of Uma in her home, in her daughter's bedroom, assaulting her in such a mocking way, filled the mother with rage and pure unadulterated hatred for the woman that had caused such dissension throughout Kortbeke and who was now threatening her daughter in their own home.

"Hello, Mrs. Hubschmid. Nice of you to come check on your daughter. Pity you weren't with her, you may have saved her. Instead, you will be witness to what I am fully capable of. What I was as a child and have now been able to fully embrace. See, Emila, I'm a killer. It's who I am and what I've always been. Suppressing my urges with silly things like wealth and sex. But no more. No, no, no." Uma giggled with smugness at the fact that there was nothing the mother could do except watch her sink her long, sharp teeth deep into the little girl's throat.

Biting her tongue, choosing reason instead of lashing out as she wanted to, Emila replied as calmly as she could, "Please, Uma. Please, don't do this. She's innocent. Let her go and you can have me, just, please not my baby." She held up her hands, insinuating that she was willing to set her knife down.

Uma smiled widely, revealing her sharpened teeth. She was glad that even in the waking daylight hours, some of what she had become remained. Her strength had certainly remained, some of it, at least. She marveled at the ease at which she was able to lift the small child up into the air. It would be all the more fun watching the poor mother weep at her feet before ending her life as well.

"Mama! Please, help me! Don't let this bad woman get me!" Frida cried out, tears running down her small cheeks onto her pajamas.

Emila moved one step forward into her daughter's room, still clenching the knife but offering it up if the woman released her child.

"If you come a single step closer, I'm going to tear her throat out," Uma uttered coldly, lifting her free hand to the girl's open and exposed throat, placing her sharpened, long fingernails against the child's soft skin and pushing against it just hard enough to cause the girl to let out a slight grunt of pain and a garbled word that sounded something like *"mommy"* from her quivering lips.

I'm going to kill this bitch, if it's the last thing I do before I die. Emila's controlled rage was at its breaking point. She saw no other option but to charge forward in the hopes that she could at least knock the child from this beast's hand and sacrifice herself instead. All while plunging her kitchen knife as far as it could go into Uma's cold beating heart and commanding her daughter to run away as fast as her little legs could carry her.

Behind Uma, a figured rose slowly outside Frida's window holding a shotgun. Emila saw her husband raise it to his shoulder, aiming it away from her daughter, toward the woman's leg.

Emila knew she was in his line of fire as he put a finger to his lips and gave her a brief glance.

"Uma, I have just one thing to say to you before you die," Emila said coldly, staring into her adversary's yellow eyes.

Her boldness caught the woman off-guard, and she let out a small laugh. "Oh, please elaborate. Hey, little girlie, your mama has something to say. Once she's finished, you will be no more. But don't worry, she'll join you shortly after, and then your father soon after that. You'll all be together again, won't that be nice?"

"You should have closed the window," Emila said, jumping to the side.

"Wha—" Uma began, starting to turn around.

Davide's shotgun erupted, instantly evaporating Uma's leg. Frida screamed in terror at the sudden loud gun blast and her rapid fall as the evil black-haired woman, in her surprise, released her from her grip.

Emila leapt forward, catching her child a split second before she connected with the wooden floor below. Her mother landed hard on her side and let out a cry of pain, cradling Frida tightly in her arms.

"Mama!" Frida cried out, terrified.

Emila rolled out of the way as quickly as she could, pain wracking her side, clinging to Frida.

Beside her, Uma had fallen to the ground as well, unable to stand on one leg.

Behind her, Davide climbed through the window into his daughter's bedroom, glaring and devoid of mercy at the intruder threatening his wife and daughter. As he did, he broke open his shotgun, expelling the spent shells and quickly fishing through his pockets for another two shells.

On the floor, Uma screamed in pain, holding onto the meat that once was her leg, now pulverized. Her eyes gleamed yellow, her teeth extended further. Her rage and pain great enough to begin her transformation into the beast she was destined to become but hadn't yet had the opportunity.

Attempting to get to her feet with her sobbing daughter in her arms, Emila was struggling with the pain in her side while Uma, seeing her prey attempting to flee, lashed out with a clawed hand, her arm extending further than any human's. Hair sprouted from it rapidly as Uma's facial features shifted. Ears pointed, nose extended and became a long snout, complete with large fangs. Her black hair seemed to be growing, covering her body as it widened, becoming less and less human in form in mere seconds. Quickly, her elegant, black slip stretched to its limit before ripping off.

Davide had replaced his shotgun with two new shells, slamming it shut and cocking the hammer back. He glanced down at the creature's shot-off stump to see it was regenerating. Bones, tendons, veins and muscle tissue were shooting out of the still functioning part of its upper leg, working their way down as if invisible doctors that knew magic were performing wonderous surgical procedures in mere seconds.

The woman that was once Uma was no more. In her place, a large wolf creature, covered in black fur, now attempted to climb to its clawed feet, even with the injured leg.

It spun around to stare at her assailant, yellow eyes bearing down on him as it hunched over, preparing to pounce.

Behind it, Emila and Frida had escaped out the bedroom door into the hallway leading to the living room.

Davide pulled the trigger of his shotgun as the Uma beast lunged at him. The spray of small projectiles slamming into her chest at such close range blasted the beast back against the small bedroom wall, a mist of blood covering it.

This, however, didn't stop Uma. The blast didn't even drop the beast to its knees. It stayed on its feet and roared at Davide, lunging forward as he frantically tried to open the chamber to reload.

Uma smashed against Davide, sending him careening onto the floor as the shotgun spun out of his hands. The large fangs of the beast snapped at his face, mere inches away, as he pushed back on its arms so it couldn't scratch him.

Beside him, the silver key Ruppert had given him back at Maximilian's had spilled out of the open chest pocket of his shirt onto the floor and slid nearly an arm's length away.

He turned to face the only hope of his survival, knowing that releasing either of the creature's arms would certainly be the end of him. He stared at the key then back up to the thing that had been Uma. It hissed and snapped viciously, trying to get to his face, and seemed to be making progress.

Outside in the hallway, Davide heard his daughter's small voice call out, "No, Mama! What are you doing? Don't leave!"

The beast's snout was now a mere inch away from biting into his face. Davide's strong arms were ultimately no match for the creature. Its own powerful arms pushed down, driving his to the floor.

Davide saw his wife's feet running toward the struggle that would end in mere seconds with him dead if something drastic didn't happen.

Emila grabbed the fallen shotgun and held it by the end of its two barrels, pulling back as hard as she could and swinging it like a club, smashing it on top of the wolf beast's head with such force, the barrels broke off from the stock, sending pieces spiraling to the floor.

The creature lifted his head, howling and snarling in pain as blood ran over its eyes and snout from the hard blow. It turned its head to look at Emila for a second and that was all the time Davide needed. He released his grip on the creature's arm and reached out for the silver key.

Wrapping his outstretched hand around the key, he grabbed it and brought it up just as Uma's head came back down to focus on him once more.

The key connected with her opened yellow eye on her right side, plunging into it with such force the eye itself seemed to pop. The creature stopped moving completely for a split second as the realization sunk in.

Emila still clung to the barrels of the destroyed shotgun as she watched her husband quickly crawl out from under the Uma beast. She reached her hand out and he took it, scrambling the rest of the way until he was beside her, standing to his feet.

The black, fur-covered creature tilted its head back and roared in pain, attempting to jump to its feet but falling backwards, smashing into Frida's bed and breaking apart the brittle boards around the mattress. It shook its head in rage at the sharp, jagged, silver key stuck in its eye.

Stepping past her husband, Emila glared at the alien presence in her home, pulled back on the gun barrel in her hand like a club, then wound up and swung as hard as she could once more. The steel barrels connected with the key sticking out of its eye, slamming it the rest of the way into the creature's skull.

Emila wasn't through. Raising the barrels above her head, she brought them down onto the creature's chest on the shotgun wound it had received a minute earlier. Over and over the barrel was lifted and came down until sinking into the fur and flesh, burrowing down into its frantically beating heart.

Satisfied, she stepped back while Davide pulled her against himself and they backed up toward the hallway door, never taking their eyes off Uma.

Uma's mind careened from one wild thought to the next. She had been given a gift. But suddenly, the few things that had meant anything worthwhile in her life had been taken away.

As her rapidly deteriorating mind processed this, she had the slightest moment of clarity. That her life was ending, and all that awaited her for a life of murder, greed, lust, envy, sloth, gluttony, and wrath was death. She had done it all. And now she would die, a fitting end to the life she had led. The last thing she thought of was the blond woman in her bedroom earlier. The wonderful, beautiful and powerful woman.

The snout shrunk, the black fur pulled back into her skin, her remaining good eye turned back to its natural color. Her human form quickly took shape and soon, she lay on

Frida's floor, naked and dying. Her chest was caved in and no longer able to regenerate itself due to the silver key that, much like Everly's blood earlier, was working its way through her system, killing off not only the invading alien blood but her own human blood.

Uma looked wearily over at Davide and Emila standing over her. She raised her hand and pointed at them, offering her final smile of contempt. "Guess you got me this time," she muttered before dropping her too-heavy hand onto her naked lap.

"Guess so," Emila replied coldly.

Uma opened her mouth as her remaining good eye rolled back into her head, releasing a low, raspy death grunt. Her face fell in on itself, skin clinging to bone. Throughout her body, internal organs failed at the same time, shriveling up and turning to dust inside her.

Uma's skin was the next to turn to dust, falling off her bones. It was all over in less than a minute. Her skeleton was all that remained of what was once the beautiful and seemingly all-powerful Uma Karlen. The silver key she had made especially for herself had brought about her ultimate demise, and it now lay beside her skull.

Davide walked over to the skeleton, bent down and picked up the key, brushing off ashes and dead skin, and put it back in his front pocket. He and Emila closed Frida's door so the charred skeletal remains were out of sight.

Frida sat quietly on the couch. As soon as she saw her father, she leapt up and ran over to him, wrapping her arms around him as he scooped her up into his own.

"Papa! Papa! I was so scared! But I knew you would save me. I knew it!" she exclaimed happily.

Of all the things he had faced in the last several hours, this innocent comment from his daughter was what nearly undid Davide. Emila joined them and together the Hubschmid's had a group hug in their living room as sunlight slowly spilled into the room.

Pulling away from her husband, Emila looked into his eyes as she wiped her tears. "Is it over?" she asked hopefully.

"I don't know, Emila, I just don't know."

They stepped outside of their house. Sunlight shone down on the town of Kortbeke. Plumes of smoke rose from St. Raphael's, the surrounding bank, and several homes. A new plume of smoke rose into the sky further away, coming from the direction of Maximilian's.

Chapter 23

"I Gave You Life!"

6:30 AM

Inside Maximilian's, Fr. Kries stood in the middle of the bar with Ruppert and Nina on either side of him, all of them prepared to do battle with what came walking out of the shadows from the back of the bar.

Leonz struggled with his restraints, his animal urges nearly taking him over completely, no matter how hard he tried to resist. Drool dripping from his mouth, he looked hungrily at the three that had their backs to him. Something caught his newly-improved keen eyesight, moving forward out of the dark shadows at the rear of Maximilian's.

A slim figure in a beautiful blue dress stepped forward, her blond hair cascading down either side of her large, perfectly proportioned chest. Bright blue eyes stared at the three humans in front of her. Her full lips parted slightly at the sight of her son, at long last, standing before her, then slowly turned to a slight smile. *I found you, I knew I would. Master will be proud of me.*

She sensed trouble from Uma somewhere else in town but shook it off, choosing to ignore it. Her dealings were with the priest and the worthless bags of flesh standing beside him.

No one spoke for a second in the stand-off. The woman was unarmed but each of them knew she was incredibly dangerous and the cause of the destruction that had befallen Kortbeke. The aura she gave off wasn't just beauty but one of utter arrogance and otherworldly evil.

"You can put that cross down, foolish boy. It won't do any good, other than repulse me, I suppose," Everly said in an almost pleasant, girlish voice.

Fr. Kries continued holding the crucifix out in front of him, his hand trembling ever so slightly.

Glancing over at Nina, then Ruppert, she added, "Stakes! Ahh, how quaint. You really think sticks will defeat me? I always knew you were a failure, Christoph, but this? These people here? It's pathetic."

"Vile woman, what you have done is an abomination to this town! To this world!" Fr. Kries exclaimed, his fear quickly turning to anger. "Why don't you show us your true self? Not this fake, glamorized version of what you always wanted to be! Come on, let us see you for who you truly are!"

Everly blinked several times. Her son seemed to have gained some confidence since she chased him away from Burnmere years ago. She sighed. "Oh, Christoph, if you only knew what I've been through to find you. How many people have lost their lives, all because of you, my dear boy."

Shaking his head, crucifix still outstretched, he replied, "Not because of me. Because of you, Everly. All because of you. I had nothing to do with the evil you have committed.

Both now and as a child. Abusing me until I was of age, then trying to lay with me. You are a vile woman, and you will be stopped!"

Ignoring him, she took a step closer and instantly noticed Nina and Ruppert raising their stakes slightly higher and gripping them tighter. She let out a small laugh. "So, let me guess: this one here, he's a drunk. Like your father. And this one, hmm…" She studied Nina.

"This one would like to ram this stake down your throat, you awful bitch. For what my Leonz has become and what you've done here! My parents are both dead because of you!" Nina spat out angrily.

Everly tilted her head, peering past the three of them, down to the man lying on the floor. "Oh, yes! You, my dear! So good to see you! I had a good feeling about you, I did. I see that my beautiful Uma got to you. Good, good. Soon you won't be able to resist my blood and will join me in putting an end to these pathetic beings. In fact, I'll see to it that this one here dies by your hand. How does that sound?" Everly's eyes went from the struggling Leonz to Nina.

Glaring at the blond woman in the blue dress, Nina uttered, "We shall just see."

"Calm, Nina, be calm," Ruppert muttered in a near whisper.

"And you, yes! Just like my husband. A loser and a drunk in his own town!" Everly crowed. "I will send him all your regards when I pay him a visit next. He and I have unfinished business. Some of which I intend to take care of here and now."

"You may try," Fr. Kries said coolly. His hand suddenly becoming still and his eyes narrowing.

This sudden shift in confidence alarmed Everly and it showed in her face. Her nonchalant demeaner disappeared and her eyes flashed brightly, her full lips turning to an angry frown. She had hoped this would have all been over in one night, before dawn broke, when she did her best work. Now, it appeared she had been hampered somewhat by her chosen ones seemingly unable to fulfill their tasks and the resistance of this small band of people.

Her mind raced once more to the two she had turned earlier, the police officer and the wife-beater, hoping for more help from them. Both were gone. And now, her assurance in Uma's assistance was rapidly waning. The fact that the other man she had seen earlier wasn't with them was troubling. Very troubling indeed. Especially considering the bad omens she was sensing from Uma.

Very well. It would fall to her. And possibly the assistance of the young man on the ground. *I need their help to turn. I need more…rage.*

Fr. Kries took another step toward her and, for a split second, she considered taking a step back. "I gave you life! And now I will take it, you belong to *me!*" she hissed.

Everly's eyes turned bright yellow as she spread her arms wide and lunged toward her prey.

"Father, look out—" Ruppert shouted as Everly's arms instantly extended, fists smashing into both him and Nina unexpectedly. She landed atop her son, knocking him to the ground as the crucifix skidded out of reach. In less than a second, large fangs pushed their way out of her gums and the once beautiful face began contorting into a grotesque mutation.

Leonz, meanwhile, snapped the steel restraints off of his wrists and leapt up. He looked over to Nina, who had spilled over backwards but still clenched the wooden stake. She stood back up and charged forward toward Everly.

Also back on his feet was Ruppert, gripping his wooden stake tightly. He lunged toward the monstrosity atop the priest who was holding her back, his hands around her neck.

Nina ran toward Everly with her stake raised in the air but was caught off-guard by her boyfriend swatting the stake from her hands with ease and grabbing hold of her outstretched arms, instantly subduing her.

Ruppert brought the stake down with both hands wrapped around the sharp wooden shard, aiming for Everly's back, but was caught in mid-swing by Everly's morphing hand sprouting fur and claws. She squeezed tightly around his left wrist with increasing pressure as he struggled. She glanced at him with yellow eyes and twisted his hand, nearly snapping his wrist. He screamed out in pain, dropping the stake to the ground and grabbing hold of his bruised wrist.

With the same outstretched hand, she raked long claws across his face. Four lines instantly tore open from the top of his forehead down past his chin, drawing blood instantly, and in the process, raking across his right eye, puncturing it. Ruppert fell over onto his back, his body going into shock from the violent assault.

Everly glanced over at Nina who was incapacitated by Leonz. She struggled in his arms and attempted to pry herself free, but to no avail. Her blood had turned him, Everly sensed it. Her mutated face smiled broadly, showing off large fangs. Her extended neck made her head seem as though it were bobbing in the air. If it had been nighttime and not the early dawn hours that had descended upon Kortbeke, her transformation would have been complete already.

Blond hair turned white while her snout pushed out and muscles rippled across her body, tearing her dress off. Breasts melded into thick chest muscle that was quickly covered by fur. In seconds, she had fully changed over to her wolf-beast self, gifted to her by her lover back in Burnmere two years prior.

Tilting her head up, she let out an ear-deafening howl. Her jaws opened wide while a thick tongue hung from it, dripping globs of saliva down onto her son under her heavy weight. She had waited for two years, hunting this son of hers. And now he would die.

Fr. Kries was unable to reach the dropped crucifix but held his head high, glaring into the beast's glowing yellow eyes.

The werewolf looked down at her prey hungrily. There would be no resurrection, this one would perish for good. A final gift from the boy's earthly mother.

The wolf's eyes peered down at the pathetic man who, in that very instant, reminded her of her own husband from many years past. He stared at her, and he was *praying*. She saw in his eyes not fear but a steady calm.

"Our father, who art in heaven…"

The wolf responded with a snarl and gnashing of its teeth, trying to intimidate the young priest. But he held his head up high and continued.

"Hallowed be thy name…" Fr. Kries said in a calm, firm voice.

It raised its right hand, opening its claws, preparing to deliver a striking blow to the son.

"Thy kingdom come; thy will be done…" Fr. Kries held fast and spoke with confidence, not budging or retreating from his mother.

Nina ceased to struggle and turned to face Leonz. His eyes were yellow, and his breathing heavy. She grabbed hold of his face and whispered, "I love you, Leonz Laurer. Help us. Help me, please!"

He looked back into her eyes, seeing and feeling the love she had for him, remembering the love they shared. He looked at Ruppert, writhing in agony on the floor. It would fall on him to help them, or at least give them a fighting chance, or all of Kortbeke would indeed fall on this day.

His eyes shifted back to their natural color as he doubled over in pain from not feeding as he had intended to do. His mutated body craved human blood and flesh and had thus far been denied it.

He leaned forward and, with tears falling from his eyes, gently kissed his love who returned the gesture.

"On earth as it is in heaven…" Fr. Kries continued, defiant and determined to bring the creature down.

The Everly werewolf had taken a step back, away from the priest that was showing no fear, but holding his ground and praying fervently. This newfound confidence was driving her back in revulsion. This was not the same pathetic son that had retreated from her countless times back in Burnmere and finally fled to save his own skin. Before her stood a confident man of *God.*

Leonz broke the kiss off and turned to face Everly who appeared to be retreating from Fr. Kries. Taking the opportunity, Leonz lunged toward Everly and landed atop the white furred werewolf clearly not expecting or anticipating his sudden attack. With the fury that had built up inside of him, he began clawing at the beast's head. Biting into its large, pointed ear with enough ferocity to tear a large chunk of it completely off.

Nina, meanwhile, grabbed her stake once more and jammed it into the werewolf's exposed side. Instantly, the creature turned to face Nina, swinging its large, muscular arm at her. She stumbled backwards, its claws missing her face by mere inches, before falling on her back on the hard, wooden floor.

"Give us this day, our daily bread..." Fr. Kries's voice increased in volume as he took several steps forward toward the white fur-covered creature.

The werewolf roared out in fury at the pain being inflicted upon it, trying to swat Leonz off of her.

Leonz, meanwhile, also begun to change as his fury was released in full force. Fangs pushed human teeth out of the way. A snout pushed itself out of the center of his face, replacing his nose, while human ears morphed into pointed beastly ones.

In less than a minute, the man that had once stood at under six feet tall was nearly as tall as the creature it was attacking. Now much stronger than before, Leonz jumped to his clawed feet, grabbed hold of Everly, and threw her over the bar.

The werewolf crashed into the back wall behind the bar lined with bottles of liquor, shattering most of them with the enormous and powerful collision.

"And forgive us our trespasses, as we forgive those who trespass against us…" Fr. Kries continued confidently, inching forward.

Ruppert looked up warily with his remaining good eye. His bruised wrist throbbed as he cradled it tightly to his chest. Near him lay the crucifix that had been swatted out of Fr. Kries's hands earlier. With his good hand, he grabbed hold of it and hastily tossed it over to the priest.

Fr. Kries looked down at the crucifix sliding to a stop in front of him. He grabbed it and raised it high, once more moving toward the towering beast.

"Lead us not into temptation, but deliver us," he paused for a second, "from *evil!*" he shouted, holding his fist defiantly in the air.

The white Everly werewolf leapt to its feet from behind the bar. It was soaked in alcohol. Once more, the Leonz werewolf grabbed hold of it, slashing at its face, instantly drawing blood on its white fur.

Fr. Kries moved courageously forward holding the cross high.

Seeing her son, a true man of God, instantly reignited Everly's rage. She grabbed hold of the Leonz werewolf by its top and bottom jaws, pulling them apart until completely breaking the top off and snapping the bottom jawbone.

Nina saw what was happening and ran toward the fight while Fr. Kries hollered out, "No! Stay back, Nina!" He held his arm out, stopping her forward momentum.

Meanwhile, with his remaining good hand, Ruppert began digging through his pockets, his face covered with blood from the deep scratches and his left hand hanging uselessly at his side.

The Leonz werewolf stumbled backwards from the jaw injury as blood poured out of its wounds. Everly took advantage of her momentum. She grabbed hold of Leonz by the throat and slammed her powerful, clawed hand into his chest, grabbing hold of the still beating heart and, in one quick yank, tearing it from his chest.

As if its body was suddenly weightless, the Leonz werewolf slowly dropped lifelessly to the ground in front of the bar.

Everly turned to face Fr. Kries and a screaming Nina.

"You *bitch*! No!" Nina shouted, beside herself with rage at what she had just witnessed.

The white werewolf snarled loudly, baring its massive fangs at the woman before turning its attention back to the priest with the crucifix.

"You will not win! Evil will not win! I've run from you my whole life and I am not running any longer, you vile, evil thing!" Fr. Kries shouted, running toward his mother, the wolf.

The Everly werewolf backed up in retreat, suddenly fearful. *He is stronger than me, and he knows it.* Her yellows eyes continued to look into his, challenging him to blink or show any sign of hesitation, but none could be found.

It was she who hesitated once more, and Kries took the opportunity, repositioning the cross with the old, tarnished silver Jesus figure atop it, driving it deep and directly into the werewolf's open jaws as far as it would go, piercing the back of its opened throat while yanking his hand out of her jaws before they could close tightly around his wrist.

Nina, meanwhile, ran to her fallen man, lying naked on the ground. Leonz's face was ripped to shreds and his chest flayed open. He was dead, and she knew it. Tears fell at the overwhelming loss she had been dealt on this, the worst day of her life.

The werewolf howled in agony at the burning in its throat while Fr. Kries quickly moved back from the flailing beast.

Everly yanked the crucifix from its jaws and, with its large claws, dropped it to the ground, stepping on it and crushing the wood. The beast's eyes narrowed to slits as it peered at its holy adversary. Blood poured from its mouth uncontrollably from the silver that had punctured its throat, spilling onto the floor already covered with the blood of the fallen Leonz.

"Nina, get back!" Fr. Kries shouted as she was now in the creature's path of destruction.

Forcing herself to her feet, Nina spat in the werewolf's direction and shouted, "You won't win! Damn you! You will not win!"

From over on the far side of Fr. Kries and Nina, the weakened voice of Ruppert called out, "Both of you, get out. Go through the back."

The werewolf bellowed out ferociously as it looked around the room, its mind no longer focused on the humans but on the immense boiling sensation spreading throughout its organs. A pain it had never felt before was coursing throughout its body. The silver image of Jesus that the creature's own son had driven deep into its mouth, piercing its tongue and throat, was spreading its own holy virus throughout its body. Killing off the tainted blood inside it.

Ruppert, meanwhile, had dragged himself over to the far side of the bar where numerous bottles of alcohol lay broken open on the floor, their contents spilled out into a large puddle of liquor. In his hand was a lit match.

Fr. Kries and Nina jumped back as the werewolf, seeing the flame as its rapidly deteriorating mind surmised what was happening, awkwardly leapt toward the bleeding man, snapping its blood covered fangs and stumbling over its own weight and failing body.

Ruppert dropped the match, instantly setting flame to the large pool of alcohol splashed across the floor. Acting as fuel, the alcohol trail led straight to the werewolf and away from Ruppert.

The Everly beast, now barely able to stand as the silver acted as a poison to its body, burst into flames, its white fur instantly singing off while it reached for Ruppert, determined to grab hold of this worthless alcoholic that had somehow got the better of her. All of them had, especially her son, the priest. *The holy one.*

Ruppert, still lying on the floor and nearly depleted of all his strength, kicked his foot out, connecting with the werewolf's chest as it reached for him. The kick connected, sending it back into the flames.

The howls turned to a woman's cries. "I'll kill you all! I'll rip the skin from your bodies! I will feast on your…" Fierce, loud and agonizing screams replaced her shouting.

Fr. Kries and Nina ran over to Ruppert who was also shouting, seeing his lower leg had caught fire. Nina grabbed a towel off the bar and slammed it against his leg, extinguishing the small flame.

The fire spread rapidly up the walls. "Another damn fire, appears to be a theme tonight," Ruppert mumbled sarcastically while Fr. Kries quickly pulled him to his feet.

"Come on, you're badly injured, we've got to get you out of here. We all have to get out of here, now, this place will soon be engulfed in flames!" Fr. Kries said firmly.

Ruppert and Nina nodded before Nina turned to look one last time at Leonz, lying dead on the floor, now covered in flames. She turned her head away bitterly from the scene.

Ruppert and Fr. Kries both looked behind the bar at the fallen Everly beast. When the fire engulfed her, she was no longer able to remain in her lycanthropic form and reverted back to a naked, burning and pathetic Everly, the same Everly that was last seen laying dying on the cold ground of Burnmere, Romania two years prior.

Her true self had lasted mere seconds before the silver melted away most of her face. This, coupled with the flames scorching away the rest of her flesh, made for a grisly picture. Made all the worse by the knowledge of what Everly truly was, a sad, evil woman that had sold herself to the devil for little more than earthly pleasures and the promise of power.

All of which was now taken from her grasp by the very son she had sworn to kill.

She lay still, no longer fighting the flames that continued eating away at her. Soon all that would remain would be bones.

"May you find the peace in death that no one on earth seemed to give you while you were alive, Mother," Fr. Kries muttered, looking away in disgust at the burning, evil woman. "Come on, this whole building is going down," he said urgently, turning his attention to the spreading fire as he and Nina tried helping a seriously injured Ruppert along. The flames continued to rise as smoke filled the building, making visibility almost impossible.

Ruppert remembered the path. "Through here!" he exclaimed.

Once outside, they hastily made their way down the alleyway, away from the smoke and fire that had quickly consumed Maximilian's.

With Fr. Kries on the left and Nina on the right helping him along, Ruppert looked back at the fire he had started and uttered, "I hope that wretched place burns completely to the ground."

Fr. Kries didn't bother turning around, simply replying, "Amen."

✝

Chapter 24

Aftermath: Early Morning

Davide stared at the smoke rising from Maximilian's far away on the southside and knew his friends were in trouble. Emila stood beside him with their daughter in front of them, looking at the smoke-filled sky.

"What happened, Papa?" she asked in a small voice, sniffling and shaken from the ordeal in her bedroom earlier.

Davide bent down so he was eye level and looking into his daughter's big, beautiful, scared eyes. "A bad person came to this town. She made several other people bad. One of them was in your room this morning. We think the bad person might be gone now but your father is going to go and make sure. It appears my line of work has changed. I am now the acting law enforcement here. Officer Lambert's final request, for better or worse. I suppose we'll see how I do."

"This town needs you. We need you Davide. And we will stand by you, no matter what. Isn't that right, Frida?" Emila said softly.

"Right!" the girl replied, peering out at the smoke.

"Well, alright then. This isn't over yet. I must go check on..." Davide began.

"Go, we'll be fine," Emila said, kissing her husband gently on the lips.

Kissing her back then looking into her eyes, he replied, "I know you will, I saw your courage back there in the face of that evil."

Giving her a brief and weary smile, he turned, hopped onto Bertha once more, and headed back toward the center of town. Along the way, he met several townsfolk heading in the same direction, and he nodded a silent greeting to each one.

Once he got to the center of town, he stopped, surveying the damage in broad daylight. The water drums had indeed proven useful in squelching the remaining fire. Already, Davide was impressed with how well the people were working together. Those that hadn't lost loved ones in the massacre were helping the grieving mothers, fathers, and orphaned children.

As he turned toward Maximilian's, he stopped once more, saddened at what he saw. In front of him lay the town doctor, his throat ripped out. Kneeling by him, looking at the wound, was the coroner.

Glancing up at Davide, the forty-five-year-old thin man with wire-rimmed glasses stood to his feet. "What, pray tell, are you doing on Erni's horse?" he asked.

"Erni's dead. So is Lambert. Their bodies are over in Fritz's house in Granhal. Everyone in that town is dead. I'm taking Lambert's spot for now," Davide said matter-of-factly. He didn't have time to beat around the bush with so much to do.

"Wha-? The police are dead, too?" the coroner said, stunned at this newest revelation.

Davide nodded grimly. "Many people are dead. Right now, we need to get the bodies of the deceased covered. Get some of those guys to help you. I'll be back soon."

"Where the hell are you going?" the coroner asked, wiping his forehead.

"Up there." He pointed to the smoke pillowing out of Maximilian's.

"Yeah, well, to hell with that place," the thin man grumbled.

"Where's our doctor's assistant?" Davide asked.

"He's over there, tending to that little boy. That damned thing ripped him apart. We're not even sure who the child's parents are, or if they're still alive. Never in my wildest dreams have I thought such evil could be perpetrated on an innocent child. And here in this very town, no less." He fell silent for a moment, shaking his head. "What the *fuck* happened here, Davide?"

"Evil came to this town, and I need to make sure it's gone," Davide said grimly as he flicked the reins of Bertha and moved away from the center of town.

He had ridden just part of the way from St. Raphael's to Maximilian's before he saw three people he knew well. All looked weary as they slowly walked in his direction. In the center was the worst off of the lot, Ruppert.

Pulling back on his reins as he approached, he quickly hopped off Bertha. "Ruppert, Fr. Kries, Nina! What happened up there?"

"She's dead. We killed her. The silver on the crucifix I found back in the rubble did it. And setting the whole place on fire finally vanquished the evil," Fr. Kries said, looking at his friend, blood caked on his face.

Noticing someone was missing, Davide asked, "Where's Leonz?"

They all fell silent.

"Oh, Nina, I'm so sorry," Davide began, hanging his head sadly.

"Don't. Just, don't. I haven't had time to process this. Any of it. My parents, Leonz…"

Nodding his understanding, he put his hand on her shoulder. At this small gesture, she caved in, giving him a hug and burying her face in his chest, sobbing.

Davide looked up to Fr. Kries then to Ruppert.

"What of Uma? And your wife and child?" Fr. Kries asked quietly.

"They survived. Uma's dead, too. It will take many years before my daughter will ever get over what she was witness to in her own bedroom. If she ever recovers, that is," Davide said sadly as Nina pulled away from him, wiping her blood-shot, tired, wet eyes.

"Come, let's go. There is much to do and none of us has had a minute's rest," Fr. Kries said.

"Ruppert, what happened to you?" Davide asked before they began making their way back to the town square.

"She got me good. I might have lost my eye. And my wrist is in bad shape. It's going to be a while before I'm of any use to anyone," Ruppert said sadly.

Putting his hand gently on his friend's shoulder, Davide responded, "You've done more this night than anyone will ever know. The town of Kortbeke is indebted to you. To all of you."

"Well, I suppose it's the first time in as long as I can remember that I did something good. I'm just glad I did my part in stopping these things, even at the great cost that came with it." Ruppert looked sadly at the still crying Nina.

Fr. Kries was silent, feeling the full weight of the atrocities that had occurred now falling on his shoulders.

Sensing the priest's heaviness, Davide turned to him. "Everyone has a choice, Father, and your mother made hers many years ago. You must not blame yourself for this. At least you all stopped her and her kind in their tracks."

Fr. Kries nodded slightly, glad Davide had been with him most of the way since they met up in Granhal many hours earlier, which now felt like a lifetime ago. He had always admired and respected the man, but now even more so after all that had occurred.

The four of them made their way back to the center of town. Very few of the injured the previous night had survived, succumbing to their injuries throughout the night and early morning hours due to the lack of medical help.

Seeing the four of them enter the ruins of the church and surrounding buildings, Kesselring, the doctor's assistant, came over to them, inspecting Ruppert and his wrist. The short-statured man cleared his throat. "We need to get you to the doctor's office. I can dress the wounds on your face and from the looks of it, you're going to need that wrist in a sling."

Ruppert nodded and said a quick goodbye to the others. "I'll catch up with you all soon." On his way out, he called over his shoulder to Davide, "Free beers for life!"

Davide smiled thinly then turned back to Nina and Fr. Kries.

"What now?" Nina asked, looking around at the death and destruction all around.

Much of the town had arrived and, while many were crying or looking forlorn, all were doing *something* productive and helping each other as best they could. Davide watched as a group of men headed toward Maximilian's with another drum of water on the back of a wagon, glad to see people taking charge. He noticed Maximilian patrons working alongside Hubschmid patrons, helping with the deceased and clearing the areas littered with debris. It made him proud of his fellow townsfolk.

"We need to let them all know what has truly happened here," Davide said.

Someone was running toward them from down the street. Upon closer inspection, they saw it was Erwin Brahms' son, Philip Brahms.

The fifteen-year-old came to a stop in front of them, breathing heavily and struggling to catch his breath as he adjusted his straw farmer's hat and exclaimed, "I don't know who's in charge here, but someone needs to come out to our farm! There's something out there I can't explain, but I think it's part of what happened last night."

"Where's your father?" Davide asked.

Nina remembered seeing the angry, accusing man hours earlier in the town square and had a sinking feeling she knew the answer.

"My Papa's dead. Killed by that wolf thing last night. My Mama's beside herself. I went to tend to our horses out in the stables and, well, you have to see it for yourself."

Davide looked at Fr. Kries. "Want to join?"

He nodded gravely.

"I'm coming too," Nina spoke out.

"Nina, with all you've been through, why don't you rest?" Davide replied.

"Leonz is dead. My parents are dead. I'm involved in this and I've earned the right to see whatever the hell is over at Brahms' farm," Nina said bitterly.

Davide looked up at the morning sun and puffy clouds filling the sky. On any other day, this would have been a beautiful sight to behold. But today it felt like a mockery of them all, in light of what they had endured mere hours ago.

"Fine, come on, then," Davide answered, running his hands through his hair wearily.

On their way to the farm, Philip Brahms looked sideways at Nina. The shy, freckle-faced boy clearly felt awkward in the presence of the town's most beautiful young woman, but he found the courage to speak. "S-sorry about Leonz. He was a heck of a guy. Always gave me a smile when I saw him in t-town. My Papa, I miss him already. Seems like a lot of us lost ones we loved last night.”

Nina glanced over at the boy, his cheeks red with embarrassment. *This boy lost his father. Numerous people throughout this town lost people. Not just me. I'm not alone in this.*

“Thank you, Philip,” Nina responded warmly, “I can't tell you what that means to me. The whole town is in mourning today and will be for what will likely be many, many years forward. But we're going to get through this. We are.”

He smiled shyly at Nina, thankful for her kind words. “There, up there!” He pointed as they neared his father's farm.

Erwin's widow Mae had several neighbors on the porch, comforting the woman over the loss of her husband. She saw them walk past as she buried her face in a large older woman's shoulder.

“Mama's been sick with grief. We all are. I was there last night. I saw my papa murdered by that wolf thing. And I think what's up ahead has something to do with it. Mama can't bear to look at it,” Philip said sadly.

In the tall grass ahead of them lay two bodies: one appeared to have been Mayor Klaus, his head flattened, the other, a naked Chadwick, also covered in blood.

“Well, we now know what happened to our mayor, judging from that overnight bag near his body. The man was likely attempting to flee, possibly on one of your dad's horses, right out of town. Chadwick got to him before he could make it,” Davide said, shaking his head in disgust at the gruesome sight.

"So, the cowardly Mayor Klaus, who had a similar dream as myself and you, Davide. This was his final act. He stopped Chadwick, I suppose. If I recall, he said that something told him that great sacrifice would be needed to stop the evil," Nina said.

"Yes, a reluctant pawn in this game of good and evil, so it seems," Davide said, staring at the remains and sighing wearily. "Come on, we need to get back to town. We'll get someone out here to take the bodies, but it might be a while, Phillip. The town's got its hands full. Chadwick's body is of great importance. The others have been burnt."

On their way back from the Brahms' property, Fr. Kries said, "These shared dreams. We know that Mayor Klaus, myself, you, Nina, and you, Davide, shared part of the same dream. I feel as though each of us were tasked in some way, to see this through and to at least attempt to stop this ancient enemy of God. And not just here."

"So, you don't think this is over yet, Father?" Davide asked.

"I know it's not," Fr. Kries said bleakly, wondering when it would be revealed to him the means by which the ancient evil was to be vanquished.

Chapter 25

†

A Town United

The first full day after the evil had descended and then been thwarted from the town of Kortbeke was a stressful and difficult one. The town had to pull together as best they could without their law officers. Davide became the one most went to with questions and concerns. He did his best in his new role, with the aid of several others in town, including Ruppert's boss, Lorin Wirthlin, from the butcher shop across from Hubschmid's, who had proven quite useful in getting the countless issues that needed to be dealt with organized.

Bodies were taken to the morgue and doctor's office on the east side of town. So many were their numbers, however, that several small businesses nearby opened their doors to house the dead until further arrangements could be made for their burial.

Davide visited Ruppert who had been cleaned up after the scrape across his face. His wrist in a sling, he wore a temporary black patch over his right eye, giving him the appearance of a fierce pirate. He enjoyed teasing the local children when he walked through town, seeing it brought them some happiness during this time of mourning.

Ruppert's condition brought forth a wave of sadness from Davide upon seeing his friend who was once again dealt a bad hand in this life. But from that bad hand, a hero of sorts had emerged, one who seemed to be rolling with the punches better than he had expected.

Resting in bed after being up and about earlier, Ruppert shook his head. "Don't you start feeling bad for me, Davide. You want to feel bad for anyone, feel bad for Nina. Feel bad for all of these people that have lost loved ones. I've got no one except for you, and you survived. Worse thing for me is a possible lost eye. Although, the doctor thinks I might regain some vision over time, which I wholeheartedly agree with. Regardless, I'm alive."

"You are. And I can't thank you enough for your hand in this. I've given you a hard time about your heavy drinking but last night you showed everyone what real heroism is. I won't forget that," Davide responded.

"Well, don't think I'm going to up and quit drinking. I meant what I said, free beer for life!" Ruppert said with a joking grin.

Davide returned the smile then saw Ruppert's face turn serious.

"Davide, what are we going to do? Think it's over? I mean, for good?" he wondered.

"Fr. Kries seems to think it isn't. For now, though, I think those things are gone and I think the town is safe," Davide said, feeling hopeful.

"What about the remains of those…creatures?" Ruppert asked.

"Good question," Davide said. "I would like our coroner to look them over. Especially Chadwick. Found his naked body out on the Brahms' property along with Mayor Klaus. It appears he was trying to flee and met his end there. But not before ending Chadwick's short reign of terror. Say what you will about the mayor, but his last deed was a good one, even if it was likely inadvertent."

"I don't mean to speak ill of the dead, and while I always thought Klaus was a cheating bastard Uma had wrapped around her little finger, amongst other things, it's good to hear he took out one of those things," Ruppert said with a sigh.

Davide nodded. "I need to address the town. Likely tomorrow morning. I'd sure appreciate it if you could be there. I think it would be good for the people to see you and even hear from you."

"Considering they accused me and the rest of us of starting that fire and possibly killing Fr. Steffen, I'm not so sure. I was given sideways glances when I checked out the rubble a bit earlier today. Seems as though some may still think I had a hand in the church's destruction, not that I blame them, I suppose. I don't have the best reputation and was seen right after things went to hell," Ruppert mused with a frown.

"This town was under a curse. A blanket of darkness that I am convinced had an adverse effect on its citizens. It's been lifted and the evil has been destroyed. Stand with me," Davide said, reaching his hand out to his friend.

Looking at the outstretched hand, Ruppert nodded, taking it into his own. "Fine, Davide, I'll be there."

They said their goodbyes and Davide left for home. He hadn't slept for what felt like forty-eight hours and could barely stand, anxious to get home after the long arduous day. Already many of the townspeople looked to him for answers to their numerous questions, and he tried to meet them all with a smile and a word of encouragement, especially after it was made known that he was the acting police force in Kortbeke. But as the long day wore on, he had simply run dry.

Fr. Kries, meanwhile, had sifted through the rubble of the fallen church, finding Fr. Steffen's bent chalice laying by his charred black skeleton. He decided it should be saved and, when a new parish was erected, placed inside as a holy object from the martyred priest who would likely, someday, become a saint.

The young priest wasn't sure what his next step would be, after the horrors of the previous night, but he felt that his time might very well be up in Kortbeke. Despite Davide's encouraging words about it not being his fault, he knew he could no longer look the townspeople in the eyes knowing he had inadvertently brought this nightmare upon them.

There was another place he felt he must return to after so many years. And that place was a great distance away from Kortbeke, or Switzerland, for that matter. He didn't know how he would answer for this to the diocese, but he would deal with that when the time arose. For now, he would do what he could for the people of Kortbeke.

He found himself back in his small cottage at the end of the day, much like everyone else in town, weary and ready for a hopefully dreamless night sleep. Before he did anything else, he dropped to his knees and began praying for direction.

✝

Davide finally arrived home after the long day and was greeted by his wife and tired daughter, both of whom gave him a hug. Emila had taken it upon herself to dispose of Uma's remains, sending little Frida to a nearby neighbor to watch over her when she did so.

Very little was left after Uma had wasted away to nearly nothing. Emila had held on to the silver key and kept it with her throughout the day. It had saved their lives and would be a reminder of all the horrors they had faced and survived. The door to Maximilian's, for which it had once been used, would no longer be needing it.

Emila had also seen to it that the bones were handed over to the coroner. "She won't be missed. Unmarked grave for this one," was all the coroner said, shaking his head and taking the cloth sack the bones now resided in.

After a relatively quiet meal, Davide took his bath while Emila read stories to Frida on the couch. In mere minutes, the child was sound asleep, much like the previous night, on her mother's lap.

Davide came out from his much-needed bath, exhausted but feeling much better with food and cleanliness checked off the list.

He looked at his two angels on the couch and his heart swelled with love followed by heartbreak, knowing there were many families that were devastated this very evening, being apart from loved ones forever. He felt the sudden urge for intimacy. Something his wife had prepared for the previous night.

"Shh, I think she's out for the night," Emila said, seeing her husband come over to them.

He didn't speak, instead, bending down and brushing her beautiful red hair out of her face and kissing her passionately on the lips.

Slightly caught off-guard, Emila returned the intimate gesture, then, as quietly and gently as possible, laid their daughter down on the couch, covering her with a hand-made quilt until she was sure Frida was comfortable and remaining asleep.

She turned to face her husband who immediately wrapped his arms around her, feeling tears well up in his eyes as he tried to push the horrors of the last days out of his mind.

As if reading his mind, Emila gently began unbuttoning her nightgown, kissing him passionately as they made their way back to their quiet bedroom.

✝

"I know this place," Fr. Kries said, looking around the dingy, filthy room that smelled of old food and unwashed linens. He barely had time to get his bearings when the door opened, and Everly Seiler walked through. Not the beautiful, fake version he had seen in Kortbeke, but the woman that had abused him throughout his entire childhood.

She looked terrible, her dirty clothes hanging from her body, her hair a rat's nest of tangles that she hadn't bothered to fix, and even her demeanor was ugly. She wore a perpetual scowl and mumbled to herself about some men in town, but he couldn't make out exactly who she was talking about. Regardless, she was angry and swearing.

Then, something caught the woman's eye. He followed her gaze to see what it was. She sucked in a gulp of stale air at the sight of a large, black wolf sitting in a doorway.

Fr. Kries watched as she followed the wolf obediently into the room. Just before the door closed, the wolf glanced back, looking directly at him, its eyes flashing bright yellow.

As soon the door closed, he found himself inside the room with the wolf and his mother. But the wolf was no longer on four legs. It was growing and changing into something between a wolf and a man.

As it mutated, Fr. Kries looked on in horror to see the woman shed her clothes and walk to the bed.

"What the hell? Wake up, Christoph! For the love of God! Wake up!" he thought desperately.

The beast stood over the bed as the woman lay writhing atop the dirty, soiled covers. It let out a low snarl, glancing back at him as its large paws climbed atop the bed. As though it wanted him to witness this.

He was unable to close his eyes when he realized what was about to take place. He turned away, toward the closed door, just as he heard the woman screaming in pain. He twisted the knob of the door and ran out, closing it behind him. As he did, he heard the screams replaced with moans of ecstasy.

Stepping outside the door, he found himself outside in the middle of the town he grew up in. It was nighttime and the buildings around him weren't nearly as nice as even the worst of Kortbeke's infrastructure. He inspected his surroundings, noticing that even the roads were in a far worse state of disrepair since he last laid eyes on them years ago.

He looked past the town up to the mountain just beyond it that loomed large and was covered in a thick fog. He squinted and saw the shape of a castle farther up and shuddered at the sight of the ominous blanket of fog that seemed to be moving, as if itself a living entity.

In the distance, a wolf howled, reminding him of the unnatural act he had just been witness to. Woman and beast, lying together. And not just a beast, something more. Something supernatural and evil. Something that could only have come from hell itself.

He heard footsteps heading his way and spun around to see his mother again, coming up the jagged street. Her rage-filled face from before had been replaced by a deranged and crazy expression. She had blood splatter on her dress and speckles of it on her face. Armed with a pistol at her side and carrying a rifle, she wore a jacket that was several sizes too big.

Everly walked past her son, not seeing him standing right in front of her, toward a house on the darkened street, heading confidently to the front door. Upon opening it, Everly was met with a gun blast to her stomach, sending her careening backwards onto the ground.

The sudden and violent act caused him to flinch, yet he couldn't turn away, nor could he awaken. It was as if something, or someone, wanted him to see this. I am meant to see this, to see what became of my mother and the evil I must still face, *he thought.*

He moved over to where his mother lay on the street, bleeding out from what would obviously be a fatal gunshot. Peering down at her, she seemed to look directly into his eyes and with an evil grin said, "Don't bother sending for the priest, I killed him."

"I don't want to see more of this, but I feel as though I must," he said to himself.

Fr. Kries turned away from the grisly image and instantly found himself awake, lying in a small bed that had belonged to Oskar Bryner, whom he had just recently administered last rites to before succumbing to his wounds at the hands of the Chadwick lycanthrope.

Fr. Kries had felt it was only fitting that his remaining days in Kortbeke should be spent in the room of a man he had personally sent to the heavens. A personal penance for his withholding who he really was to the good people of Kortbeke since arriving in their town three years prior. A fact he planned on sharing with the town soon enough.

Sliding out of bed, he dropped to his knees and buried his face into his hands, weeping at the mother who had given him birth only to embrace evil. He wept for the lost souls of Kortbeke and Granhal, along with his hometown of Burn-mere, and every place in between that she had likely visited and committed further sinful acts of violence and destruction in her pursuit of the son that escaped her clutches so many years prior.

"Lord, my burden is heavy, but you will be with me." His mind went to a Bible verse he thought of often due to the horrible events of his past and now, his present. "Fear not, for I am with you; be not dismayed, for I am your God. I will strengthen you, yes, I will help you, I will uphold you with My righteous right hand." He finished with, "Isaiah forty-one, verse ten."

Fr. Kries continued to cry softly as he pulled out his rosary and climbed back into bed. He began to run his hands over the beads as he prayed silently until sleep once more washed over his weary body, welcoming him into a dreamless slumber for the remainder of the night.

Fr. Kries wasn't the only one that was visited with unpleasant visions that night.

✝

In a distant land far from Kortbeke and Switzerland, Nina walked through a forest on a narrow dirt path. Her travels led her upwards farther and farther. The skies above were covered in fog and visibility was poor, especially at night. Thankfully, she held a torch to guide her way.

On her lonely travels up the mountain, tree cover hung overhead, as if wanting to keep her trapped inside its looming, winding trail, until she came across a large clearing that appeared to be covered in rubble. Large, shattered stones spread out across the relatively flat area of the mountain in all directions.

Near the edge of the destruction stood two shapes that appeared to be actively chanting aloud in what sounded like some sort of séance.

The two human forms, shrouded in the cover of darkness, one of which spoke in a language unfamiliar to her. They raised their hands above their head. In front of them burned a small bonfire, crackling and popping beside a flat slab of stone with writing on its side as the concealed individuals continued on in the odd dialect.

Charred bones were spread out around the fire. "We have brought the bones to you, master," the tall, cloaked, male voice uttered.

Covered in complete darkness, a hiss from beyond the fire spoke. "Good, soon all will be made right. Her work is not done, you need her. She failed in the retrieval of her son, but her usefulness is not over. She will bring about the rise of the great Pricolici once more. Her bones will be placed atop the sacrificial altar. Foolish humans below go about their days and nights, eating, drinking, working, fucking. They will soon see what it is to live in the darkness. They will know, and they will bow."

Blackness filled her vision. Alone in the darkness and still in a dream state, another voice, much softer, almost calming spoke. "Make haste to the origin of the evil," it said, then paused before finishing the sentence, "my good and faithful servant."

Nina gasped, sitting up in bed. Catching her breath, she looked around the room. Night had turned to morning, the second day since the attack on their town. She shook her head and crawled out of bed, trying to shake off the terrible dream. This one seemed more pronounced than the one with Everly Seiler being shot and making taunts about a dead priest while bleeding out on the ground.

She paced the floor, back and forth, speaking her confusion aloud. "What are you showing me? Whose bones were those being thrown on the fire? And who was that cloaked man? I feel as though I must learn the answers to these questions! To see to it that those responsible for the murder of my parents and my dear Leonz come to justice. I will see this through to the bitter end!" she exclaimed, realizing suddenly she was praying.

She hadn't truly prayed in a great while, leaving the "religious stuff" to her mom and dad. But now, it was just her and her God. The finality of her deceased loved ones hit her once more as she hung her head and made a sign of the cross.

"In the name of the Father, the Son, and the Holy Spirit, help me, Father, my burden is heavy."

With that heavy heart, she cleaned up and got dressed. Davide would address the town today and she wanted to be there for it.

✝

The entire town assembled in the morning hours near the destruction of the church. Atop a large piece of rubble stood a revitalized David Hubschmid. Beside him, his friend Ruppert was bandaged up but holding his head high. On his other side stood Fr. Kries who had woken early in the morning, still clutching his rosary from the previous night's gruesome dream.

The townspeople talked among themselves until several loud claps from Emila, standing off to the side near her husband, got their attention and a hush fell across the crowd.

Davide began, "People of Kortbeke, I am not going to mince words and you will hear only the truth from me. This town was visited by a lycanthrope not two days ago. Thirty-four are dead, not counting the creature that was the cause of this destruction. Granhal is wiped out, completely. Our police force is gone, as is our church."

He paused, looking out over the crowd, as many gasped in horror and others hung their heads sadly.

Fr. Kries looked uneasily at Davide, knowing that soon his secret would be revealed for all to know, and he would have to deal with the repercussions and fallout of it.

Davide continued, "As some of you may know by now, Lambert's last order of business before he perished in Granhal was to make me acting Chief of Police. I certainly didn't ask for the job, but until things are better organized, you'll have to put up with me. Fr. Kries can corroborate my story, as he has been doing already, since the incident." He fell silent, waiting for pushback, but none came. Not after the horrors that befell them all less than forty-eight hours prior.

"I can tell you this," Davide said. "The thing that came to this town is dead. And its accomplices have also perished. We will bury our dead with dignity and respect. And then we will set about the daunting task of rebuilding our parish and bank along with the houses that have been lost to the fires."

"What of Maximilian's?" someone in the large crowd shouted out.

"Maximilian's is closed, permanently," Davide said matter-of-factly. Then continued, "I realize I am the owner and operator of Hubschmid's Pub, but my time there has come to an end. My time is better suited at home with my wife and child in the evenings. And helping this town recover, I suppose."

A murmur from the crowd kicked up.

"Fr. Kries would like to have a few moments of your time. Father, go ahead," Davide said, gesturing for him to say his piece.

"People of Kortbeke, you may know me as Fr. Kries. However, my real name is Christoph Seiler. Son of Marco and Everly Seiler, the woman that visited this town." He paused as many once again gasped, taking a deep breath and glancing over at Ruppert, Nina, and Davide before continuing.

Fr. Kries then explained everything to the people of Kortbeke. He spoke in detail of the physical and emotional abuse at the hands of his mother. Of the sexual abuse he narrowly escaped when he fled Burnmere, and of finding himself later in Austria in seminary and later becoming a man of the cloth.

He told the crowd who was responsible for the horror that had befallen Kortbeke and that a part of the evil itself, like the roots from a tree, had been ripped out and destroyed from their town after being burned to death inside Maximilian's. The tree however, still existed, and had to be destroyed. It was up to him to go to the source of that evil and try and stop it, once and for all.

At times, angry words were hurled at Fr. Kries, but he held fast, continuing on with his story until its completion.

"What now?" a woman from the crowd asked when he had finished.

"Now, I must go home, to meet this evil head-on. I must face my past and reconcile with my father. I feel as though the key to it all ending and bringing about true redemption for those that have perished at its hands, lies in the town of Burnmere, Romania. I will be travelling there within a day's time."

Ruppert saw the crowd growing restless with the information Fr. Kries had given. He stood to his feet and hollered out, "Listen, everyone! We've all lost something, but this evil will not destroy this town. We're going to band together and repair it. And we're *not* going to point fingers! I've been pointing fingers most of my life, and it cost me my family. No more! We are a decent people in Kortbeke, and we *will* overcome this!"

The crowd fell silent, looking at the man who was quite obviously scarred for life and would likely never see out of both eyes again. All knew him as the town drunk that couldn't keep his wife and two boys. A dead ender and a loser. But not today, and not any longer.

Davide raised an eyebrow at his friend's well-articulated speech.

After the meeting, when most everyone had gone back to their homes and businesses, Davide spoke with Ruppert, Nina, and Fr. Kries alone. "Are you truly leaving tomorrow?" he asked the young man of the cloth he had come to admire even more over the last couple of days.

"I must. As I said, my destiny now lies many miles away from here and I likely will not return. Contact the diocese and you will be granted another priest. But they must know of this tragedy," Fr. Kries answered resolutely.

"Certainly, Father. What do you expect to find in this town you are heading to?" Davide asked.

"I'm expecting to do battle with something much stronger than what we dealt with here. 'You shall be shown the means to defeat the evil that spawned her. You must be strong.' Those are the words etched into my mind. I can't shake them, no matter how hard I try! I don't know how to defeat the evil that spawned my mother, changing her into the wolf-beast she had become, a lycanthrope, but God…or whomever has communicated with me, will show me when I am ready. It must be me that ends this."

"You're not in this alone, Father. I'm going with you," Nina said.

"Oh, no, Nina. You cannot!" Fr. Kries exclaimed.

"Everyone in my life is dead," Nina retorted, then told them all about the dream she had the previous night. About the bones and the man shrouded in a black cloak. "The man said her work is not done! Who? Your mother? Or more of those things that rained death and destruction down on our small town? Regardless, the words continue to play out in my head: 'Make haste to the origin of the evil.'"

"This is certainly unexpected, and not good news," Fr. Kries said grimly.

"But, don't you see, Father? Whatever is speaking to you is also speaking to me, I believe. And I feel as though I need to go along with you. My destiny lies with you for a time, it seems," Nina said.

"Very well," Fr. Kries sighed, resigned to the young woman travelling along to an undetermined and likely quite dangerous future.

Ruppert, who had been uncharacteristically silent until now, spoke up. "I think I shall come along, as well. I believe we make a good team, and I could certainly stand to get out of Kortbeke for a while. These last few days have made me reevaluate a good bit of my life, or lack thereof." He paused, then added, "I, uh, had been considering ending it all. I was a washed-up drunk living in a tiny loft above a meat packing store. Wife and kids gone, a laughingstock in town with a one-way ticket to an early grave. I was planning on hastening that one-way ticket. Hell, I even had the noose wrapped around a beam on my ceiling if I ever got liquored up enough to actually do the deed. Until these events that transpired in Kortbeke. Now I know I have more to live for. Perhaps I can do some good yet in this old world."

Davide, stunned by his admission, looked into Ruppert's remaining good eye and placed his hands on his friend's shoulders. "I'll always be here for you. There's a good man," he paused, "no, scratch that, a *great* man standing in front of me, and he proved that. The good Lord isn't done with you, it seems."

Ruppert smiled and nodded his appreciation for his friend's kind words.

Fr. Kries felt the weight of responsibility for these two who would be joining him on a journey likely to be fraught with much danger, unknown challenges and the very real possibility of death. "I cannot promise any of us will survive what evil waits for us in the distant town of Burnmere, deep in the mountains of Romania."

Nina and Ruppert nodded their understanding, neither one taking back their earlier words.

Davide breathed heavily. "So be it. I will take care of things here. I advise you leave early in the morning tomorrow, before people are up. It will be easier. I will go to Mae Brahms' and see if her son Philip might be willing to take you to Leipzig. That would be the nearest train station to continue on to Bucharest."

They all agreed to this and went their separate ways to prepare for the trip.

Davide watched them leave, holding his head high, fighting back tears knowing that after their departure the following morning, he would likely never see any of them again.

He then turned and headed home to tell Emila about this unexpected turn of events.

Later, as Emilia heard the news, she clenched the silver key that had saved their lives earlier, recalling how it had brought about the evil Uma's demise. Just as the silver Jesus atop Fr. Kries's crucifix brought about Everly's end. And, from what Davide had told her, a silver bullet was found lodged in Chadwick's body.

God, or *something* supernatural, appeared to have visited the dreams of Klaus, Nina, Fr. Kries, and her own husband. They were all involved in a purpose far greater than she could understand. Klaus hadn't survived it. She hoped and prayed for their safety in what lay ahead in their undetermined futures.

"This key doesn't belong to me," Emila said quietly to Davide before wrapping her arms around him, scared for her friends and their perilous journey ahead.

Chapter 26

✝

A New Journey Begins

The next morning came quickly and, at first light, right as the sun began peeking up over the tall snow-capped mountains surrounding the town, Fr. Kries, Ruppert, and Nina met at the front entrance to town on the northside, along with Philip Brahms and his father's largest horse hitched to a covered wagon.

Philip had agreed to take them to the railroad station in Leipzig, Germany. From there, they would take the train to Bucharest, Romania, Fr. Kries's hometown.

Davide reached them, nodding at Philip who sat atop the covered wagon, ready to take his passengers to their next destination.

"Take this," Davide said, handing Ruppert Deputy Erni's revolver.

"You sure?" Ruppert said, taking the six shooter and looking it over.

"As long as you only need one hand to shoot, I think you should take it. I got it from the station," Davide said, half-joking while helping his friend strap on the holster and belt around his waist.

As Ruppert nodded his thanks, Davide looked the man over. An eye patch covered his right eye, scratches across his face, his lower arm in a cast. "Are you sure you're up for this trek?"

Ruppert looked up at the clear sky, breathing in the fresh air. "Yes, I am. My wrist shall heal, and I am confident I will regain some of my eyesight. They need me and I need them. I feel called to do this, even if I'm not having those dreams. Before this, I was aimless. You know it and I know it. I'll miss our nights at Hubschmid's, but my destiny lies with these two many miles from here. If it's the last good thing I do in this life, I want to help put an end to the evil that visited this town, once and for all. For the first time in a long time, I have purpose. Been a long damn time since I've felt this way, Davide."

"Well, then, take care. You're a good friend and I shall miss you. If you do return to us, Hubschmid's, or whatever it's called at that point, will give you that free beer. Hopefully, that may entice you to come home," Davide said, shaking his right hand.

Ruppert chuckled at this. "I'll hold you to it, although I'm not sure how much drinking I will be doing in my future. And, hey, my right hand works just fine, if I ever do need to use this." He pointed to the revolver.

Leaning in, Davide said quietly so only Ruppert could hear, "I always knew you had it in you. You're a strong man, stronger than you may realize. Keep that strength, you shall likely need it where you're heading."

Ruppert's face turned serious. "Thank you, Davide, for… everything."

Davide smiled at Ruppert then moved to Nina, putting his hands on her shoulders. "I've said it before, but it bears repeating, I am sorry for your loss. Your immense loss. I hope you stay safe out there. Hubschmid's will not be the same without you and your spunky attitude."

Nina threw her arms around Davide, then pulled back, smiling, holding in tears she figured she had run out of over the past several days. She contemplated staying for Leonz's funeral rites but couldn't bear it. She would morn his loss in her own way, on her own time. Everything about Kortbeke reminded her of loves she lost. Of her dear mother and father, wiped out in one night. Her lover, turned to evil before sacrificing himself for good. She knew, beyond the shadow of a doubt, she was destined to go with the priest to Burnmere for reasons unknown to them. Yet. *Make haste to the origin of the evil.* The words were burned into her subconscious and haunted her, becoming the new driving force in her life.

Finally, Davide's eyes fell to Fr. Kries. "Father, I wish I could guarantee your safety." He sighed heavily. "But I can't, not after all we've been through."

Fr. Kries put his hand on his friend's shoulder. "I wish you and the rest of Kortbeke would not have had to lift the heavy burden that has been my life. I will bring God's justice to the suffering this town and its people have endured. Our journey will not be easy, and I cannot guarantee our success, but we must try to end this evil that still lives in the Carpathian Mountains. I feel it, I know it still exists and there are people there that will suffer greatly if I do not go there. It is my calling. My whole life has led me to this moment, preparing me to take on what awaits us."

They all fell silent, knowing the end had arrived and a new chapter awaited the three former residents of Kortbeke.

"Oh, Father, I almost forgot!" Davide said. He reached into the pocket of his jacket on the chilly morning and pulled out the small silver statue of Jesus that had been on the crucifix. Most of the wood from the cross had been destroyed in the fight with Everly inside Maximilian's but a thin silver cross with Jesus crucified on it remained. "This belongs to you. A keepsake of St. Raphael's and a little something to remember Kortbeke by."

Fr. Kries took it into his hands and inspected it gratefully. "I don't know what to say, Davide. I figured this was lost to the fire. This crucifix means so much to me and to have little more than this image of our Lord with His hands outstretched, it means a great deal to me. Thank you, my friend."

At the same time, both men embraced. While squeezing each other tightly, knowing this was likely the last they would see each other in this life, Davide whispered, "Take care of them, they are your flock. I believe in you, and I believe in your quest."

They pulled back from each other as Fr. Kries gave a nod of understanding, placing the silver image of Jesus into the breast pocket of his clerical jacket where it would be safe and near his heart.

Emila stopped Nina just as they were turning to board the wagon. "Wait, I also have something to give you," she blurted out.

Nina turned to see Emila with her hand outstretched. "What is this?" she asked, curiously.

"It's the silver that was used to destroy…what Uma had become. I was planning on keeping it as a reminder of what we vanquished. But you three need it more than me. It may come in handy once more," Emila said, extending her hand with the silver key in it.

Nina looked down at the beautiful item, realizing it was the same key Leonz had driven into Uma's foot days earlier, then looked back up to Emila as fresh tears welled up in her eyes. She glanced over to Davide who nodded his approval.

"Very well. But if I ever return to the town of Kortbeke, I shall return it to its owner. Thank you, Emila," she said, graciously taking it into her hands and looking it over.

"We've got to get a move-on if you're going to make that train. We've got a ride ahead of us," Phillip said from the awaiting wagon.

Giving one last nod to Davide and Emila, the three turned toward the new lives that awaited them. A life filled with uncertainty and, likely, fraught with danger. But they had each other.

Davide and Emila watched as the three travelers climbed onto Philip's wagon. With a smile and a nod, Philip cracked the reins and rode off into the early morning sunrise, the two of them watching until he and his passengers were out of sight.

Emila continued looking at the beautiful sunrise spilling over the mountains. The weather had been like this ever since the dreary night when the evil had arrived. Almost as if it were washing away the stain that had blanketed the entire area.

She turned to Davide, looking into his eyes, searching his thoughts. "My dear, do you think they will succeed? Whatever it might be that they are heading into?"

Davide didn't answer. Instead, he kissed her gently on the cheek, then, taking her by the hand, walked back toward home.

The day went on as the previous one had. People pitching in and cleaning up the town. Today was a day of great sorrow though as many bodies would be laid to rest. Tim Von Almen, the priest of St. Mary, Mother of God Parish in Salzben, had been notified of the tragedy that had occurred in Kortbeke and the nearby Granhal and would be arriving shortly to spend time with the loved ones of the deceased as well as lead in the burial rites of the numerous dead.

The fifty-seven-year-old had quite liked Fr. Kries and regretted not being able to say goodbye to the young man and, more importantly, get more information on what had occurred in Kortbeke as well as the priest's history that now appeared to be in question.

Davide, however, made sure that didn't happen. He didn't want an informal inquiry of Fr. Kries to take place. Not in Kortbeke, at least. Davide had filled the priest in upon his arrival on some of the gorier details of their towns attack, primarily, that the attackers were similar to that of a pack of rabid wolves.

Much of the town knew about Fr. Kries's departure along with Nina and Ruppert and while sad to hear the news, many had figured it was for the best. While Fr. Kries had indeed not been entirely forthcoming about his past and his real name, he was a good man that had been dealt a bad hand. A bad hand that had followed him all the way to their town. But it was over.

✝

Night fell across Kortbeke. The burials had taken place and the long, somber day had come to an end. Those that had perished in the massacre, including the bodies from Granhal, were buried together in the location where the small-town bank had once been before it burned down, beside what would soon be a rebuilt parish where St. Raphael's once stood. The town would never forget what happened on that fateful night.

Davide made sure that the only three people *not* buried in the cemetery were Uma Karlen, Chadwick Kern, and the woman named Everly. All three were buried in unmarked graves outside of town near the foothills on a nearby tree-covered mountain, and it was decided that no mention of the gravesite would be given, for fear of it being desecrated.

The coroner inspected the skeletal remains of all the infected bodies, what little was left of them, and found the only ones still mutated in appearance were the bones of Everly. The rest appeared to be human.

Each set of bones was placed in its own sackcloth and then buried as dusk fell across the land. Two local farmers tasked with the job had agreed to do it, as well as keep their mouths shut about its location, with the promise of a night of free ale at what had been known as Hubschmid's Pub but was now simply, "The Kortbeke Tavern," a name chosen by Davide himself.

Arles and Mikel were more than happy to toss the remains of the murderers haphazardly into the shallow holes dug for each. Once the holes were covered just enough so the sacks the bones were placed in were no longer visible, Arles wiped his sweaty forehead and looked over at Mikel who was taking a swig of water from the canteen he brought along. Arles reached his hand over and Mikel handed him the canteen.

"Piss on these lousy, murdering sods," Arles said bitterly, pulling a cigarette from his shirt pocket and lighting it. After a long drag and exhale of the much-needed nicotine, he continued, "I don't see why we couldn't have just thrown the remains into the trash bin instead of trudging out here. Guess the free ale will be worth it. But any amount of energy given to this lot after what happened is too much."

Nodding in reply, Mikel scratched his unshaven, dirty face, peering up at the beautiful mountain at whose base they stood. "To think they're buried here, surrounded by this beauty, it doesn't seem fair."

"Yeah, well, they're rotting in hell, where they belong," Arles replied.

Mikel glanced around and seeing no one else, uttered, "Hey, let's give 'em a right proper send-off, shall we?" He pulled his trousers down and let loose a spray of yellow piss atop the dirt.

Arles let out a laugh at this and quickly joined in the fun.

Once they were finished relieving themselves, the men slung their shovels over their shoulders and began making their way back to Kortbeke, roughly a quarter mile away.

Silence fell over the land as the voices of the two men faded into the distance.

Across the rapidly approaching night sky flew a winged creature, unseen by human eyes. It swooped down the mountain, mere inches from the highest treetops. Its large wings gently flapped in the wind that carried it forward.

Once it reached ground level, it flapped its batlike wings forward to slow its speed and gently come to a halt on the soft grass beneath its feet. With a quick twitch of the back, both wings curled up and pushed into open flaps of skin.

The animal, shrouded in darkness, sniffed the air. It knew the scent it was tasked with picking up and knew that the location was nearby from the strong odor that filled its nostrils. It smelled something else. Human urine. Someone had marked the site. The bones and the urine smell combined made them all the easier to locate. However, the bat-winged creature thought of how it would enjoy ripping the hearts out of those that had desecrated the grave site.

But that wasn't its task. Not this time.

With bare feet, the figure walked to three shallow holes that barely covered what could easily be seen, even with human eyes, to be cloth sacks. A pale hand with long, pointed fingernails reached down, pulling two bags out. The third one was pulled out last, opened, and its contents sprinkled into each of the three graves.

Several kicks of its bare feet and fresh dirt covered the bones back up. Bones across all three graves. Three graves, three partial skeletal remains. In case anyone decided to go snooping.

It held up the two sacks of bones, bringing its nose against the sack cloth. Smelling past the stale urine and soil sticking to the sack, it smelled the remains inside. One belonged to a woman recently turned. The other it had been tasked to retrieve. That is, if she failed in her quest to vanquish her offspring as her master had ordered.

Looking at the bag holding Everly's remains, the voice holding them hissed, "You don't deserve a second chance. But I suppose I was given one, as well. If not through your son, then the great Pricolici shall live through you. Then, long live the darkness! Long live...the *master!*"

Holding the two sacks of bones, Ingrid Brassard stepped into the moonlight that cast a glow onto her naked body. Her eyes gleamed yellow and her full red lips pulled back to reveal a smile with two rows of pointed teeth.

A slight twitch of her back opened up the thin slits running down her skin, producing a set of large, flesh-covered, bat-shaped wings which she instantly started flapping, sending her spiraling upwards into the night sky before vanishing completely.

✝

The young priest stood inside a church nothing like St. Raphael's in Kortbeke. This church was significantly smaller and not decorated with the more lavish display of holy items in Kortbeke, such as stained glass and chiseled statues of saints from years past. But it did have a cross hanging above the altar, one that Fr. Kries remembered well from his youth when his father would, at times, take him to Sunday morning Mass. Beneath it stood an old man wearing priestly vestments.

Fr. Kries didn't recognize the priest. It certainly wasn't Fr. Jannick Gustloff, the priest that had been Burnmere's pastor when Christoph had taken off, escaping Everly's wrath, or so he had hoped. This man was old and overweight, and what hair remained atop his head was thin and white. He wore small, round, wire-rimmed glasses that he pushed up his nose as he spoke to a woman and two men.

"You've searched for your son for nearly two years. We don't know what's come of him. But something is happening on the mountain, the wolves have returned, and the villagers speak of shadowed figures in the night on the hills leading up to the ruins of Castle Visimar, human forms shrouded in the cover of night. It's as if we're being watched…studied, looking for a weakness, perhaps," the priest said solemnly.

The woman, a beautiful brunette, stood close to the larger of the two men. "Father, since we came to this town, after the incident in the castle and here in town, things have gotten much better. Is she coming back? That is our main concern."

"Since the events of two years ago, there hasn't been any activity at all, on the mountain or anywhere in the surrounding region. We were just informed by the police force over in Crownhaven that an infant is missing. The police are looking into the parents, but all clues are pointing to an abduction," the younger, handsome man said.

"An infant goes missing in a nearby town. I'm not trying to sound the alarm bells just yet, but that has all the hallmarks of the work of vampires. Babies and small children missing,

followed by adults trying to find rational explanations for the abductions where the only true explanation here in this region of Romania is...vampires," the large man said with authority.

My father! That's my father, Marco! *he thought with excitement.*

His father continued, "I know that woman and I know well the supernatural powers that inhabited that castle. We all do. The evil infestation that spawned from up there was stopped but not destroyed completely. The scrolls are up there buried in all that rubble. As is the demon we thought was vanquished. We haven't seen the last of Everly and we haven't seen the last of the ancient evil that has plagued this land for countless years."

The woman said, "The doctor shot her dead outside his house, but later we saw her condition. She was healing. Lying on the coroner's table and healing! And then she vanished."

"And when she, or anything like her, returns, we'll stop them like we did before, by fire and by stake," the younger, handsome man said, glancing at the woman and the man she was apparently in a relationship with, judging by their close proximity to each other and the way she looked at him.

"I must get back to school. My students will be arriving shortly." She leaned in and gave the large man a quick kiss on the cheek.

He smiled back lovingly at her as she made her way out of the church.

Once the door was closed, the two men looked at their priest once more, who spoke in a more urgent voice.

"Evil is at work as we speak, and it will show itself soon. Somewhere out there, more powerful than Everly, more powerful than Visimar and his vampire and lycanthropic minions, it will come for us and we must be prepared. Call it intuition, call it divine intervention, but the devil's work isn't done. I fear many have perished and many may still meet their ends at this evil's hands if it isn't stopped."

"What can we do?" the young man asked.

"For now, we pray. Not just for us here in Burnmere but for all that may cross this great evil's path. Most especially, your son, Christoph, because if Everly is alive, she will no doubt hunt him down." The priest looked at the large man. "We will defeat this evil that still lives on the mountain, once and for all, but we aren't yet prepared. A key piece of the puzzle in stopping this has not been revealed. We must have patience and, more importantly, we must have faith!"

"I don't know if wooden stakes, holy water, and flames will be enough to send it back to hell, not this time," the large man said grimly.

"I have asked the Lord to send us help, to send us an answer to bring the evil down once and for all." The priest paused, then pointed behind him. "We must have faith in our Lord and the gifts he bestows on us. He will show us what must be done at the right time."

Fr. Kries looked up in the direction of his pointed hand. Attached to the tabernacle where the blessed sacrament was stored, right in its center, was a beautiful ruby-red gemstone. He hadn't seen it before but now couldn't look away from its incredible beauty. It seemed as if the stone showed itself only when directly pointed out. Otherwise, it blended in with the other, smaller stones and gold adorning the tabernacle, nearly vanishing from sight unless singularly focused on intently.

Whatever it was, it was hidden in plain sight and of great importance to his father and the others. Maybe to us as well, Fr. Kries wondered in awe.

Suddenly, the men were gone and he was alone in the church. It was just him and the tabernacle, and the dazzling stone.

Still dreaming, but no longer in the small church in Burnmere, Fr. Kries stood at the foot of what appeared to be the ruins of a large castle. It was nighttime and a fog appeared to have surrounded him. He wasn't alone, beside him was Nina and Ruppert. All of them stared at the enormous pile of stones scattered wide up on the mountain.

Something was happening under the rubble. A vibration had started and was growing more intense by the second.

"What is happening?" Fr. Kries exclaimed.

Ruppert and Nina remained silent, either unable to speak or too frightened.

The vibrations continued as the rocks shimmied in place then began splitting open.

Fr. Kries attempted to turn and run but found his feet unable to move. You want me to see this. To see what we're up against, he thought as he forced his eyes to remain open, looking on at the further destruction.

Behind the piles of stone stood what appeared to be several figures shrouded in the dark of the night sky. At their feet were several animals, which, from their shapes, looked to be wolves. He counted two but was unsure if there were more as the dust from the stones was making visibility difficult.

A feeling of dread fell over him, the likes of which he had never experienced before. Worse than his encounter with his lycanthropic mother, than his horrible upbringing. This was something much, much worse.

"Show yourself, you infernal beast!" he managed to shout at the top of his lungs.

Several larger piles of stones crumbled, sending rock and debris plummeting into the earth underneath them, yet Fr. Kries and his fellow travelers remained in place, witnesses to something being birthed.

Out of the rubble, an enormous arm emerged, the size of a small house with thick claws adorning its hand. Flames appeared to be rising up out of the arm, as if the appendage itself was made of fire.

"Oh, Lord, have mercy! Oh, Lord! Hear me! Save me!" Fr. Kries muttered as tears fell from his face at the ghastly sight before him. Behind the rubble the two figures appeared to be bowing in front of the monstrosity emerging from the ruins before being sucked up into the flames.

Smoke hissed from beneath the ground. Fire exploded upward. In between the massive arms, the tips of two wide horns began rising from the earth as the arms worked to push forth what lay under the destroyed structure.

A hiss fell across the mountain where they stood, coming from the emerging beast.

"I...live..."

Fr. Kries's eyes fluttered then opened wide. He sat bolt upright and immediately looked around the small compartment, seeing both Ruppert and Nina slumped on the opposite bench in their train compartment, both sound asleep. *We're on our way from Germany to Romania, that's right.*

He looked down at his watch. 1:00 AM. One night removed from his previous dream in which he was made witness to the horrors his mother had wrought across the town of Burnmere. He shook his head, further waking himself up and replaying the events of both dreams over in his head. He felt nauseous and contemplated visiting the washroom, but quickly drinking a bit of water provided for their train ride calmed his sour stomach.

He contemplated waking up his travelling companions as he looked at them both. Flawed and damaged people, outwardly and emotionally, but they were here, seeing this through with him. And now that he had a much clearer vision of what needed to happen and what they were truly up against, he felt not less but more afraid.

Fr. Kries gripped the small silver statue of Jesus attached to a small silver cross with the rest of the wood having been burned away in the fire inside Maximilian's tightly in his hand. Thinking back to how it had helped him vanquish the creature that was once his mother, Fr. Kries uttered quietly, "The gemstone on the tabernacle. Our answer lies with that, in order to bring about the beast's destruction. I know not how just yet. But it will play a role in defeating this great evil. The priest prayed that our Lord would send help. Well, Father...help is on the way."

He thought of the awful thing crawling from the fiery pits of hell and pushed the thought out of his mind. He needed to think on better things. His mind wandered to the large, dark-haired man in his dream who was standing in the church with the others. The man who had tried desperately to do the right thing for his son growing up but was cut down by his wife every chance she got.

Fr. Kries thought on these things, anxious to deliver the news that the woman who was neither a wife nor a mother, but a beast, chosen to do the devil's work, had been destroyed by his hands. He hoped it would make his father proud of him.

He wondered about this father he barely knew. What stories did the man have to share, and would he welcome back his prodigal son or turn in shame at the coward who fled, leaving him to deal with the vile woman for so many years on his own?

He knew the road ahead would be perilous. His mind filled with uncertainty as doubts tried to take over. Would he make it out of this alive? He supposed, at this point, that was of little concern.

There is a great evil loose in the world, and you, Lord, have called your faithful servants forth.

"Father, I'm coming home."

✝

About the Author

Eugene Weaver was born on August 8, 1974, in small town, rural Ohio. He and his wife Joani have been married for 20 years and have two boys. They currently live in the Canton area of Ohio.

Eugene has been an avid lover of movies, music, and the arts nearly all his life. At 12 years old, he wrote his first novel, *Pivoron Mountain,* in longhand cursive. At the persuasion of his boys thirty-six years later, he decided to take up writing once more. His first novel, *Thunder Stone Realm,* and its two subsequent sequels were published in 2023 and 2024. After completing his *Thunder Stone Realm* trilogy, he followed it up with another science fiction tale, *Battle for Quadrant 8304.* Next, up was the tropical island zombie story, *Crimson Paradise,* his fifth novel, released in early 2025. *The Amulet of Visimar was next, published in early 2025. Night of the Wolf* is the second book in the Visimar trilogy.